A Song
for the Stars

OTHER PROPER ROMANCE NOVELS

Nancy Campbell Allen

My Fair Gentleman

Beauty and the Clockwork Beast

The Secret of the India Orchid

Kiss of the Spindle

Julianne Donaldson

Edenbrooke

Blackmoore

Heir to Edenbrooke (eBook only)

Sarah M. Eden

Longing for Home

Longing for Home, vol. 2: Hope Springs

The Sheriffs of Savage Wells

Ashes on the Moor

Josi S. Kilpack

A Heart Revealed

Lord Fenton's Folly

Forever and Forever

A Lady's Favor (eBook only)

The Lady of the Lakes

The Vicar's Daughter

All That Makes Life Bright

Miss Wilton's Waltz

Promises and Primroses

Becca Wilhite

Check Me Out

Julie Wright

Lies Jane Austen Told Me

Lies, Love, and Breakfast at Tiffany's

A Song for the Stars

PROPER ROMANCE

ILIMA TODD

SHADOW
MOUNTAIN

Library of Congress Cataloging-in-Publication Data

Names: Todd, Ilima, author.

Title: A song for the stars / Ilima Todd.

Description: Salt Lake City, Utah : Shadow Mountain, [2019]

Identifiers: LCCN 2018029474 | ISBN 9781629725284 (paperbound)

Subjects: LCSH: Hawaiian women—Fiction. | Sailors—Fiction. | Culture conflict—Fiction. | Hawaii—History—To 1893—Fiction. | Hawaii, setting. | Eighteenth century, setting. | LCGFT: Romance fiction. | Historical fiction. | Novels.

Classification: LCC PS3620.O3175 S66 2019 | DDC 813/.6—dc23

LC record available at https://lccn.loc.gov/2018029474

Printed in the United States of America

LSC Communications, Crawfordsville, IN

10 9 8 7 6 5 4 3 2 1

For my children
Emma Mililani, Parker Makana,
Stirling Kaʻopuʻulani, and Hailey Haukealani.
This is your story, too.

John Harbottle's Journal
4 February 1779

I fear we've overstayed our welcome.

My relief when the captain orders the ships ready to depart is palpable. Our duty is to search for the Northwest Passage, after all, not indulge ourselves in the pleasures of this paradise.

Yet what a paradise it has been.

Never on our previous two voyages have the natives been more accommodating, more praising, than here in this protected bay. Even the captain, whose demeanor has been despondent of late, has emerged a new man while ashore, as though the water here is a life-giving elixir. One must only drink to become transformed—translated into a more celestial state.

The natives revere the captain as divine, much to our advantage. Even as we make preparations to leave, we are inundated with such quantities of food and gifts that we haven't the room to hold it all. But perhaps the captain has seen what some of the sailors have as well—the natives grow impatient. Suspicious. What they expect us to do or say I know not, but after a month's recovery on the island, it is past time we take our leave.

After enjoying a gift of song and dance from the natives, their double-hulled canoes adorned with feathers and flora out upon the water, we cast our sails and veer from the bay. We head again in search of the elusive passage to the Atlantic. This is our purpose, the cause of our voyage.

Yet as I stare longingly at the Sandwich Isles shrinking on the horizon, I wonder if the other sailors feel as I do—a small sliver of regret that this may be the last time we see these shores. Our time here will be but a memory, a dream. One that, perhaps, I may one day question had ever been real at all.

ʻekahi

Chapter One

I sink lower into the hull of the canoe, pressing my back against the *koa* wood along the base. My eyes close, eclipsing the stars in the night sky above me. I relax and try to feel the rhythm of the sea. She rams against the side of the vessel like a stubborn child, sending a salty spray of water over my face, refusing to be ignored. A moment later, she cradles the canoe, wrapping her arms around it like a trusted friend, rocking it softly. She's erratic and fierce, soothing and mild. She is unpredictable. But there's a pattern here that longs to be understood. So that's what I do—attempt to comprehend what she's trying to tell me.

"What do you feel, Maile?" Ikaika asks. His voice is soft but carries easily in the crisp night air.

"I feel . . ." I pause, considering the question. "Distracted. Stop talking."

He laughs briefly then says nothing more.

I think of the first time Ikaika brought me out on a canoe like this. We were children, and I begged him to teach me the skill of wayfinding, the method of reading the clouds and stars and water to navigate on the ocean. He'd been training to become a navigator, and I was jealous of everything he was learning.

Girls aren't allowed to navigate. I'm the second daughter of Kalani the high chief, and I'm not even granted that privilege. But Ikaika was never one to pass up a chance to show off, and we paddled out into the bay on a small outrigger so he could teach me what he knew.

It was the first of many training sessions and the start of a lifelong friendship. My father tolerated our jaunts, mostly because he'd already arranged for Ikaika to be my husband one day and he hoped our time together would prove beneficial. Now I'm eighteen, and our wedding is only a month away. As the chief's prime navigator, Ikaika is an honorable choice for me. One I'm grateful for.

I focus on the ocean again, pressing my palms against the base of the canoe the way Ikaika taught me, spreading my fingers and trying to feel the water. She moves uneasily. The canoe drifts with the current, but it's hesitant. As though it's unfamiliar with this path and moves with trepidation.

I feel Ikaika's mouth against my neck, his warm breath tickling my skin.

"No distractions," I say, feigning annoyance.

"But I didn't say anything," he teases.

I open my eyes to see him grinning above me, kneeling at my side. I shake my head at him, knowing this training session is almost over.

He moves his mouth to my ear and whispers, "A navigator must be prepared for a variety of distractions while upon the water."

"Is that so?"

He nods against the side of my face. "It's only appropriate that I provide such distractions. For training purposes, of course."

"Of course," I say, this time giving him a small laugh.

He presses his nose and forehead flush against mine, his hand cradling the back of my neck. We breathe in and out, exchanging our breath, our *hā*. He moves his nose to the right of mine then shifts to the opposite side. It is our *honi*, our kiss, and it leaves me breathless.

"Maile," he says, pulling away slightly. "What do you feel?"

I can't tell if his question is meant to be romantic or part of our training, but it makes me think of what I felt a moment ago from the water, and I know I can't ignore it. I sit up and look at the ocean surrounding us as though I can find the source of my unease in the darkness.

"The storm is gone," I say, referencing the squall that pushed through our island a couple of days ago. "But something is still amiss. She doesn't feel right."

Ikaika sighs and leans against the side of the canoe. "You're not still thinking about those white sailors, are you? They've been gone for eight days."

"How could I not think about them?" I ask. "Their arrival changed everything."

Ikaika shrugs and fingers the iron dagger hanging on his belt cloth, one of the many metal weapons and tools our people traded the white men for. "You're letting it muddle your instincts. The sea is calm. Steady. It is you who is turbulent, not the water."

Maybe he's right. Maybe it's all in my head. There's no reason for me to question James Cook or his intentions for our people. His ships, the *Resolution* and *Discovery*, had been skating along the shore of our island for days before they entered our bay—Lono's sacred bay. We'd been honoring Lono during our yearly *makahiki* celebration when the ships arrived. Lono is our legendary white god, the god of peace, destined to return to our shore one day. James Cook came at just the right time to just the right place, and with his pale skin and head of white hair, it wasn't long before our priests declared him to be the god himself.

James Cook never denied it. He participated in the sacred ceremonies honoring him, frequented our *heiau*—our temples— and allowed our people to prostrate themselves before him whenever he walked by.

And of course, there was the iron. His sailors freely traded their abundance of metal for food, supplies, and women. I glance at Ikaika's dagger again. I'd never seen anything like the substance before. None of us had. Harder than lava rock and molded into whatever form the sailors needed, it was virtually indestructible. Surely such a thing had come from the gods.

Yet one of Cook's crewmen died while on shore—obviously a mortal. How could that be? And there seemed to be no end to the amount of food the sailors could eat. I'd seen some of our people patting the crews' stomachs in awe of their appetite. Did they come from a place where the food had failed? How could Lono live in such a place?

I wasn't the only one who questioned Cook's divinity. There were many relieved expressions among my people when the white men finally sailed their ships out to sea. There are only so many pigs one can hunt on an isolated island to give as gifts to the foreigners. I was beginning to worry we wouldn't have enough supplies for our own needs.

"Besides," Ikaika says, drawing my attention back to him. "The season of Lono is over. James Cook wouldn't return now that it's the season of Kū. Not unless he wants to start a war. They will not be back."

His reasoning doesn't make me feel better. Kū is the god of war. This is the season when challenges can be made to the chief and his royal status, when a lesser chief of the island can wage war on us if he seeks a higher rank. My father has maintained peace for most of his years as high chief of our island. Though his men are trained to fight, they haven't had to for a long time. If James Cook really is the god Lono foretold, he will not return.

But what if he isn't Lono?

"Come here," Ikaika says, motioning to the spot next to him.

I move to his side and lean back against the edge of the canoe, letting him drape his arm over my shoulders. I run my hand over the large white whale tooth that hangs at his neck, sitting on his collarbone.

"I know you didn't like them being here." He squeezes my arm, trying to comfort me. "You avoided them as much as you could, stealing me away to the water just to get away." He smiles. "Not that I'm complaining about spending more time alone with you. But, Maile, they were a blessing."

I harrumph, not seeing how foreigners depleting our food stores was a blessing. We were doing just fine without them.

"They *were* a blessing." He nods, as though trying to convince himself, too. "Of all the beaches on our island, of all the beaches on all the islands that exist, Lono chose our bay. He chose to bestow the gift of metal on *us*. Think of the advantage our people have over all others now. We are a chosen people."

I try to see the white men as he does. As revered guests. As a blessing. But there's still a part of me waiting for the trick to reveal itself, the proof that they're really a curse in the end.

"Change can be a good thing." Ikaika squeezes my arm again. "We'll both be changing in a month. That's good, isn't it?"

I smile, thinking of our wedding day. "You will not change," I tease. "You'll still be arrogant."

"Yes," he agrees.

"And reckless."

"Well . . ."

"And stubborn," I say. "Defiant. Irreverent. Selfish."

"You speak as though these are bad things."

I laugh. "You will be the same haughty boy who has sought to best me in everything, always."

"Yes." He runs his fingers down the length of my hair. "But I will be yours."

I look up at his dark eyes, a lock of black hair falling in front of them. I brush it away and say, "You've always been mine."

"I know." He holds my gaze. "I'll still be handsome, too. That won't change."

I swat him on the chest, scolding him for teasing me so readily. But at least he's made me forget about James Cook and his foreign sailors. For now.

"Twenty degrees," he says, bringing me back to the lesson I thought was over.

I hold my hand up in front of me, stretching my thumb and little finger as far apart as I can, one full handspan. It is exactly twenty degrees—one-eighteenth the distance around the entire sky. With my arm outstretched, I superimpose my hand against the sky.

"And ten degrees," he asks, testing me.

I clench my fist, my arm still outstretched. The width of my fist measures ten degrees in the sky.

"Five degrees?"

I hold up three fingers.

"One."

I hold up my little finger. The width of the very tip measures one degree.

"Good," he says. He holds up his hand as well, extending his little finger like me. But because his arm is longer than mine, it's farther away from us, making up for the fact that his hand and fingers are larger as well. It's a trick he taught me many years ago. The measurement holds, even for children, because the length of our arms is proportional to the size of our hands.

He hooks his little finger with mine midair before pulling my hand toward his chest and holding it there. We've been out here most of the night. Dawn approaches on the horizon. I close my eyes and try to feel the calmness he said he'd felt from the ocean. But all I feel is the steady beat of his heart against my head as I rest against him. It lulls me to sleep after an entire night awake.

I dream I'm walking through the high forests of our island, following a well-worn path likely carved out by boars. A mild rain shower has just passed through, leaving droplets on the large green leaves of the trees surrounding me. The sunlight scatters down between the greenery, brightening the corners of the forest as its rays reflect off every wet surface. The constant *drip drip drip* of the water running off the high leaves and splattering onto lower ones creates a song that makes me want to raise my arms and dance to its melody.

A soft trill sounds, like that of a bird caught in a trap. I follow his cries, finally finding him on a high branch near a tube-shaped lobelia blossom. He's a golden finch, the only bird on the island able to reach the sweet nectar of lobelia thanks to his long, curved beak. Bird catchers like to brush a layer of breadfruit paste along the branches next to those blossoms, hoping to trap the birds—like this one—and collect a golden feather.

I reach up and carefully free him from the branch, gently

removing the residue from his feet. Bird catchers pluck one feather from every bird they catch before they let the bird go, collecting another feather another day. They use the feathers for capes, head-dresses, *lei*, and other adornments. I don't have it in me to steal a feather, so instead I stroke him once, my touch sliding off him as easily as a drop of water. I open my hand and let him fly free. He disappears from my view so quickly, I regret not holding onto him a little longer. I know he doesn't belong to me, but there's an emptiness I feel now that he's gone. It makes no sense, but the feeling is there all the same.

"Where are we?" Ikaika's voice invades my dream, making me startle.

"What?" I blink my eyes open and lift my head from his chest, reality coming back to me.

"Did you fall asleep?" He tucks a length of hair behind my ear. Without waiting for my answer, he asks again, "Where are we?"

I rub at my eyes and look to the horizon, knowing the question is part of my training. I stretch my arm out again, my palm turned away from me. With my fingers close together, only my thumb is outstretched, parallel to the horizon. The fixed star in the north sits just above my index finger.

"We are in Hawai'i," I say. "We are home."

Ikaika lowers my hand and sits tall, looking out to the horizon I just measured. He blinks as though he, too, is waking from a dream. I strain my eyes to see what he does; his vision reaches farther than mine. All I see is the thin line of orange touching the surface of the water as the sun begins his daily climb.

"What is it?" I ask. The moment the words are out, I see it. Calmness abandons my body, leaving behind a turbulence that was hiding all along.

This time, I know those white clouds low on the horizon are not clouds at all, but the large white sails of James Cook's *Resolution* and *Discovery*. And this time, I know he will not be welcomed.

John Harbottle's Journal
11 February 1779

The storm was mild at first. The winds blew moderate enough that we reefed the topsails for a while, though some of the men became seasick as the Resolution tossed about. As the winds increased, the fore topmast sail split, so we lowered all yards to the deck. Unfortunately, our luck continued to decline.

In the early morning, a crack appeared in the foremast. All sailors stood in shock, as did the captain. It was the same foremast that had caused us trouble two years ago. The foremast we were certain had been fixed. An old leak began to haunt us as well, but no misfortune was as bad as the topmast moving unsteadily when it should have held rigid, even tipping as the ship rolled. The wooden supports we'd installed at Nootka Sound had failed. The lower mast was the only thing we had to set our course.

The captain assembled an emergency meeting, and the decision was unanimous: the entire mast assembly would need to come out. Which meant we needed to find a beach. A protected one. There was only one answer, but none of us wanted to voice it. We'd traveled along the coasts for days upon first arriving in the Sandwich Isles, and there was only one bay we knew of that could accommodate both ships for a repair that would likely take weeks.

After dismissing the other officers, the captain inquired of me what I thought our return would signify to the natives. Serving as a translator naturally made me more attuned to their opinion of our presence. I told him I was confident our arrival wouldn't be celebrated as it had before, but that the natives would hold no animosity toward us. I suggested we anchor far from the chief's beach but still well within the safety of the bay.

I know the captain's frustrations stem more from the added delay to our voyage than potentially unreceptive natives. We've dealt with unfriendly islands in the South Pacific before. It's the Northwest Passage that continues to elude us.

Disinclined to return but with no other choice, we are heading back toward the familiar bay mere days after leaving. Notwithstanding my assurance to the captain that all will be well upon our arrival, I've little understanding of what awaits us when we do.

ʻelua

Chapter Two

Ikaika gives me a paddle and takes one for himself. Soon after we begin rowing, I realize we're trying to move in opposite directions.

"We have to tell my father," I say. "We must return to the village." The chief needs to know right away that James Cook has returned so he can decide what to do.

"Kalani already knows," Ikaika says. "Or at least he will soon." He lifts his paddle out of the water and uses it to point toward Cook's ships. No, not the ships—to a group of canoes heading toward them, already halfway there. "We weren't the first to spot them."

"What do you intend to do when we get there?"

"Find out why they've returned," he says, beginning to paddle again toward the towering ships. "Determine what their intentions are."

I hesitantly lower my paddle into the water and help maneuver our outrigger toward the foreigners. Though our people paddled out to Cook's ships almost daily during their month-long stay, I'd never been near them. My desire to stay away burns even stronger now, but perhaps learning what the captain's objectives are before he and his men have a chance to get comfortable will prove an advantage.

The *Resolution* casts a long shadow in the water, the ship backlit by the rising sun in the east. When our canoe reaches the shade of the vessel, a chill runs through me in reaction to the sudden decrease in light and temperature. The other canoes are already here. Our people scramble up the side of the ship and onto the deck. There's no animosity in their excitement to reach the top, just curiosity and anticipation. Some carry offerings of food; most scale the ship as though they've done it dozens of times. They probably have.

"Wait here," Ikaika says.

He drops his paddle in the canoe and knots his hair back before jumping into the water, swimming toward the base of the ship, and taking hold of the wooden slats. I watch as he ascends the side and disappears from view at the top. I let go of a breath I didn't realize I'd been holding.

I look around at the canoes near me in the water. There are only six of them, and most are abandoned, their occupants on the much larger ship above us. I wonder what the sailors think of their welcome party today. Scant offerings, half a dozen small canoes, and none of the royal family. Except me, of course. But they wouldn't recognize me thanks to how much I avoided contact with the white men. Those of us who have gathered today are a tiny fraction of the hundreds who paddled elaborate canoes out to greet Cook the first time he was here.

But I know my people look on from the cliffs, the undergrowth, the tree line. Their minds likely race like mine, trying to make sense of why Cook has returned. There's an ominous feeling in the bay—the sailors must feel it, too.

I spot one of my people attempting to pry an iron fitting from the side of the ship. Disgusted with the blind obsession we have for the metal, I realize that's the reason most of them are here this morning—to bargain for more iron. Or steal some, apparently.

I lift my gaze to the deck of the ship, wondering how much longer Ikaika will be. Wondering if he's safe. A white sailor stands at the edge, looking toward the coastline, perhaps troubled by the lack of hospitality today. He wears a dark, large-brimmed hat with three corners and a deep-blue coat. I know enough of the foreigners' clothing to know those who wear blue are leaders within their ranks; the rest of the sailors wear red or white. It's not Cook, but he has white hair with curls above each ear like the captain. This man is younger. If it weren't for his white hair, I'd guess he wasn't much older than Ikaika and myself.

The sailor's gaze moves from the coast to the canoes gathered at the base of his ship, eventually landing on me. I look away, embarrassed to have been caught staring at him and uncomfortable with how boldly he stares back at me. Looking directly at a member of the royal family without permission is a punishable offense, except for Ikaika and members of my father's court. I'm used to heads angled down and eyes averted in my presence. But this man is not one of us, and he doesn't know I'm the daughter of the high chief.

I look back at him, determined not to be intimidated. He's the one trespassing in my home. He's the one who doesn't belong, who invites trouble by returning to our shore during the season of Kū. He continues to look at me, his eyes narrowing slightly. I can't tell if it's in anger or if he's trying to comprehend something—he's too far for me to decipher details.

Shouts erupt from the far side of the *Resolution*, and the sailor turns and rushes away from the edge. I stand in the canoe, hoping to see what's happening, but I'm too close to the base and see nothing. Several of our men begin jumping off the ship into the water, climbing into their canoes and paddling away. I pray to the gods Ikaika is safe.

A moment later, he appears at the edge where the white sailor had been standing not long ago. He dives into the water and slips into our canoe in front of me.

"Hurry," he says, ordering me to paddle as he does the same. Away from the ships and toward home.

"What happened?" I ask.

"I'm not sure," he says, out of breath. "One of our priests was there. On board. I was asking him what he'd learned from the captain. About why they're here." He pauses to catch his breath, making a few hard strokes with his paddle before continuing. "One of our men started running across the deck with a satchel in his hands. The sailors grabbed him before he could get away." He turns to look back to me. "Maile, they took him and bound him to the rigging. Raised him into the air. Punished him with lashes against his back."

I stop paddling, too stunned to think clearly. In all the time Cook and his men were anchored here, in all the time they spent among our homes, our people, I'd never heard a report of them acting violently. This is new. And now during our time of war . . .

"What was in the satchel? What was he trying to steal?" I ask.

"I don't know."

I look behind me to the ships anchored at the outer edge of the bay. The only vessels moving in the water are our own canoes, everyone hurrying home like we are. Just us—and one small skiff belonging to the foreigners. There are no white sailors in that boat, just our own men. My gut fills with dread. Our people have stolen one of their boats. How will they retaliate?

"Why are they here?" I ask Ikaika.

"What?" he shouts back at me.

"You said there was a priest. That he knew why they came back."

"A part of their ship was damaged in the squall. They've come back to repair it." He shakes his head. "How could Lono's ship break? It wasn't even a strong storm."

"Because he is not Lono," I say.

Ikaika doesn't argue because we both know it must be true. It's the only explanation for their swift return, for their disabled ship. Cook is not as powerful as he led us to believe, and if Cook is not Lono, if he is not the white god we'd been looking for, then his presence here, now, isn't good.

We remain silent the rest of the way to the beach. Once on shore, we pull the outrigger onto the sand, out of reach of the tide. When all the other canoes are on shore, Ikaika runs to help with the skiff, pulling it out of the water as well. I wait by the small outrigger, not wanting to be a part of the crew that stole the foreign boat so brazenly.

The foreigners seem to view the possession of property much differently than we do. I know a person can't really own anything—all things belong to the gods—but we've always traded for what we wanted. To take without permission, combined with the distress of Cook's unexpected return and what it means for us . . . I'm not surprised it's come to this.

I shield my eyes and look out over the bay. Several smaller boats are being lowered to the water from both ships, but they don't head to shore. Instead, they paddle out to the narrow opening of the bay, a line of boats blocking the open water. Are they trying to seal us off?

One small boat turns toward the beach and heads for us. It's hardly a war party, and I can't tell how many people are in the boat, but there's no doubt they want to retrieve what was taken. I think about the man strung up in the rigging of their ship, whipped as punishment. If that's the result of someone's failed attempt at theft, what will they do to someone who actually got away with it?

I look toward Ikaika. He's helping to move the skiff inland past the tree line and is too far away to hear me. They must have noticed the incoming sailors as well and are trying to hide what they stole. I can't bear to think of Ikaika being caught—captured, tortured, or even worse. I curse under my breath and hurry inland to see where they are taking it.

A crowd gathers at the far side of the homestead where Ikaika and the others are moving past the huts into a grove of bamboo. I follow, pushing my way through the throng. When the people realize who I am, they step to the side and let me pass, careful not to touch me. I reach Ikaika and the others, now hidden behind a thicket of green and golden bamboo stalks.

"What are you doing?" I ask.

Ikaika turns toward me, his face flushed from exertion. "Hiding the boat."

"I see that," I say, motioning to the skiff. "But why?"

"I told you what happened to the man they caught," he says. "I don't want anyone else to be treated that way."

I had the same worry, but he doesn't seem to realize he's now an accomplice. "And I don't want *you* to be treated that way," I say. "They saw the stolen boat on the water. They saw you carry it inland. They're going to find it. And then what? It would have been better if you had left it alone on the beach with those who stole it in the first place."

"They won't find it," he says simply. His thoughts are in the right place—he wants to protect our people. But who will protect him?

I look around at the grove of bamboo. The stalks are thick and dense. Ikaika is right: unless the white men send out an extensive search party, they might not find it. But our people gathered here isn't exactly an exercise in stealth.

"*Ho'i*," I say, loudly and with authority.

The crowd scatters, leaving me and Ikaika alone with the boat. It's both wider and shorter than our canoes, and the base is flat, not rounded. Several slats of wood span the width, edge to edge, creating space to sit on. The slat in back is the largest of them, expanding to the very rear of the boat. A thick white dye or paste of some kind flakes off the wood, and a pair of oars rest along the base.

Ikaika sits on one of the slats, which creaks beneath him, before resting his head in his hands. "They won't find it," he repeats. "They've limped into our waters on a broken ship. They're not smart enough to find us."

I hold back a wince, realizing I'm now an accomplice as well. In my haste to disperse the crowd, I sent away those who actually stole it. I turn toward the beach, squinting as though I can peer through the thick bamboo and see what's happening on shore, but the thicket is too dense.

Their single boat in pursuit must have reached land, and if my father didn't know about Cook's return yet, he does now. He's likely been summoned to the beach. I grasp two stalks of bamboo, squeezing the smooth, rounded canes in my hands, my knuckles turning white as we wait.

When I hear a rustling ahead of us, I step back. At the same time, Ikaika jumps to his feet and moves in front of me, ready to protect me from a potential threat. But then we see my father and two of his guards stepping through the narrow path, and we both relax. I don't know what mood the chief is in, but I desperately want to know what happened.

"Is everything all right?" I ask Father.

"I don't know." He looks me over, as though making sure I'm well. He seems relieved to see I am unharmed, but then he notices the boat behind us and he clenches his jaw.

"It's not her fault," Ikaika says, defending me right away.

"It's not Ikaika's either," I say. "Yes, our people stole it, but Ikaika only helped them hide it to protect them from Cook's retaliation."

Father's eyes narrow, as though puzzling through something.

"What did they want?" I ask, anxious to know if we're in danger.

The chief runs his hand down his graying beard. "It was a couple of sailors. They wanted us to return the items we stole—a boat and some kind of navigation equipment in a parcel. I promised them I'd find the items and return what was taken. They'll be back in the morning to collect them." He glances toward the boat, empty except for the two oars. "Was there a parcel, too?"

Ikaika relates everything he saw happen on the *Resolution*, including the satchel that one of our men had tried to steal before he was caught and punished.

"That could be what they're looking for," he adds. "But it never left the ship."

Not unless someone else took it, I think. In one of the other canoes.

There's not a lot that happens on our island without my

father's knowledge, which is probably how he knew where to find us and the skiff. If navigation equipment was taken, he'll find it. But I'm confused about why the foreigners need navigation equipment in the first place. A navigator uses signs from the world around him to determine where he's been and where he needs to go. No man-made tools can do that.

"I want our men armed tonight," the chief says to his guards. "On alert. I don't trust James Cook."

It's the first time he's ever called the captain by his foreign name and not addressed him as Lono. Father must have his doubts about Cook's divinity as well, which means he's preparing to defend our people should the foreigners attack. He may be concerned about the stolen items, but he is more distressed over why Cook has returned. Suspicious. And rightly so.

"Do you think they will come with force?" I ask.

Father doesn't answer, just turns and looks through the thicket like I had earlier, straining to see the ocean beyond. Deep creases mark his brow. He is confused. Uneasy. Distraught. There is no precedence for this, and I pray the gods will grant my father the wisdom he needs to deal with people he's not even sure are his enemy.

John Harbottle's Journal
13 February 1779

The captain has asked me to accompany him ashore in the morning. He wants his request to be clear when speaking to the natives, with no misunderstanding due to faulty translation: we need the navigation equipment returned or measures will be taken to secure it.

I'm not certain what measures the captain is referring to, but he instructed all of us to fill our rifles with musket fire rather than shot. The order is unsettling, to say the least. The captain's standard practice with all indigenous peoples thus far has been to use shot as warning fire. It leaves no lasting injury and has minimal impact on the welfare of the people. He's never even had to use shot in this place, the peace exhibited by the Hawai'ians unrivaled until now. But musket fire? They have no knowledge at all of the harm our weapons can inflict.

I fear the request is a result of the captain's lack of patience—both with the thievery and the loss of time due to the broken masts. Perhaps his temper was kindled further by the fact that a native made it into the officers' quarters and stole not only the captain's plane table frame, a magnifier given to him by a dear friend, a backstaff, and a sextant, but also a detailed—and irreplaceable—world atlas.

The thief who stole the items likely has no idea of their worth let alone their function, but the act itself was an invasion of that which is most precious to the captain. The last thing we should want is to start a war, yet it seems even the sensible James Cook has a breaking point, and that point has been reached.

I only hope the chief, Kalani, is able to recover not only the skiff but the navigation items I asked him for on the beach so we can end this quarrel peacefully. I fear the temperament of the captain, should things not go his way, will worsen. Given his orders for the men to arm themselves accordingly, it's obvious he's willing to kill to get what he needs.

'ekolu

Chapter Three

I keep pace with my father as he hurries from our weapons hut to the beach. He is juggling an armful of clubs and knives. "Let me fight," I say.

Cook approaches on the water in a skiff with two additional boats filled with red-coated sailors behind him. They hold weapons made of wood and iron at their sides. I've no idea what their weapons do, but the white men are obviously anticipating a dispute.

"Back to the homestead, Maile. A battle is no place for girls." His voice is sharp and commanding. He speaks as Kalani the chief, not Kalani my father.

I stop and press my tongue against the roof of my mouth, quenching the fire of words that long to escape. I'm to be married soon; I'm no girl. Besides, I can do boy things better than most of the men. Like navigate by the stars, hunt boar tracks, and wield a bone knife faster than lightning flashing on water.

My father hurries past the copse of trees toward the shoreline without me.

An arm slips around my waist from behind. "Someone's

angry," Ikaika whispers. I feel his warm breath on my shoulder. "Tell me how to fix this."

I turn and lean my forehead against his chest and exhale. Having Ikaika near usually lifts my mood, but my insides pull at me like a rip current, threatening to drown me in worry with everything that happened yesterday.

"Father ordered me to return home," I say. "He says battle is no place for girls."

Ikaika harrumphs. "You are *no* girl."

I smile against his chest, but it doesn't feel right, so I let it fade. "Maybe I should have ordered our people to return the boat yesterday, the moment I saw them paddling in the water. I shouldn't have allowed it to even touch our shore."

"None of this is your fault," he says. "They shouldn't have taken it, but Cook shouldn't have come back. It's war season, and the sailors' presence here isn't right." He pauses. "If there's to be a battle, it's not because of anything our people have done. It's because the white men disregard the sanctions of the gods."

I nod. He's right. They shouldn't be here.

He backs away just enough to slip something off his belt cloth and into my hand.

"My knife."

I turn the slashing weapon in my hand. It's made of a half circle of *koa* wood with a slot large enough for my fingers to slip into and grip. The curved end is lined with tiger shark teeth lashed on with coconut fibers. "Thank you."

Ikaika shakes his head and runs his thumb along my cheek. "I knew I wouldn't be able to keep you away from the beach. I decided you might as well be prepared." He fingers the iron dagger at his waist before gripping his spear. He knows me well enough not to offer me one of the foreign knives; he knows how much I despise them. The irony is that my father likely held several weapons of metal in his arms as he rushed to the beach. Our people will be fighting the sailors with their own weapons.

I slide my curved knife into my own belt and pull my wild dark hair into a high bun on top of my head, the way the men do. I can't enter the battlefield topless like the others, but maybe amidst the chaos I'll go unnoticed.

"Let's go," I say, pulling Ikaika behind me toward the beach.

As we step onto the sand, he slides in front of me with his fingers to his lips. I don't need the reminder to be silent. I'm speechless at the scene before us.

Men from our village line the shore, their weapons held high, itching for an excuse to use them. Some hold rocks or slings, others have iron daggers like Ikaika, but most wield clubs or spears of varying lengths, lined with shark teeth similar to my knife. This is no training exercise. They intend to fight to the death if needed.

The *Resolution* and *Discovery* are still anchored at the mouth of the bay, and three of Cook's smaller boats are still approaching. I can see more clearly the strange wood-and-metal weapons his sailors hold in their hands.

Our people traded many precious things for the foreigners' iron objects—feathered capes and headdresses that had been passed down for millennia, bark cloth pounded for hundreds of hours, adornments made of the hair and teeth of our ancestors. Items that had *mana*—power. But no matter how many iron tools or objects the sailors gave up, they never traded away these strange, long weapons they carried. My stomach twists with uncertainty.

Father is in the water at the far side of the beach, giving orders. He wears his red-and-gold feather cloak and helmet that identifies him as the ranking chief of the island. Several men surround him, and I doubt he'll notice me for a while. The skiff my father promised to return sits on the other end of the beach, ready to be given to the sailors. Perhaps the day will end in peace after all.

Ikaika and I make our way toward the crowd. Their shouts grow by the second. I pull my weapon out of my belt and slide my fingers into the well-worn slot. My hand shakes, so I flex my wrist, twisting it from side to side.

"Don't worry," Ikaika says, sensing my anxiety. "He is not Lono. He's just a man with a strange head of curly white hair." He sticks out his tongue, and I can't help but laugh, my tense shoulders relaxing a little.

I look out to the boats heading toward us and see several men with the same white hair, though I can't see any faces. One of them must be Cook, and I remind myself he is just a man. He must be.

I follow Ikaika into the water until the waves hit just above my knees. I can't see past the crowd in front of me, and Ikaika hikes me onto his back so I can get a better view. My father stands waist-deep in the water in front of his men as the first of the boats arrive.

I recognize James Cook immediately. The captain stands at the front of the eight men in his vessel. Two other boats fall in behind him with about twenty-five in each. Cook wears the blue-colored coat of the officers.

"Lono." Father's voice rises above the others. I'm surprised to hear him call out that name. I know he has his doubts that Cook is a god; perhaps he doesn't want the foreigners to know of his suspicions.

"Kalani." Cook's voice is imposing, a good match to my father's. They stand with heads high, shoulders back. It's clear that they've both spent the majority of their lives as leaders to others. I study the captain's face. His brows arch in slight surprise, but his long nose reaches a disappointed mouth, his chin tucked in sharply, as though he's readying himself to discipline a wayward child. I remind myself again that he's just a man beneath his elaborate clothes.

"Why have you returned?" my father asks. I hear him, but can only see the top of his helmet from where I stand in the water. "You are not welcome here any longer."

Another man rises to stand next to the captain on the boat. He has the same white hair as Cook, tied back with tight curls above his ears. Except this man is younger. Much younger. He's the one I saw at the edge of the *Resolution* yesterday. The one who watched me. I recognize him even without his three-cornered hat.

"I am Lieutenant John Harbottle," the younger man says.

My arms tighten around Ikaika's neck in surprise. This John Harbottle speaks in our tongue, though his accent is strong. I knew Cook had a translator, but I'd not seen him before. Our words coming from his mouth sound so strange, even more foreign to me than if he had spoken in his own native language.

"I will speak for the captain." John's eyes scan the crowd of my people and land on my face. He narrows his eyes at me for a moment, then turns to Cook at his side.

The captain says something to John so low I can't hear the sound of his voice.

"Your people have stolen valuable items from our ship," John says. His eyes find mine again, a question in his expression. He's trying to place me, perhaps confused why a woman is in a crowd of male warriors.

I don't want to draw any more attention to myself, so I slip off

Ikaika's back and hope John can't see me anymore, even though I can still see him and Cook standing in the boat.

"We don't want to hurt anyone." John pulls his wood-and-metal weapon tight against his body. "We just want our things returned."

"Your boat is ready for you." Father points to the skiff on the beach. "But we have nothing else of yours." He raises his wooden club to his shoulder. "Leave our island now, and we will let you go unharmed."

John rubs the side of his face and sighs. "We were caught in a storm, and our foremast was torn. We've returned just long enough for repairs. We will not inconvenience you any longer than we must." He turns to speak with Cook for a moment, and then continues. "But there are things your men have taken. A compass. A sextant. An atlas."

I don't recognize the words, but I try to imagine what they could represent. Are they things to help them interpret the water and the sky? Are they small enough to fit in a satchel?

"Maps," John continues. "Equipment. Important ones to help us navigate. These things can't be traded. We must have them."

"No." The chief steps closer to Cook's boat in the water. My father doesn't want to fight, but he's already given them a warning. He has already shown mercy. Any more leniency he offers the sailors will make him look weak, especially when they're accusing him of lying. He can't risk that—not in front of his people, not this time of year. He must leave no doubt in the minds of his people that he's capable of handling unexpected threats like this one. Lesser chiefs and noblemen are watching; they could challenge my father for the role of high chief.

"You are mistaken," Father says. "We don't have the items you have lost. Turn and leave. Now."

John argues with the captain before speaking again, louder this time. "P-please." His eyes turn down, and he stutters, as though he's trying to stop the words from being said even as they fall from his mouth. "We . . . we are prepared to take hostages if we have to. Use force. We cannot leave without our things."

Father stands firm and says nothing. The men at his back tense, ready to fight.

I look out to the horizon where a line of boats blocks the mouth of the bay. I thought it was meant to intimidate us, but now I think they're keeping us prisoner until we return their things. Prisoners in our own home. I don't understand why they won't leave. We're returning their boat, and we don't have the items they need.

After waiting for what feels like a slow crawl of the sun across the sky but couldn't have been longer than the lap of a wave, Captain James Cook waves his hand to the sailors behind him. Suddenly, fifty red-coated men are in the water with their foreign weapons—and they all head straight for my father.

"The chief," I whisper.

Ikaika nods. He sees it, too. They mean to kidnap my father.

Boom.

The sound is deafening, leaving a hollow ringing in my ears as though I'd been knocked to the ground. I see clouds. Only, they're clouds of smoke, and they rise from the surface of the water, not the sky. No, not from the water—they come from the end of one of the white men's weapons. And a body floats in the sea next to my father, blood flowing from his chest into the water.

What kind of magic is this?

When the smoke finally clears, a strangled cry leaves my throat.

They've taken my father and pulled him into Cook's boat. He

fights with a ferocity befitting a great warrior, but there are too many red coats, and he can't hold them all back.

"Father!" I push my way through the fighting men. There are so many of them it's like trudging through the muddied riverbanks after a rainstorm, and I can't move fast enough.

Boom.

My hands fly to my ears against the sound. It's so loud it makes my head throb, eclipsing the endless shouting of those engaged in the fight.

Ikaika pushes past me and runs his dagger through a man on the boat. A few of our warriors fight off the sailors on the other side of the boat, and Ikaika climbs on board. Between him and my father, and the fact that Cook's men seem to struggle with their weapons in such close quarters, they manage to ward off the white men and jump back into the water.

I help Ikaika pull Father to the shore. I finally get a chance to use my knife, slashing at two sailors who attempt to grab the chief again. I spin and use the momentum to slice one through the stomach and the other across the throat. A gush of blood pours over my knife and hand. I pause, watching the warm liquid drip from the tiger shark teeth, as if I'm a sea creature that has just torn the flesh of the man, not a woman in her first kill. I feel a strange detachment from what just happened, as though I'm witnessing it from a distance. But I don't have time to think about it more.

"Maile!" My father's face burns red, and I don't think it's because of the struggle in the ocean. "What are you doing here? I told you to stay away."

"You're hurt," I say, fingering a knife wound in his side with my clean hand. I move my other arm behind me, trying to ignore the blood that runs along my skin in streaks.

"I'm fine." He brushes my hand away and stands tall to take in the battle.

Ikaika and I rise next to him and see Cook and his men advancing onto the sand. The booming sounds from their weapons continue to create a smoke that obscures my vision, and I don't know which side is winning. The three of us rush into the crowd, determined to stand firm against the foreigners.

"They tried to kidnap your chief," Ikaika shouts into the smoke, raising his spear above his head. "They will not get away with it."

A roar erupts from the water, and as some of the smoke settles, I see the three small boats heading back to their ships, filled with sailors abandoning the battle. Cook and his remaining men run down the beach toward the stolen skiff pulled up on shore. John Harbottle is at his side, repeatedly looking back as if to determine how many men are in pursuit.

Ikaika and I rush in that direction, splashing into the shallow water in front of the boat to block their escape out to sea.

Cook moves to the other side of the boat and attempts to launch the vessel with the help of his sailors. But soon there are several of our men, pushing back, and the small boat remains in place.

"Time to move," says a shaky, heavily accented voice.

I look up to see John with his weapon of smoke pointed in our direction. I hesitate, remembering the man floating in the salt water, the wound in his chest. Whatever this weapon does, there's no doubt this man intends to kill us with it.

They want to retreat like the others. Maybe we should let them go. Avoid further bloodshed. But they've killed so many. They tried to kidnap my father. That alone demands punishment. Where is the chief? I'm not sure what to do.

I glance to Ikaika at my side, and he shakes his head at me almost imperceptibly. We can't give in to the foreigners. This is our land, our home. They are the ones who don't belong—no matter if their captain is the one foretold or not. We can't surrender.

I turn back to John and raise my bloody hand across my chest to touch my shoulder, my knife angled and ready to strike at anyone who tries to move or hurt us. My hand drips with thin, salty blood that stains the bark cloth on my torso.

John lowers his weapon slightly, staring at me with the same, questioning look he had earlier, as though reasoning something out.

I look past him and feel my eyes go wide. I nearly open my mouth in warning, but snap it shut in an instant. I silently watch one of our men connect a large wooden club with the back of Cook's head. The captain's body twists at a strange angle before falling to the sand, his face landing in the white, frothy water. The tide recedes, and all goes silent, as if the world is standing at the precipice of a sheer cliff, holding its breath and waiting for the wind to tell it what to do next. Then a hand appears, holding an iron knife. It falls into Cook's back, and the world exhales.

Boom.

Sound returns to my ears in one terrifying crash, and the water rushes up the sand once more, disappearing from my view behind more thick, white smoke. I cough as I move out of the water and onto dry sand. As the clouds clear, John Harbottle is the first person I see.

"Where is he?" he yells, and I think he's speaking to himself, because there's no one here but me.

I look toward the line of trees beyond the sand and see our men dragging a blue-coated man with white hair inland. I know it is James Cook. And I know what they will do with his body.

Is this how a god dies?

But John doesn't see it, and I turn away to gauge what's left of the battle. The beach is lined with fallen men from both sides, white men in red coats and my people in brown bark. The rest of the sailors who abandoned the fight are almost to the *Resolution*. Do they know their leader is dead? The stolen skiff is still halfway on the sand, the lapping waves making a hollow sound each time they run into the hull.

"Where did they take him?" John is yelling at me now. He grasps my chin with one hand and presses hard while holding his weapon with the other. Smoke drifts from the thin metal end of it, moving as slowly as a sea turtle on sand. It reminds me of Father's smoking pipe.

"Please," he begs. His eyes brim with tears, and his hand falls from my face. His expression is full of sorrow—for his lost leader? "Where did they take him?"

I shake my head, and that's when I see it—floating in the sandy white shallows at the edge of the water just a few steps away.

Ikaika.

No.

I run to the body in the water and collapse to my knees. "*Auwē*," I cry. A circular puncture wound in his stomach spills blood into the water surrounding him.

I press my head to his chest and feel for his heartbeat. I press my hand against his mouth to feel for his breath. But it's not there. Ikaika's eyes are open, looking up into the sky, staring into the afterlife.

I cry into his chest and pound my fist into the sand. I pull at my hair and yank the bark cloth on my torso in frustration, in mourning. I look up in search of Father. He'll know what to do.

Because I don't. I don't know how to move or breathe or live after this.

But my father isn't here. Only one man is. John Harbottle. He glances across the beach like I did a few moments ago, rubbing his forehead as though tired and defeated, confused about how quickly things disintegrated into this. Then he looks at me with an expression of shock and sadness before dropping his foreign weapon to the sand, smoke still winding from the end of it.

And that's how I know what he did.

John Harbottle killed Ikaika. My betrothed. My love. My life.

My hand tightens around something hard, and I look down, surprised to see I'm still holding my knife.

John Harbottle's Journal
14 February 1779

Along the beach, there is a line of seaweed and driftwood that forms a barrier between the wet sand and the dry. This border marks how high the tide reaches each day; the water will not move past the debris it has washed ashore in the past. It's unchangeable, and a measure for how far one must pull up a boat or place other possessions to ensure nothing will be swept away by incoming waves.

When we first arrived in the bay in early January, our welcome was unrivaled. We were met by a kind people who were generous and happy and peaceful. It was not the dark and brooding welcome of the natives in New South Wales, who were elusive and hidden. Unwilling. Indeed, I speculated that the Hawai'ian people knew nothing of hate. The only hint of war was found in their weapons stores, though even those items seemed to be a collection of historical artifacts, unused for centuries. Perhaps from wars in the long-forgotten past.

But there was a barrier in the sand. A line of understanding. As long as we stayed within the safety of that perceived border, followed their rules and expectations, we had nothing to fear. We respected their gods, their beliefs, their traditions. We behaved cautiously in all matters, always quick to acquiesce to their governing laws. It was our measure of safety.

That line was washed away by the storm. We all felt it. The captain, the sailors. Even the natives. We didn't know what to think about the absence of their hospitality. They didn't understand the difference between trading and stealing; they didn't believe that some things can't be bartered. The captain armed us with musket fire while the indigenous came to the beach with weaponry I thought were useless relics.

I was wrong.

I was so wrong.

Our men fired. They injured and killed. But the natives didn't stop. They charged, fueled by their rage. Our men couldn't reload. Some escaped in the smaller boats, but the rest . . .

The losses were numerous on both sides.

I don't know how to bring the line back. I can't draw the barrier or build it. Not with tangible materials, at least. The mere act of trying to restore the line could simply break it all over again. I'm at a loss of what to do without James Cook at my side.

Oh, my captain.

'ehā

Chapter Four

"*Wahine.*" John's voice is a whisper as he falls to his knees in the sand. "*Wahine.*"

Woman.

John's word means he realizes I'm female. I think he finally recognizes me as the girl in the canoe he saw at the base of his ship. Was it only yesterday?

I brush away my hair that I'd pulled loose and stand with a cry. I march toward him, my knife in the air. When I reach him, he looks up at me, the expression of sorrow unchanged on his face. He must know what I intend to do, but he doesn't attempt to defend himself. I hesitate, not sure if I have it in me to kill an unarmed man. I kneel in front of him, my back to the water, and put the teeth of my knife to his neck, pressing it into his skin. A desperate sound escapes my lips as I think of Ikaika only a few steps behind me. Dead.

I want to end this man's life in front of me. Why won't he fight back? He doesn't even lean away from my weapon. He just looks at me with those sad eyes. I grit my teeth together, willing him to move, to speak—to do something that will give me an excuse to slice his neck.

Tears fall down my face, and I can't tell if the salty, bitter taste in my mouth is from them or the ocean water. Or maybe it's the sour tang of regret of everything that has happened today. Father was right. Battle is no place for girls, and right now, that's how I feel—like a little girl who doesn't know what to do. I look at John Harbottle's face, see the grief in his eyes, and my hand starts to fall from his neck.

Boom.

The sound comes from the ocean, and I spin around. A red-coated sailor stands in the water and aims his foreign weapon in my direction. He shouts something at me, but I don't understand his words.

John answers, yelling something back in a language I don't know. But his voice sounds off. Jumbled. I turn to see him on his back, a line across his chest where the white and blue cloth has been ripped. And beneath it, blood soaks into the fabric and spreads as though from a deep wound. I look to the knife in my hand, now fresh with blood, then back to John on the sand. It hits me in one solemn moment: I sliced him across the chest when I turned to see where the booming sound came from. A mixture of satisfaction and anger churns inside me. I feel sick to my stomach as guilt takes over, and I want to say something to John but don't know what.

John's eyes go wide as he sees something behind me, and I turn again just as the sailor walks out of the ocean toward us, his weapon still pointed at me. John and the sailor exchange heated words, and I would give anything to know what they say. But all I can see is the weapon coming closer and Ikaika in the corner of my eye, his body floating slowly in and out with the waves.

I scramble backward, behind John, as though he could defend me from this man. The sailor yells at John, moving his weapon back and forth between the two of us, like he's trying to argue his point.

I do the only thing I can think of to spare my life. I wrap my arm around John's neck. I pull him back toward me, so that his entire body is blocking mine, and I hold my knife to his neck again. This time, my hand trembles, and John's painful groan makes me flinch.

In a shaky voice, I say, "Tell him to back away."

John says something to the sailor, slow and clear.

The sailor yells at me, and I press the knife into John's neck again, praying to the gods I don't have to push any farther.

John yells at him again, and the man lowers his weapon.

This is my chance. "Stand up." I pull John to his feet, and though he's a head taller than I am, I manage to drag him along with me as I back away from the sailor and toward the stolen boat. My foot catches on something, and I look down and gasp. It's Ikaika's body in the shallow water. I bite my lip until it bleeds, trying to stifle the scream that wants to escape.

I force John into the skiff, trying to gather the bravery I earlier wanted to prove I had, when I headed straight into a battle I wasn't prepared for. I push the boat into the water then settle between two of the wide slats with John in front of me, laying him back to protect my body from the magic weapon the soldier on shore still holds.

"Don't move," I tell John, though I don't think he could move if he wanted to. The entire front of his coat is saturated with blood. I take a deep breath and grab one of the oars from the base of the boat. Pushing away from shore, I never take my eyes off the man on the beach. He's the only person there; everyone else has either died or run off.

I paddle south, away from the beach and away from Cook's massive ships. I paddle until the sailor is just a speck of red on the sand. I wonder how far his foreign weapon can reach. I paddle until my arms lose strength, and I realize I've no idea where I'm going. John's eyes fall closed, and I don't know if he's sleeping or dead. And then I think of Ikaika on the shore; I *know* he's not sleeping. I stop paddling and cry until sleep overcomes the pain.

Through no effort of my own, our vessel washes up on shore, and it's the scraping sound of the boat against the sand that brings me back to awareness. It's dark out. I look up to the sky and squint at the stars, trying to adjust to the dim light. The constellation of the canoe-bailer sits just above the horizon in the east. It's not midnight yet.

I'm wet and cold, and I long for a fire. But my limbs will not move. They feel heavy. I look down and wish I hadn't. John Harbottle lies across my body. It reminds me of another man, the one he killed, perhaps still lying dead at the meeting of water and land among a throng of others who have passed this day. I squeeze my eyes shut, pushing away images of Ikaika's body—swollen, cold, and lifeless.

I want to wail in mourning, but now is not the time. I shove John off me, then step out of the boat and scramble to the dry sand out of reach of the tide. The steadiness beneath my feet is a relief. I draw strength from the solid earth below me—I yearn to be firm and unyielding, not a disjointed mesh of emotions that will fall apart with a silent gust of wind. I shout out loud into the night. I want this day to be over. Forgotten.

John groans behind me. He's still alive? I stumble back to the boat and tighten my fingers on the rim. I should push it back out to sea. Make him disappear along with the memory of him killing Ikaika. Release the reminder of how he wouldn't defend himself against me, or the way my knife sliced across his chest without me realizing it.

I bend over next to the boat and vomit, upheaving my disgust. Disgust with him. With myself. I wipe my mouth with the back of my hand and look at John. His breathing is labored. Scratchy. He probably doesn't have much longer to live anyway. It wouldn't be cruel of me to end his life here, right now. It would be merciful, really. I could slice his throat—intentionally this time—and spare him the pain of a slower death. Besides, it's my right, isn't it? He killed Ikaika—the chief's prime navigator and my future husband. Who else but me has the right to end his life? This is war, after all.

My curved knife sits on the floor of the boat, and I reach for it, but I can't make my fingers slide into place. Instead, I let it hang from my fingers, holding it away from me like a diseased animal. I grit my teeth. *Do it, Maile.*

Before I have the chance to grip the knife properly, a hand grasps my forearm, and the weapon falls. I gasp in surprise and look at John. His eyes are wide, focused on mine with such clarity, I feel like he could slice me with his look alone. It makes him seem even younger, despite his white hair. Still holding onto my arm, he reaches across his body with his free hand and grabs my weapon. I tense and try to pull away, but John's grip is surprisingly tight and burns my skin. I watch him lift my weapon.

I steady myself for impact. I'm not afraid, though I thought I'd be. Instead I exhale a long sigh. Resolve fills my body, and I relax against his grip. Perhaps this is the release I need. Not revenge on this man for what he took from me, but a release of my own life, a permanent escape from the despair and uncertainty that has haunted me this day. A misery I know I'll never be rid of. I look into John's wide eyes and wait for my own death, ready to welcome the journey to my afterlife. A small smile forms on my lips in anticipation of meeting Ikaika there.

But the knife doesn't connect with my body. Instead, John tosses it behind him into the ocean. Away.

My eyes grow as wide as his, and his hand against my arm begins to shake.

"Help," he says in my language. His voice is a whisper, barely there in the heavy night air. "Help me." He drops my arm and squeezes his eyes tight against the pain.

I back away and spin around, hoping there's someone else here. Anyone else. That he's not talking to me but begging another to save him.

"*Auwē*." I look to my right and left, trying to determine where we are. The beach curves out to sea on my far left and continues north after a short bend inland. On my right, a series of black rocks sit in the water, forming a barrier for a shallow pool against the beach. Beyond them are more rocks, pushed up against an imposing reef with no sand to walk along, even at low tide. We are far south of my homestead, but still within the boundaries of my father's land. I remember there's an abandoned hut nearby, used by the men when they go boar hunting.

I curse as I pull the boat farther up the sand, far enough so it will be safe from the incoming tide. I stand over John and kick the side of the boat. The vibration rattles his eyes open.

"Can you walk?" I ask. I can't carry him through the forest by myself. I silently hope he's immobile so I have an excuse to leave him.

But he sits up and manages to stand in the boat, though not without another painful groan. He stumbles out and falls onto my shoulders. It takes all of my strength to hold his weight. And even though his body has been sprawled across mine for the last several hours, I still cringe at his touch.

"I . . . can't," he mumbles, starting to sink toward the ground, sliding down my body.

I grab one of his arms and yank him back up, surprised by my own strength. "Yes, you can." I drape his arm across my shoulder and wrap my arm around his waist, supporting him as much as I can. "You have to."

John's head bobbles in what I think is a nod, and we stagger inland. Once we're beyond the sand and onto hard ground, our steps become surer, and I'm pleased with the progress we make. After stopping to rest a few times along the way, we finally make it to the clearing. A simple hut is tucked into the side of a small, open field. Coconut trees outline an area just large enough for a fire and a few temporary shelters.

Kicking open the door to the hut, I drag John across the floor to a pile of woven mats serving as a bed. I'm too tired to find wood or build a fire. I'm not sure I could carry him back outside to warm up by it anyhow. Instead, I gather as many blankets and mats as I can from all corners of the room and drape them over his body. I save a couple for myself, and after rolling into a length of fabric, I collapse to the floor on the other side of the room, not wanting to be near my enemy.

Long after I think John must be asleep, I hear his voice from across the room, muffled by the layers of blankets.

"Thank you."

I begin to sob and welcome sleep, part of me hoping I never wake up.

JOHN HARBOTTLE'S JOURNAL
14 February 1779

I write these words by moonlight. Is it fortuitous that I carry my small journal with me always? Perhaps time will tell. But for now, amidst pain, sorrow, and, to be truthful, a little fear, I write what I can while my mind is lucid enough for transcription. And while my captor is asleep, unaware.

I don't know her name or why she fought in the battle today, but I'm certain she's the woman I saw below the Resolution *less than forty-eight hours ago. Her cries of anguish have pierced my heart in a way nothing else ever has. She mourns for her companion on the beach. It is a verbal manifestation of the turmoil I feel inside, and it makes me feel connected to her somehow.*

Can grief do that? Make you feel a common bond with a stranger, even an enemy? It doesn't explain the unexpected pull I felt when I first saw her, though. I wasn't grieving then.

My mind is beginning to muddle.

I'm not a man of many regrets. I regret the death of my parents and the death of my captain—for I've no doubt James Cook is dead by now—but those were events out of my control. Of the things I could control, there is only one I wish I could take back. Though trained in the skills of war like every naval officer, I had not killed anyone before him. He was my first and, God willing, he will be my last, but I wish he were my never.

Maybe then her cries wouldn't haunt me so.

Maybe then I wouldn't feel connected to her in a way that defies all sensibility.

ʻelima

Chapter Five

I wake to the sound of chattering teeth and realize it's not me. I'm too warm, so I roll out of the layers of fabric that envelop me. Sitting up, I see John on his side, shivering in his blankets. I move closer and feel his skin, pulling away from the heat of it. Using one of his blankets, I wipe the sweat from his forehead. A tuft of brown hair escapes the mound of white on his head.

Drawing my eyebrows together, I pull at his white hair. My mouth opens in disbelief as it comes away easily, revealing a head of dark brown hair tied loosely with a string in back. The white hair was a lie. What a strange custom—to wear false hair when your own is perfectly fine. I toss the fake hair aside. It makes the burning heat radiating from his body worse.

John mumbles something I don't understand. His eyes are scrunched tight, and he tosses his head back and forth, still asleep. He's probably in the depths of a fever nightmare. I'm not ready to face him yet. I stand and grab a water gourd from a table in the corner and leave the hut.

Sunlight filters sideways through the trees in the east. It's early still. I hike to the spring that flows just a thrown spear's distance from the clearing, the reason this site was chosen for habitation years ago. Filling the gourd with water, I pour it over my head, gasping at the coldness of it. I rub at the blood staining my hands and arms. I rub harder at my face and neck, wondering about blood I can't see. How much of it is the blood of the sailors I killed? How much is Ikaika's, or even John's? I'm not sure. All I know is it's too much, and I cringe at the sight of it on my clothing. It will take more than the rinse of water to erase those marks.

I untangle my hair with my fingers, knotted from a night of restless sleep, and then gather it into a braid that sways just below my hips. Filling the water gourd again, I pluck the *nahele* weeds growing near the spring before hesitantly walking back to the hut.

After being outside, the interior of the hut is dark to my eyes, so I open the window flaps that line the walls. I take in a deep breath, realizing how trapped I'd felt in the darkness. The light and air help.

I kneel next to John and wonder again why I'm doing this. Saving him is not going to bring Ikaika back. But I can't let him die. If it weren't for John, I would've been killed by that sailor's weapon on the beach. I'm not sure if John was trying to convince that man not to hurt me, but if that's the case, I have a feeling it may have something to do with my being female. So much of yesterday is confusing, and I don't know what to make of it.

I soak a cloth in the cold water and wipe at John's head and neck before rolling him onto his back. I lay the cloth on his forehead and hold my breath as he opens his eyes. They are a blue-green color, like the shallow water near the reef at midmorning. I decide he's not a handsome man. His nose is too pointy, the skin beneath his eyes bulge, which makes his eyes look too large, and his lips are so thin and taut they rival the horizon in straightness. Now that I can see his real hair in the daylight, I realize it has a slight wave to it, and small, curly, dark-brown wisps gather around his hairline.

When I look back at his eyes, I exhale and gather my courage to examine his wound. I unfold the blankets covering him. I feel him watching my face, so I avoid making eye contact and instead focus on his chest in front of me. After I clumsily push around the shiny contraptions that hold his coat together in front. John, his face twisted in pain, slowly shows me how to detach one of the connections. I follow the line of them down his chest and undo each one the way he did. After opening the blue coat, I tear at the white cloth beneath. At least I think it's supposed to be white. It's dark now with dried blood.

The slash across his chest is deep but clean. I've not mended such a serious injury before, but I've seen my sister, Haukea, do it often enough. I soak another cloth in water and wipe away the dried blood from the skin surrounding the wound. When I begin to clean the cut itself, John flinches.

"How bad is it?" he asks.

I don't look at him, just stuff a few *nahele* weeds in my mouth so I don't have to answer. As I chew, I think about how his voice sounds much stronger than it did the night before. I hope it's a good sign. When I'm done cleaning the skin, I pull the weeds out of my mouth and lay them carefully over part of the knife wound.

"What are you doing?" John lifts his head to look at his chest, but I shove him back down and stuff some of the weeds into his mouth to shut him up. "What do I—?"

I push his chin up to close his mouth and say, "Chew," before placing more weeds in my own mouth. After a moment, I slide my finger between his teeth to scoop out the medicine and then apply it across the injury along with my own bitter mouthful of weeds. There is just enough to cover the deep slice.

I lift John's head and slide my leg beneath it to prop him up. He opens his mouth to say something again, but before any words escape, I press the water gourd to his lips. "Drink."

He does. Greedily. This is another good sign.

"Thank you," he says when I pull the gourd away.

I move my leg too abruptly, and his head hits the mat, followed by a painful groan. I ignore it, stand, and leave the hut without looking at his face.

Once outside, I pause and bite my fingers to keep them from trembling. *What am I doing*? I follow an abandoned pig trail on the far side of the clearing, gathering passion fruit and mountain apples that grow at my shoulder level. I pause at the spring again and peel at my fruit, enjoying a moment of solitude while I eat my breakfast.

I need to get home. Father will be worried, and I'll be expected to help with the injured. And the care of our dead. My stomach lurches at the thought. I don't want to see Ikaika's body. With the gods' mercy, his family will have finished with him by now, and any evidence of his death will be wiped away. I wish it were as easy to deal with my memories. I long to scrub away at my mind, erase the terror I have seen. The heartache I still experience.

How could things have turned out so wrong in so short a time? Everything was going perfectly. I was born a daughter to a chief, so I've known since my first memories that I was destined to wed. To be given in marriage. My younger brother, La'akea, as the only male child of my parents, will inherit a portion of the island to rule as his own. My older sister, Haukea, has been reserved should a special marriage be necessary, like to the son of an allied chief, or to an enemy if peace is needed.

But me? I am second daughter to Kalani the chief. My engagement to the chief's navigator may not have been a political union, but it was honorable, a showing of respect for Ikaika's ability as a trusted leader in the ranks of my father's royal family and a tribute to Ikaika's skill with the chief's canoe fleet. It was a match I'd thanked the gods for on more than one occasion. A childhood friend turned welcome lover—any woman would be a fool to discard such a blessing.

How quickly that ideal life had been torn from me. And by the man in the hut a short distance away. Why hadn't I killed him when I had the chance? Why hadn't he killed me when he had the chance? Perhaps we are both fools.

I walk back to the hut with an armful of fruit. Inside, I place them on the table in the corner.

"What is your name?"

I turn to see John sitting up and watching me from the bed. Ignoring his question, I grab a small roll of cloth from the table and kneel next to him. "The medicine can't work if it's not directly on the wound." I readjust the weeds and wind the cloth around his torso, holding the medicine in place. I keep my head down, avoiding his gaze. When I'm done tying off the cloth, John grabs my wrist and pulls me gently toward him.

"Your name?"

I finally look up at his questioning face. "Maile."

"Maile," he repeats. "Why were you on the beach yesterday?"

I slam my teeth together in an audible snap. "I . . . what do you mean?"

"There were no other women there," he says. "I didn't think it was a common practice of your people to have female warriors."

"It's not our way," I say, feeling like I have to defend my people and my own actions at the same time. "I just . . . I don't know." I had wanted to prove to Father I wasn't a little girl. How wrong I was.

"That man I . . ." John's voice falls to a whisper. "Was he your brother?"

I take in a sharp breath but manage to shake my head.

"Your husband?"

My hand flies to my mouth to stifle my cry. I shake my head again and feel tears fall down my face. I stand and step backwards. "One moon." I wipe at my cheeks and raise my chin. "We were to be married in a month."

"I'm sorry."

I turn away from him and look out the window to the vegetation beyond. It's a blur of green because of the tears in my eyes. I can't tell where one leaf ends and another begins. The hues blend together in a mass of chaos. I want it to clear, to show me a distinct path. Because right now I feel like I'm stumbling this way and that, unsure of the right way to go.

John clears his throat behind me.

I turn and see him biting his lip, hesitant before he speaks.

"This is going to sound terribly rude and insensitive." He looks down. "And I know my timing isn't ideal, but I don't think I can walk, let alone stand on my own."

I'm not a fool. Even the strongest of men wouldn't be able to walk under similar circumstances.

"I need to relieve myself."

I draw my brows together, not understanding.

"Urinate. Use the head. *Hanawai*."

"Oh."

"Yes. Oh."

I don't understand why he's embarrassed. I help him to his feet. He cries out in pain so loudly a flood of guilt washes over me for being the cause of it. We slowly shuffle outside and take a few steps toward a coconut tree. I stand and wait for him, but he clears his throat again.

"I don't think I can do it with you standing right here."

I roll my eyes and prop his arm against the tree before stepping away. When he calls for me again, I pull his arm around me.

"Thank you," he says.

I wish he'd stop saying that. Because every time he does, I think of the wound across his chest. He can't be grateful for that.

Settling him back on his bed, I give him the water gourd again and make sure he drinks enough. I retrieve the fruits from the table and spin around. "I need to return home. My father's homestead is an hour north of here. I'll be back this afternoon."

"You're the chief's daughter?"

I can't believe I let that slip. I square my shoulders and try to exude dignity, ignoring the bloodstains on my clothing. Dismissing his question, I say, "You need to rest. Try to sleep so the medicine can work."

"Why are you doing this? Helping me, I mean." John lies back on the woven mats. "Don't misunderstand; I am extremely grateful. I just . . ." He pauses and looks at me with his blue-green eyes. "I killed your—"

"Ikaika," I say, interrupting him. "His name was Ikaika."

"Maile." His eyes are sad, the lids drooping with exhaustion.

I'm not sure telling him my name was the right thing to do. My stomach twists every time he says it.

"Maile," John says again, his eyes finally falling closed. "Thank you, Maile."

I grunt and drop the fruit next to him on the bed. He can figure out how to eat them later if he wants to. I'm leaving. And after a minute of watching him sleep, I storm out of the hut.

I march toward the beach along the path we hiked last night.

It's much easier now that my energy is back and I'm not dragging a dying sailor with me. I find the boat easily, the oar I used in our escape sitting next to it in the sand. When I slide the oar into the boat, it catches on something beneath the large wooden slat in the back. I yank on the oar and hear a ripping sound. I draw it back carefully, and a satchel slides with it, snagged on a splinter of wood.

The oar falls from my hands, the handle slamming against the boat with a loud knock. I flinch, spinning in a circle to make sure no one is around to hear it. Because I know exactly what that satchel is—it's the navigation equipment Cook had been looking for. The items he said we stole; the items we denied were in our possession.

I look beneath the rear slat of the boat. A swatch of fabric remains wedged in the wood. The satchel must have been hidden back there the whole time. Cook was right—our people did steal it. We could have given it back. We could have prevented so much bloodshed.

Ikaika could still be alive.

I take a deep breath and open the satchel, revealing clothing, small iron tools, rolls of what look like thin bark, and several metal items I can't begin to guess the function of. I lift a large, sun-colored device. It's much more complicated than the small weapons we've traded for, its triangular shape awkward to hold.

I set it down and pick up a hard, rectangular item. The outer portion is stiff and echoes when I knock on it. It's filled with a material that reminds me of bark cloth pounded impossibly thin, yet it is so uniform I wonder what tree was used to make it. Odd tiny symbols fill each layer of identical cloth, and it's all bound together on one side with what must be an invisible gum paste. The symbols don't look like the figures our people carve into stone, and I wonder what they mean.

It's impossible for me to return these things to the sailors. If word spread that we had the equipment and the chief didn't return it, didn't even know about it, he would lose the respect of his people. It would guarantee threats to his position, challenges from lesser chiefs. War. I must hide it—somewhere no one will find it. I have to protect my father's honor.

After shoving the items back into the satchel and cinching it closed, I push the boat into the water far enough that it catches a deeper current and won't return to this shore. Perhaps the red coats will find it. Perhaps it will be lost at sea. Either way, I'm glad to be rid of the reminder of so much pain. So much death.

I lift the satchel. It's heavy, but I have no choice. I head in the direction of my homestead, but rather than enter the village, I turn toward the higher hills, away from prying eyes. I climb for almost an hour until I reach the forest and find an open spot on the ground. With nothing to dig with, I rifle through the pack of stolen items. The rectangular bound cloths and golden device are no help. The small round items with a clear surface are of no use, either. They seem almost as hard as iron, but the edges are too smooth to help me dig. I find another strange tool, though: sanded wooden sticks lashed together into several connected triangles. It should work.

I slam the wooden tool into the soil and begin to dig, working to expand the hole until it is large enough to hold everything. After carefully placing each item in the hollow, I cover it with the excavated dirt and pat it down. I have no idea what any of the objects are or their specific functions, but I know they are vital to John and the sailors. But it doesn't matter. I have to protect the chief.

Looking around the clearing for something to mark the site, I gather several green coconuts that have fallen from nearby trees. They likely fell in the squall that passed a few days ago, since they're not yet ripe. I place the coconuts on the freshly turned soil, forming a small rainbow shape over the spot. It's not noticeable enough to stand out should someone pass this way, but I'll find it easily if needed.

I only hope I'll never have to.

John Harbottle's Journal
15 February 1779

I've never met a member of the chief's royal family until now. The chief was selective about who was allowed to engage with him in those early meetings, and as Cook's translator, I was permitted to attend. But no matter how many of the chief's priests or advisors accompanied him, he never brought members of his immediate family. I'd always wondered what they were like.

The children of the village often laughed when I spoke, not because of my humor but because of my accent and the way my words sounded. I know this because often a child would mockingly repeat something I had said, followed by an outburst of giggles from the other children surrounding him. I didn't mind. The sound of children's laughter was a welcome sound indeed, especially after years on a ship with only the coarse banter of the crew to fill my ears.

Though many of the adults seemed impressed with my attempts to master their language, I could tell some wanted to laugh as well when I talked, but they kept their amusement to suppressed smiles, measured in their teasing as a show of respect. That restraint was manifest tenfold among those in the chief's court—guards, holy men, advisors. They were so convincingly indifferent toward my efforts to communicate, I wonder if they can hear at all.

But I remained curious about the chief's family, speculating what their demeanor might be like. Would they laugh at my words? Perhaps turn away to keep me from witnessing their amusement? Or would they remain stoic in their response as though I had never spoken?

The chief's daughter, my captor, seems to favor the latter. I doubt she has any concern for the way I pronounce words in her native tongue given our circumstances, but her communication with me thus far extends only to what is required and nothing more. Whether this

is a common practice for her or merely a result of the strained begin-
ning to our acquaintance, I can't say.

    Maile.

    Her name is Maile.

'eono

Chapter Six

The smoke of several fires surrounds my home. There's a stench in the air that churns my stomach—the smell of burning flesh. Considering the number of dead on the beach yesterday needing to be incinerated, these fires will continue for at least another week. I head for my father's hut but am stopped before I reach it.

"Maile?" My mother's familiar arms wrap around me. "Maile, where have you been?" Her voice breaks into a sob. "I thought we'd lost you."

The strength I'd managed to conjure in the last day finally leaves me, and I collapse into her arms. She holds me in place, her embrace supporting all of me, and I cry with her.

After a moment I feel two more arms around us, and I know it's my father. I pull away to get a good look at him. When relief fills my entire body like a tidal wave, I realize I wasn't entirely sure he was alive. I touch the bandaged knife wound in his side.

The chief grunts and brings his rough hand to my face. "Where have you been?" he asks, echoing my mother. The slow release of his breath tells me he was more worried than his controlled expression lets on.

"I escaped the battle in one of the foreigner's boats," I say, looking down to avoid his eyes. Father has an innate ability to determine if a person is lying, his children included. It's part of what makes him a strong ruler. He already disapproves of me fighting in the battle yesterday; I don't know what he'll do if he learns I'm hiding one of our enemies in the forest. Or that I buried the items stolen from the sailors.

I point north, away from the direction I'd just come. "I spent the night . . . in the coconut grove just beyond the fishponds." I nod, as if that will confirm the truth of my tale. "I was so exhausted from yesterday." My shoulders fall, and I try not to cough, the smoke from the fires stinging my eyes. "I decided to rest for the night before returning home this morning."

Father doesn't respond; he's focused elsewhere. I follow his gaze and see Ikaika's parents a few huts away. His mother is shaving the hair off her husband with a bone blade as a symbol of mourning. She leaves a strip down the middle of his head. When she finishes, she cries a slow, sad chant of regret. It's a sound I will have to get used to these next days—the sound of grieving. A part of me feels like turning around and heading back to the hut of an injured white man, even though he's the cause of all this.

Father squeezes my shoulder, and I return my attention to him. I can't hide my grief. He can tell I know Ikaika's dead. That I've known it since the battle. He drops his hand and says nothing else as he walks toward Ikaika's parents.

I'm not sure if he intends for me to follow him, but I don't. Instead I shiver and walk into my hut, disgusted with my weakness that I prefer the company of Ikaika's murderer to the anguish of those who lament his death. At least with John, I'm in control.

Of his fate, his life. Here, I feel anything but in control. Here, I'll crumble into a thousand pieces the moment someone says Ikaika's name aloud. I fall onto my bed and cry into the mats, my eyes overrun with the smoke of the village and the sorrow it holds.

An hour later, someone shakes me awake. I open my eyes to see Haukea looming over me.

"Maile, wake up." She tugs on my braid. "It's time."

"Time for what?" I yawn and roll onto my back, blinking up at her. She's just a year older than I am, and some have mistaken us for twins because we look so much alike. But while I enjoy fishing, navigating, and going on hunts with my father, she prefers to keep company with the women and paint elaborate designs on bark cloth, reveling in the gossip of the village. The women in those *kapa* huts are like squabbling geese, nipping at each other about things I couldn't care less about.

"It's time for you to visit him," she says softly, her brows lowering at an angle.

For a moment I think she's talking about John, and my heart races, wondering how she found out about him, but then I understand the sorrow in her expression.

"No," I say. "I can't." I'm not ready to see Ikaika's body.

"It's expected." She stands and reaches for my hand, pulling me from the ground. "Father sent me to get you . . . Oh."

I follow her gaze to my clothing, stepping back in surprise. I forgot I was still wearing the bloodstained cloth.

"I'll change first," I say. I wonder if my parents noticed the stains.

"Good idea." Haukea nods. She moves past me and gathers a fresh wrap from the corner. "I'll help you."

I untie the belt holding the soft bark against my skin and peel away the fabric, dusting off the thin layer of salt and dirt that is leftover from the events of yesterday. Haukea helps me with my wrap, securing it tight at my waist. Then she frowns at my hair.

"May I?" she asks, pointing to my braid.

"Yes." I'm fine with any excuse to prolong having to see Ikaika.

Haukea undoes my rough braid and brushes through it until all the tangles are out. She braids it again, but this time, she brings the end up, twirling it on my head into a bun. Securing it in place, she pulls a white gardenia from her own hair and pins it in mine. After rubbing something off my chin, she steps back and looks me up and down.

"You look beautiful," she says, a little surprised.

I'm not offended. It's no secret I've never paid much attention to how I look, or tried to refine my manner the way she does. As the first daughter of the chief, Haukea has lived her life knowing she's meant to marry for a political purpose one day and will represent our family and our people. She's always had the pressure of being perfect. It's a responsibility I've thanked the gods was never mine.

But Haukea fills the role naturally. She's beautiful and poised, and she takes pride in her obligation to our father. While I would have pushed back against every attempt to mold me into what was needed, Haukea considers it a privilege.

"In fact you look like you're about to—" Haukea cuts her words short, turning her head away. She didn't do it quick enough, though; I saw the tears in her eyes.

"About to be married?" I finish for her, wiping my own stray tear. I'm surprised I have any left after sobbing through the night. "You lie," I say, trying to lighten the mood. "My eyes are red and swollen, my voice is raw, and you've already seen how clean my hair and skin are after . . . after everything that happened."

"No," she says, stepping closer. "You look perfect. It is perfect for him." She leans forward and presses her nose against mine, breathing in deeply before wrapping her arms around me and embracing me. "I'm so sorry, Maile."

I hug her back, grateful for her kindness. "Thank you."

She steps away, fixing the flower in my hair. Then she nods. After a few deep breaths, I'm ready for the mourning ritual. Haukea links her arm with mine and walks me to Ikaika's hut. When we get there, I squeeze her arm in gratitude before letting her go and pausing at the threshold of the hut, waiting to be invited in.

"Maile." Ikaika's mother waves me over.

I slowly walk toward her and kneel in front of Ikaika's body. His torso and loins are covered by a bleached cloth. He won't be burned like some of the other bodies. Cremation is reserved for those without honor, like the enemy soldiers or those who failed to fight valiantly. But because of Ikaika's rank and the *mana* that exists in his body, he'll be treated differently. They'll take his limbs and preserve his bones, forming them into jewelry or other relics that will be passed down for generations in his family, protecting them and giving them his strength.

I rise to my knees and bend over his head, pressing my nose to each temple. His face still looks like him, though the color is off. I know he's gone, though parts of him will always be with the flesh that remains. I can't hold back the tears anymore, and I begin my slow chant of sorrow and grief, a lamentation I have a right to bestow as his betrothed. I run my hand along his bare head as I sing. His hair has already been cut off and stowed away; it will be preserved like his bones will be. I sing of his strength, his wisdom, and his devotion to me. He always treated me with respect and love, and I'll forever be grateful for his kindness.

When I reach the end of my chant, Ikaika's father brings something to me.

"His body will be buried in a cave," he says as he places the large whale tooth in my hands. "But a part of him needs to go back to the ocean."

"Of course."

Ikaika wore this necklace, a gift from his grandfather, for most of his life. Because of that, it contains some of his *mana*, and it's only right it is returned to the sea where Ikaika was most at home. I swallow hard as I stand, trying to exude honor but feeling inadequate. After taking one last look at Ikaika's body, I head to the door.

As I step out, a holy man waits with stripped *kī* leaves and, while brushing them over me, offers a cleansing chant on my behalf. After spending time with the dead, I must be purified before joining the living again. When he's done, I hurry toward the beach and find Ikaika's small outrigger canoe. The beach is clear and peaceful, so different from yesterday when crowds of warriors battled. After carefully placing the whale tooth in the canoe, I push the vessel into the water and paddle out past the break.

I can see the downed sails of the *Resolution*, which is farther out than it was yesterday. The foreigners retreated but haven't left. There's enough distance between us that I won't be bothered on my errand. When I determine I'm out far enough, I stop paddling and carefully drop Ikaika's necklace into the water. This will be his last voyage. He'll never follow the path of the stars at night or manipulate the sails of a canoe to best harness the wind. No more memorizing where we've been to determine where we are and where we need to go. Because this is it. He's never going anywhere ever again.

I lie along the hollow of the canoe, my back flat against the hull. I pretend I'm in the middle of the ocean, no islands in sight. No humans, no birds, nothing to clue me in to where I am. The sun is too high to determine where it rose and where it will fall, so I close my eyes and listen to the water as it sloshes against the small canoe; I can feel the ocean breathe. I spread my fingers along the wooden sides to sense the pattern and speed of the wave crests, the way Ikaika taught me. Land is near. The water tells me that much. And not just land—our land. Home.

But it doesn't feel like home anymore. Not without Ikaika. And not when there are strangers here. The wind hasn't just shifted. It's a new wind altogether. I don't know how to decipher this wind. I don't know the pictures in this sky, or the pattern of this water. Nothing I've been taught will help me navigate this new world. One with strange weapons, new languages, foreign clothing. One where a man refuses to defend himself against me, tries to protect me, thanks me . . . all after killing the man I loved.

I sit up, dipping my hand into the water and feeling the warmth, the push and pull of the current. I wish it were later in the year, when the humpback whales return from their migration. As my 'aumākua, my ancestor spirits, the whales' presence always gives me confidence things will be right.

This is my island, my world. And I'm not going to let that man—these men—push their way into our lives without fighting against it. They need to leave and never come back. We may not be able to erase the damage they've already done, but perhaps we can prevent something worse from happening.

At dusk, I walk into the hut without warning, startling John, who is sitting against the wall next to the pile of mats. His hands drop to his sides when he sees me.

"What are you doing?" I point toward his chest, now covered with his stained shirt and blue coat. Had he been trying to fasten it closed? I amend my question. "Where are you going?"

Guilt flashes across his face, knowing he's been caught trying to escape. He clears his throat. "I need to return to my men." His voice is weak, and I step closer to get a better look at him. He's still sweating, feverish. I reach for his neck, my hand burning before it even makes contact with his skin.

"You're not going anywhere," I say, kneeling before sliding his coat off his shoulders. The added heat from the fabric will make his fever worse.

"So am I to be your prisoner?" John's face is still, his mouth impossibly straight, revealing no emotion. But his eyes tell me he's confused about what his being here means. I don't want him to stay, but the sooner I can heal him, the sooner he and his men can go.

"Not my prisoner. I'm not going to kill you," I say. "Or hurt you." I pull off another layer of his clothing. The wound on his bare chest is red and irritated. "I won't hurt you again, I mean." I step away and put both items of clothing on the small side table. Maybe I'll mend them at some point. "But you've no idea where you are. You have no means to communicate for rescue." I motion toward his chest. "You won't get far in your condition."

"A prisoner," he repeats.

"No, because I don't want you here!" I spit out the words quickly, with too much emotion behind them. *This is my home,*

I remind myself. *I am in control.* "The moment you're healed, I'll take you to your men. Then you can all leave and never come back." The healthier he is, the more leverage we'll have in returning him to his men. Besides, I owe him for sparing my life.

He breathes out slowly. "The small boat we came here in—the one your people stole and that you used to get away. Where is it?"

"It's gone," I say. It's the truth, though I don't add that I'm the one who pushed it out to sea. Away. And I definitely don't tell him what I found hidden in the rear of the boat. He doesn't need any encouragement to attempt another escape. I narrow my eyes, daring him to accuse me of lying.

John just nods and asks, "And the captain? What have they done with him?"

"I don't know." Another half-truth. James Cook was a man of strength, a respected leader. Though he ended up being an enemy, he was still revered by our people. Perhaps he was not a god, but he commanded his men, introduced us to metal, showed us a civilization we'd never known. I may not know where his body is, but I know he won't be burned with the other sailors. My people will protect the power that remains within his bones.

I think of Ikaika—of visiting his body and mourning his loss both in public and in private. I see a similar sadness in John's eyes. He mourns for his captain. And though I may not understand him or his ways, I understand his sorrow.

"But I will find out what they've done with him," I add. Perhaps John needs to say goodbye to his captain in his own way, too. I'm not sure he deserves the chance, but I know the pain of grief can be much more powerful than a knife wound.

John looks up at me, his eyes wandering to the flower in my hair. "Thank you, Maile."

John Harbottle's Journal
16 February 1779

This fever makes it hard to determine how much time has passed. I keep slipping in and out of consciousness, not knowing if it's still the same day. Has Maile come and gone without me realizing it? Perhaps she will never come back and I will die in this abandoned hut, forgotten.

In one of my bouts of fever-induced sleep, I dreamt of a night spent aboard the Resolution not long ago. The captain was irritated, frustrated at facing yet another winter of waiting for the ice to thaw enough for us to continue searching for the passage. Combined with the constant deterioration of the ship and the amateur inspection it received before leaving port, his temper was the worst I'd seen. I'd been with him through two other voyages, so I knew this was not his common disposition, or at least it never used to be.

I sat in the officers' quarters, our meal nothing more than flat cakes and sauerkraut since our salted meat stores had run out. As I glanced through the windows into the hall that connects to the galley, I saw a line of men waiting for their portions. They peered into our quarters as they waited, as they did every day. It's an arrangement the captain had always insisted on: If the crew sees the officers are not above eating the pickled cabbage the men claim to detest, they will eat it, too. It's why no man had ever died from scurvy on any of James Cook's ships, a feat unheard of.

The captain's legacy will be more than the lands and peoples he's discovered or the instruments he's invented. It will be more than the detailed maps he's made to improve the inaccurate shorelines of several continents. Despite the deterioration of his spirit at times, he will always be remembered as one who cared for the men under his command—for their health, their happiness, and their safe return home.

Will the world know what happened to him here? Or will his memory be lost like his body, dying somewhere on this island, perhaps in another abandoned hut? A secret kept by a people more wondrous and unrestrained than any I've before encountered.

ʻehiku

Chapter Seven

I brace myself against the waves, one foot deep in the sand beneath the water, the other pressed against the black rock face to prevent me from slamming against it with each crest that comes. With a small bone knife, I pry the sea snails from the rock one by one, depositing them into a woven basket. *Scrape* and *plunk*. *Scrape* and *plunk*. The rhythm of the movements and sounds, combined with the ebb and flow of water against the rock face, soothes my mind into emptiness. The morning passes this way for an indiscriminate length, until the basket is full and there are no snails left.

I carry the basket to shore near my homestead and debate finding a new basket and location to harvest, when I see something white on the horizon. Instead of numerous square-shaped sails atop a massive ship, there's a single triangle above a small canoe simple enough for one man to maneuver. It's one of ours.

With my full basket in hand, I hurry to the homestead and find the chief.

"Someone approaches on the water," I say. "From the southeast. I think it's Makana."

Father moves wordlessly toward the beach, and I follow, curious about what news Makana brings. He's more a scout than a spy, navigating through nearby islands to gain information about possible threats. He left after Cook and his ships did, almost two weeks ago at the start of war season. The fact that he's back so soon isn't a good sign. Once on shore, he heads straight for my father.

"'Eleu, ranking chief of Wai'ole, is planning an invasion before the dry season." Makana takes deep breaths, trying to recover from the exertion of hurrying back to the island. "It could be sooner. I only know he will hit on the south end." Makana looks briefly at me then back to the chief. "He plans to take the entire island."

My father steps backward and crosses his arms, and I nearly drop my basket. The entire island? I've never heard of such a thing. A chief might declare war for food or resources, even the need for women and children. But for an island? As ranking chief, 'Eleu already has control of Wai'ole, a large island just south of us that is bigger and more populated than our own. What need would there be except greed for power? It's not sanctioned by the gods.

"We're in no condition to fight," my father says. "Our resources are depleted, and we've lost too many men."

"Lost men?" Makana looks past the trees inland, as though he could determine which men are no longer here. "What happened?" He knows we've been short on food and supplies after we gave so much to honor Cook and his sailors. It's one reason I've been out harvesting sea snails. As daughter of the chief, I don't usually have to work at such menial tasks, but in an emergency even the chief himself will join his people in preparing and cooking the food. But Makana wasn't here for the battle with the foreign sailors.

Makana points toward the *Resolution*. "And why has Lono returned?"

"They came ashore," I say. "They tried to kidnap the chief."

Makana's eyes widen. "And we fought back?"

I nod. "Their captain was killed."

"Lono."

"Ikaika, too."

"No." Makana pulls me into an awkward embrace, the basket of snails between us. "I'm so sorry, Maile."

I look up at my father. "What will we do?"

"We can't fight," he says. "With their numbers, they would likely overtake us." He turns back toward the homestead. "We'll have to solve this another way."

I lower the basket of sea snails to the ground and fall in step behind him, knowing exactly what he plans. He's going to offer my sister in marriage. If the foreigners had arrived in 'Eleu's bay, would it be his supplies diminished, his men who'd been lost? Why would the gods allow this to happen to our people and not his?

I wait in the council hut with my father while Makana gathers the rest of my family. A tall, thatched roof sits high above an open-air shelter. The chief sits at one end on an elevated platform, but I can't make myself sit on any of the woven mats set in front of him. Instead I pace the room, grateful for the breeze that passes through, easing my nerves and silencing the warning voices in my head. If a marriage arrangement doesn't work, I don't know what we'll do.

My mother walks in, followed by my sister, Haukea. She sends me a questioning glance, wondering what this is about.

Suddenly my nervousness shifts from the fate of our island to the fate of my sister. She's known this was what she was saved for, but it's different now that it's here.

Our younger brother, La'akea, runs in. He moves to sit next to my mother, Amai, but not before sticking his foot out to make me trip in my pacing. At fifteen years old, my brother still acts like a toddler sometimes.

Father repeats Makana's message to the rest of the family, explaining the threat from the island just south of us, 'Eleu's plans to attack, the current condition of our warriors and supplies, and how we'll be slaughtered if we choose to fight.

Haukea glances at me again before our father has a chance to say what he proposes, because she already knows.

I stop pacing and take a seat next to her. While our father explains his plan to present Haukea as a wife to a member of the rival chief's family, I run my hand through her long hair. It's something she's always loved, something that's always calmed her whenever she is sick or nervous. She leans into my fingers as I press them against her scalp, and I imagine brushing away her anxiety at the same time.

"We'll leave right away," Father says. "In one hour."

So soon? It's midday, and I realize he probably wants to take advantage of the daylight. I pull Haukea closer and lean in, pressing the side of my cheek against hers.

"It'll be fine," I say. "They'll love you."

How couldn't they? She's always been the pretty one, the well-behaved one. She's prepared for this her entire life. Now that it's here, despite my fear that I may never see my sister again, I know she's ready for this.

Haukea exhales slowly, shaking her hands out to calm her nerves. "Help me get ready?" she asks me.

I smile and nod before turning back to Father as he finishes his instructions.

"I want to make an impression," he says. "We'll take the entire royal court, including myself, Haukea, and Amai."

So my mother is to go as well.

"We'll go in full dress, with a set of guards, a holy man, and my advisors." Father glances toward me. "Maile, you're still in mourning, so you will stay. La'akea will be in charge of the village while we're gone."

My mouth falls open. La'akea? My immature brother?

Father holds up a hand, as though expecting me to protest. "With the recent battle, I don't think the sailors will pose a problem for a while, especially after losing their leader. La'akea will see that the harvest continues so our stores are replenished and make sure the rest of the dead are taken care of."

"La'akea is a child," I say. "He can't even remember to bathe regularly, let alone run the entire village. I'm more than capable of—"

"You're capable of a lot of things, Maile." The chief's nostrils flare. "Including restraining yourself from arguing with your father."

I snap my mouth closed and try to smother the fire inside me. I can't seem to keep it subdued, so I stand and begin pacing again, trying to stomp it out.

"Your brother will be chief one day, and he's old enough to do this. It will be good practice for him." Father pauses. "And you."

He means it will be good practice for me in being subservient.

I stop pacing and look at my brother, who makes a face at me. Sometimes being born female feels like the most unjust punishment the gods have bestowed on me. Especially when I'm older, an adult, and my own father trusts a child over me.

"That is all," Father says before standing, essentially dismissing us.

I help Haukea from the ground and lock arms with her before heading to her hut. I don't know if I'm trying to support her or if I need comfort from my older sister. Maybe both.

I help her get dressed in her formal outfit. First is a smooth, white bark cloth covering her from chest to knees with a black linear pattern stamped along the neckline. Over that I secure a skirt woven from the leaves of a *hala* tree, tied at her waist with a thin rope of coconut fibers. A belt of opalescent shells covers the rope, with an accent of yellow finch feathers above each hip. I tie a decorative braiding of *kī* leaves to each wrist and ankle, and I slide a smooth turtle-shell bracelet onto the upper part of her left arm.

After brushing through her hair with a comb, I say, "I have an idea," and I hurry out to find the nearest *'awapuhi* bush. Plucking several of the small blossoms, I return to my sister and hold them in my cupped hand. We both bend over to inhale the fragrant scent.

"What are those for?" she asks, speaking for the first time since we left the council hut.

"I'll weave them into your hair, hidden inside the braids." I grin like a child about to play a trick. "They'll smell the fragrance but won't know where it comes from. They'll think you smell like that all the time and will be smitten immediately."

She offers a tiny smile and nods once.

"The scent should last several days," I add. The journey shouldn't take more than a day and a night, but I don't know how long they'll be gone. Negotiations could take days. And if they decide to proceed with a wedding right away, then . . .

I try not to think about it. It's what we've been born to

do—be given in marriage. It's our lot as daughters of a chief. I don't know what will happen to me now that Ikaika is gone. Perhaps Father will find another husband for me. But Haukea will become the property of another, live in a new place. I don't know if the advantageous position we'll gain is worth her sacrifice, but she's willing to do it. That makes her truly royal.

When I'm done braiding the flowers into her hair and pinning the braid atop her head like a crown, I give my sister a long embrace. The scent is sweet yet calming, perhaps tricking my mind into accepting what's happening. I welcome it, whether it's an illusion or not. With everything that has gone wrong here the last days, I need some semblance of right.

We walk to the shore where men are loading food and supplies into the royal canoe. Two large hulls are connected by several beams, and a large mast supports several sails, ready to harness the wind. They've enough manpower and paddles to arrive at their destination should the winds fail, and enough guards to get my family to safety quickly if needed.

My mother wears her formal outfit as well, and I lean in to give her a *honi*—a kiss—nose pressed against nose, before she boards the canoe with my sister. My father squeezes my shoulder before he steps onto the canoe. His helmet stands out against his dark skin, and the red and yellow feathers of his cape make him look not only like someone important, for the clothing is beautiful, but also powerful and commanding. As though he could sprout wings and take flight if he willed it.

He moves to stand between the royal *kāhili* stationed at the back of the canoe. The tops of the royal standards are decorated with the same red and gold feathers that indicate my father's rank. I hope the sight will intimidate the enemy. I remind myself we really are important, and we really are powerful—it's not a lie or trick. And as the canoe drifts farther away from shore, I pray the gods will grant something in our favor.

My brother says something to me, but my mind is on arranged marriages and impending war so I don't hear his words. But I can tell by the look on his face that he meant to mock me. When he disappears from the beach and heads back to the homestead, I hear the familiar wail of grieving of my people. Bodies are still being chanted over. Burned. I haven't yet discovered what happened to James Cook, but I don't want to linger to find out. I want to leave this place.

I'm sure La'akea doesn't want me around to criticize his every decision. Maybe I should have petitioned for Father to take me. They might need a navigator, and I'm the best there is now that Ikaika's gone. But Makana is with them, and he knows exactly where to take them on this trip. Besides, Father would tell me navigating is for men, and I shouldn't worry myself over such important duties.

I don't want to be here, and I can't be out there, on the ocean with my family.

I grunt and pick up the woven basket I'd left earlier, popping one of the sea snails into my mouth. At least there's one person on this island who—though he might not want my company—still needs me.

John Harbottle's Journal
17 February 1779

My fever is gone, the wound on my chest continues to heal, and I'm feeling much renewed. It's still a struggle to move, but I manage short trips outside the hut to relieve myself. The majority of my time is spent resting on this bed of mats, as my full strength has yet to return and I'm burdened by weakness. Boredom has begun to set in as well. I'm grateful for this journal—not only to record all that has happened and provide an outlet for my observations, but also to offer a distraction from my disability and the monotony. I've especially enjoyed reviewing my linguistic notes.

There is no doubt the native language here is related to that of the other Pacific islands we have visited. The vocabulary and syntax are so similar, in fact, that speaking in the tongue of the others would serve as basic communication here. This naturally made my study of their language much easier than I had hoped.

One would predict, then, the various peoples either stem from a common ancestor or place and then set forth on the waters toward separate lands, or they settled one group of islands before moving on to another, their language slowly changing through the millennia into what it is today.

Given the relative remoteness of the Sandwich Isles, if the latter theory is true, it's quite possible these were the last islands to be inhabited along that chain of voyages. The language here is softer than the other Pacific tongues. The consonants are not as harsh and abrupt, the vowels flow through each word like water, drowning each sound yet buoying it up at the same time, as though the miles of sailing through sea and sand has shaped it into the smooth, polished literation it has become. I could not imagine anything more pleasant to experience after such a rough journey.

ʻewalu

Chapter Eight

When I reach the clearing in the late afternoon, I'm surprised to see John sitting outside near the empty firepit.

"I grew tired of lying down," he says with his strong accent, guilt painted across his features. "And the sun felt nice."

"You're not hallucinating, are you?" I place the basket of snails next to him and feel his forehead. It's cool.

"I don't think so." He shades his eyes from the afternoon sun and looks up at me. "Unless I'm *not* shipwrecked on an island paradise and being held prisoner by a beautiful native woman. Then perhaps I might be hallucinating after all." He smiles at his joke.

"Well I don't know about the prisoner part," I say, unwrapping the bandage from around his chest. "But the beautiful woman . . . yes, that's real."

He tosses his head back and laughs. His entire body participates in this laugh, his chest heaving, his shoulders moving up and down. Even his legs stretch in front of him as though making room for his joy. I don't know whether to be offended that he thinks my claim to beauty is outlandish, or surprised that he's capable of such humor when all I've been surrounded by these last days are grief, hatred, and fear. I feel a tug at the side of my mouth, a smile wanting to join his contagious happiness. That's an indication I need to leave.

"I'll get more water and *nahele*," I say, avoiding his eyes. I'm worried his smile will unravel me. I kick at the basket on the ground. "Eat."

I turn and hurry away, remembering my purpose here. I need to heal him so he can leave with his men—and that's all. I splash my face with cold water from the spring and snag a few more weeds before heading back. It might be the last batch he'll need.

When I return, he's holding the basket to his nose, inhaling and making a sour face. He sees me approaching and lowers the basket to his lap.

"What are these?" he asks.

I raise one eyebrow. "Sea snails. Have you never had them before?"

He shakes his head. "I'm afraid I've never encountered them in England or anywhere else in the Pacific."

I know England is the name for his home, but I don't know why they wouldn't have sea snails. "'*Opihi*. They cling to the rocks near the water. A delicacy, really." I sit next to him and pull one of the black shells out of the basket. Holding it to my lips, I slurp out the flesh then toss the shell to the ground, reaching for another. "They are one of my favorites."

He takes that as assurance and picks out one of the shells. When he tries to suck out the flesh, a dribble of orange streaks down his chin.

This time, I let a small smile escape. I scrape the flesh out of the shell in my hand and hold my finger to his mouth.

"Don't worry," I say. "We usually have to shuck it first for the children, too."

He grunts and eats it from my finger, leaving a slight flutter in my stomach.

John chews for a moment and then swallows. Raising one eyebrow, he says, "That *is* delicious."

"Did you think I was lying?"

He grabs another and practices slurping it himself, and soon we're both eating through the basket without saying anything. When it's empty, I give him half of the *nahele* weeds. He knows what to do with them, and we both chew before applying the paste across his chest. I bandage him again to keep the medicine in place. Though the wound will heal, he'll have a sizable scar for the rest of his life. Something to remember this paradise by.

"Why are you here? And I don't mean in this clearing—as my *prisoner*," I quip. "Why did Cook bring you and your men to our island?"

"To find the Northwest Passage to the Atlantic."

"I don't know what that means."

John leans over, his face twisting from his injury, and grabs a few rocks near the firepit. He drops a small stone in the ash toward the left.

"This is England," he says. As he places larger stones on the ground moving right, he adds, "Africa, Europe, the Asian Empire, New Holland, and the Americas."

The words mean nothing to me, and he notes my confusion.

"Large masses of land and people," he explains. "Much larger than the Sandwich Isles."

"The Sandwich Isles?"

"Your group of islands—that's what Cook has named them. After the Earl of Sandwich."

I narrow my brows. "What right does he have to name our home?"

"He doesn't." John pauses, as though conjuring an apology. "It's just a name for the purpose of our maps."

"Maps?"

"A flat representation of our world that we keep on the ship," he says. "So we can see where each section of land and water is. It helps us navigate."

I wonder if one of the items I buried in the forest is this map he's talking about. But I'm more curious about the stones. I point to the first one.

"You said this is England?"

"Yes. Where I am from. It's small compared to most places on Earth." He picks up a stick and moves it through the ash between the stones. "We traveled on our ships through the ocean, around the coast of Africa, cutting under New Holland, and making stops in the Friendly Isles and Tahiti—places we've been to on previous voyages. But the Sandwi—" He stops himself. "Hawai'i. This is our first voyage here." He plucks one small shell from the sea snails we discarded earlier and places it in the middle of a large span of ash—of ocean. "This is you. Us. Where we are now."

"So small?" I whisper, glancing around the large stones on his 'map.'"

"Yes," he says. "A tiny dot in a huge world. It's almost a miracle we found you here." He scatters a handful of tiny shells on the ground farther down in the ocean-ash. "Most of the islands in the Pacific are congregated down here, in the south. But you are virtually alone and separated from everyone else in the world, here in the north."

No wonder John feels like a prisoner, shipwrecked on our

island. He and his men are so far away from home, so far away from everything else they've known.

"And here." John draws a line to the top of the stones he called the *Americas*. "We've been searching for a path through the water to get to the other side. To the Atlantic Ocean. With no luck yet."

I lean over and draw my finger along the same path he did, the path that brought him from England to my home. How did they find us? The ocean is massive; the other lands are vast. We really are just a few specks of sand on an endless shore. A tiny star in an endless sky. I sit back on my heels, my head spinning.

"It's a lot to take in, I'm sure." John sits next to me, our knees touching the bottom line of his map. "We've been trying to discover the world we already know is out there, and you're just discovering that there *is* more."

"I knew there was more in the world than our little island," I admit. "Our stories go back for generations, to the voyages of my ancestors, to the lands they discovered and the lands they originated from. I've just never seen it laid out like this before." I touch the small stone of England. "Do you think we all started in one place and became explorers—like you are now?"

"That's a whole other topic in itself, I think." John rises from the ground and stumbles slightly, finding his balance. "One I'll leave up to the missionaries who are sure to follow the moment word of this place reaches England."

I don't know what a missionary is, but . . . "More people will come?"

John cringes, and this time I don't think it's from pain. "The world seems suddenly smaller, doesn't it? I'm sorry, Maile."

I rise and take his arm to lead him back to the hut. Inside, I lower him to the mats and make sure his head is elevated. I run my hand along his bandage to ensure it's still in place, then I sit beside him in the opposite direction, so that I'm near his waist with my legs outstretched by his head.

"Have you been to all those places on your map?" I ask.

"No. This is my third voyage with Cook." He looks away. "And my last, I suppose. But thanks to him, I've traveled to more places than most sailors. More places than I'd ever dreamed. James Cook was . . ." John shifts and looks up at me. "He was sort of a father to me, I suppose, after my parents died. And he trusted me."

Cook didn't seem like the kindest of men, not like John. I wonder if John saw something in the captain others didn't. Still, it sounds like a harsh life, traveling for such long stretches of time.

"This map of yours," I say. "If you haven't been to all those places, how do you know they exist?"

"Other men have gone there. They record it. Write it down."

"Write?"

He looks at me long and hard. "They . . . make pictorial representations. Words. And they share it with others. On paper."

"Paper," I repeat.

"Like your *kapa*," he explains, reaching for the hem of my bark skirt. He pulls his hand back at the last second and rests it on his stomach. "Only thinner. And lots of it."

I remember the bound cloths I found in the boat. And the rolled bark, too. Things I've hidden. Things he supposedly needs.

"Do you not have any kind of writing here?" he asks.

"Pictures?" I ask. "We have pictures carved into the rocks. But no maps like you speak of."

"But your people—they navigate, don't they? From island to island?" He narrows his eyes. "If you don't record what others have discovered in the past, how do you remember where any-thing is?"

I give a small laugh; the question is ridiculous. "We chant."

"Chant?"

"Sing. We share the songs with our children, and they re-member it and pass it on to their own children. We don't lose anything. It's all in here." I point to my chest. "We carry it with us. We don't need maps to tell us what we already know."

"Amazing," John whispers. "So you memorize the paths from island to island?"

"Yes." I pull my knees to my chest and lean forward. "We use the stars. The weather. We sing of my ancestors and where they are buried. I can tell you of my father's father and his father and on and on for hundreds of years. Stories of where my people originated from. How they came to be."

"What else?" John's eyes are wide, full of interest.

"The history of our wars. Medicinal practices. The works of our gods and demigods. The precise depths where certain fish swim. Anything. Everything."

"Tell me."

"I just did." I could sit for a full day and tell him all the things we chant, all the songs I've memorized since I was a small child, but it would be the most boring day in the world.

"No," he says, looking back and forth between my eyes. "I mean sing to me. Sing me something. One of your tales."

I don't say anything, certain he's making fun of me and my people. Of our silly traditions. We may not have his paper or maps or bound cloth, and we may not have written down the discoveries of other men with complicated symbols and passed them on to future explorers, but our chants are important. They are sacred, *kapu*, and the last thing I want is for him to tease me about them.

I shake my head, refusing to sing.

"Please, Maile." His voice holds no sarcasm, no teasing. "I want to hear about your family. About your history."

I wait, still feeling vulnerable. "This is important."

"I know it is." His blue-green eyes are light and clear, as though I can see right into him. No malice. No judgment.

Finally satisfied he will listen, I begin to chant. *"I ka lā i hala iho nei . . ."*

I sing of Maui and his magic fishhook. About how his brothers made fun of him, and how they took him out on their canoe to fish. I sing about his hook catching the land beneath the sea, and him telling them to paddle as hard as they could as he fished the land to the surface. And how their curiosity got the better of them and they turned around to witness his catch—our chain of islands. Hawai'i.

My voice rises and falls with the story, echoing the sadness, the triumph, the adventure, and the power of the event. I sing it the way my grandmother did, my voice getting louder and softer in the same rhythm as hers. I can't help but let my hands and arms rise to form the waves of the sea as Maui and his brothers paddled and the peaks of the mountaintops as they emerged. The awe in my voice echoes the awe of Maui's brothers upon discovering not only their brother's worthiness, but what he accomplished.

When I finish, I look at John. He stares at me without saying anything. I brush off my skirt and pretend to study the trees outside because it feels so awkward in the room. Just as I'm about to stand and walk out from embarrassment, he clears his throat.

"There are a lot of things I love about your island," he says softly. "The sensation of the humidity on my skin at the same time an ocean wind rustles my hair while I'm sitting in the shade. Flowers that smell so delicious I wish I could eat them like sugar-coated confections. The freshest water I've ever tasted, and the lush forests filled with the sweetest fruits. The sea snails." He smiles before smoothing his expression again. "But my favorite thing about this place? It's you singing that song."

I feel heat rise to my face, and I know it has turned a dark shade of red. I press a palm against my cheek, as though I can push my blush away. I hope John can't see it in the shadows of the hut. His words are the nicest compliment I've ever received, and I don't know how to react.

"Will you sing me another one?" he asks.

"Yes." As I begin to chant about the fragrant vines that grow on our highest hills, John closes his eyes and drifts to sleep with a slight smile on his face. When I'm done, he doesn't move, though his chest rises and falls with deep breaths.

A part of me wishes John were a brutal man, angry and tempestuous, arrogant and condescending. Mean. Then I wouldn't have this confusion inside me twirling around like a building storm, wondering what to do with him.

Why did he have to be kind?

John Harbottle's Journal
18 February 1779

Maile sang to me. It was like nothing I'd heard before—raw, unpretentious, and filled with emotion. It was the perfect ending to what I perceive as a significant day.

Until now she has been reserved and stoic toward me, guarded. Besides a grief she couldn't control and a short-lived bout of anger I ascribe more to impatience than anything, she hasn't allowed herself to open up around me. Not even the slightest crevice.

But she smiled for the first time. She made me laugh so hard I forgot who I was for a moment, an injured naval officer turned prisoner of war. She was inquisitive and eager to learn about my world. She was frustrated, overwhelmed, afraid, content, shy, determined, embarrassed, and confused all within a few hours. I witnessed the same range of emotions in her song. She felt it so deeply, it was a wonder to behold.

It reminds me of the Hawai'ian concept of hānai. When a child is orphaned, he is given to another family. They care for him, raise him as their own. There is no distinction between him or any of the parents' other natural-born children. He is welcomed as though they had always been his stewards. The wide acceptance of this practice of informal adoption is poignant to me, as I lost my own parents when I was young.

But that is not where hānai ends.

Sometimes, families will give a child to a couple who are unable to bear their own children, or to a grandmother who could parent a child, or to a friend who has lost a child. And age is not a condition. If an adult needs a loving support system, he could be welcomed into an extended family of strangers who share with him the standard warmth usually reserved for those bonded by blood.

While I suspect this practice may lead to confusion in the genealogical history of their people, the generosity and community-focused concept of hānai not only expands the narrow definition of family I'd previously believed, but also stretches my understanding of the capacity humans have to love unconditionally.

I see that same capacity in Maile. Not just to love, but to understand, to trust. I feel like a line is forming again, a barrier of protection in the sand that will help define our peoples' relationship and widen our understanding of each other. It gives me hope that we can make our way back from the indignation born in our recent battle to find a semblance of peace we can all accept. My only desire is that neither I nor my men make a choice that will erase that line again.

'eiwa

Chapter Nine

I walk along a path through the ashes that remain of the dead. A few fires still dot our village in the open area near the taro fields. I can't get a full breath of air; it's as if the dead are clinging to me, wanting me to join them. The ashes will eventually be buried in the orchards, the remains of the dead helping to fertilize new life. But for now, faint smoke rises from the black and red coals that are dissipating, reminding me of lava as it flows into the ocean, the steam blinding and suffocating with the clash of hot and cold, life and death.

I see my brother with a piece of sugarcane protruding from his mouth. He rips off a piece and chews it, sucking the sweetness from the fibers. How can he eat in this place?

"La'akea." I wait for him to turn toward me.

"Sister," he says. "Where have you been? I need your help with the burial ceremonies."

"No, thank you."

He stomps his foot like a little child. "Father said you were to support me."

"He also said you're more than capable of taking care of the dead yourself. I'm supporting you by letting you do just that."

He spits out the wad of fiber and bites off another piece of sugarcane from the stalk in his hand. "I thought being a chief would be easier than this."

I slap him on the shoulder. "First of all, you're not chief yet. And second, the chief is probably the hardest working person on the island. He has to make sure everyone is contributing, everyone is healthy, and no one is fighting. And he participates in the work as well."

La'akea makes another face.

"It's fine." I pretend I'm doing him a huge favor and sigh. "I'll help with James Cook. Do you know what's become of the captain?"

"I wanted the men to burn him like the others, but they refused." He points down the valley toward the north end of the bay. "A number of them are taking what's left of his bones to the sailors as an offering of peace."

"What? When?"

"They just left," he says, nonchalantly. "They're taking the north trail to the ships."

"And you let them?" It's been ten days since the battle. While any physical wounds the foreigners have sustained may be mending, it's likely too soon for the recovery of emotional ones. I'm not sure how our men will be received.

La'akea shrugs as though he's not concerned. "A chief should want peace. Our men are getting peace. What's the problem?"

"You are *not* chief," I say through clenched teeth. "Father left with the impression that the white men would leave us alone in his absence. Now you've gone and prodded them with a stick."

"A bone," he says. "I've prodded them with a bone." He laughs at his joke.

I turn away in disgust and hurry down the hillside to the trail that leads north. As I run along the path, I try to think of every possible outcome that could result if our men encounter the foreigners before I can stop them.

The best scenario would be that the sailors accept Cook's bones and recognize their return as an overture of peace. Forgiveness or an admission of guilt is unlikely from either side—not yet. But perhaps gratitude will follow if we show them that we remembered them in their grief and gave them back a piece of what they lost.

There are too many things that could go wrong, though, and each scene my mind invents ends with smoking weapons and more of my people dead. It's not worth the risk. Especially when my father isn't here.

The trail ends in an open meadow overlooking the ocean. There are no beaches here, just a cliff at the edge. The shore is lined with boulders smoothed from years of water erosion. A winding trail leads down the face of the cliff to the shore where the *Resolution* and *Discovery* are anchored. The cliff isn't very high, but I'm still surprised that I can see the tops of the ships from where I stand on the far side of the field.

There's no one here. Perhaps our men descended the trail, or maybe they changed their minds and turned back. I should walk to the cliff to search for them below, but I'm distracted by what I see in the field.

This is a holy place, a location separated from the rest of the villages and meant to honor the gods. A *heiau* stands in the center on a foundation of black lava rocks. The temple is small and simple—a wooden frame covered in layers of *pili* grass. Outside stands an altar meant to hold offerings for the gods. A short wooden fence surrounds it all, marking the place as sacred. Forbidden. This temple is dedicated to Lono. Our priests brought James Cook here to honor him as a god. He insulted us by allowing it to happen and tempted the real gods with his mockery.

But that disgrace was nothing compared to this. I spin in a circle, trying to absorb all I'm seeing. The door to the *heiau* has been ripped away. Have the foreigners entered the temple? That is strictly forbidden. Only our holy men are allowed in. Pieces of the exterior altar and extended lengths of the wooden fence have been torn down. Sitting across the threshold of the temple is a giant beam of wood from one of the ships.

There are unfamiliar tools sprawled along the ground, and discarded heaps of wood litter the entire area. They've been using materials from the temple—Lono's temple—to repair this broken piece of their ship. They have desecrated a holy place.

I march across the field to the path that leads below, angry at their cruel behavior. How could they do something so blasphemous? As soon as I'm to the edge, I hear shouts coming from the shore below. Then—

Boom.

I drop to the ground and crawl to the edge to get a glimpse of what's happening without revealing myself as a possible target for the sailors.

Boom. Boom. Boom.

Fear roils through my body. The worst is happening. I'm too late to stop it.

Boom.

More yelling, this time closer. I see a line of warriors running up the trail towards me. Loose rocks slip beneath their steps, causing them to stumble in their haste. There are six of them, but I've no idea how many came. Are they all here, or . . . ?

There's a crowd of white men on the ships, weapons pointed toward the cliff's side. A layer of white smoke rises around them, dissipating the higher it gets. They yell words I don't understand, but they don't pursue our men. It's a small relief in what was obviously an unsuccessful attempt at diplomacy.

I back away from the edge just as our warriors reach the top of the trail, running into the meadow. A couple of them pick up rocks in the field and run back to the head of the cliff trail, hurling the stones over the edge to the ships below. Before they have a chance to pick up more stones, I stop them.

"*Pau*," I yell. "That's enough."

All six men turn to me, noticing me for the first time. They lower their heads, and some drop to their knees when they see who I am.

"We need to leave this place," I say. We can't give the soldiers an excuse to follow us and bring their deadly weapons into the village.

They rise and move quickly to the path that leads back home. I run behind them to keep up with their pace. After we are a safe distance away, we slow, but we don't stop moving.

"What happened?" I ask.

With eyes averted out of respect for my rank, they relate to me all that transpired.

"We brought the remains of the captain," one says. I recognize him as one of our canoe builders, Puna. He lifts a small woven basket in his hands. There are only a few bones in it, the rest likely stolen by others in the village greedy for Cook's *mana*. "But when we got to the clearing, we saw what happened to the temple."

"The four sacred idols of our gods were missing," says another. "With the altar and the fencing destroyed, it wasn't hard to know who took them."

Only now do I notice one of the other men, Keahi, holds a wooden idol in his hands—or at least a piece of one. I recognize the fierce expression of Kū, god of war. The pearl shell eyes have been pried out, leaving empty sockets sitting over the familiar pig-shaped nose. I reach out a hand and trace the detailed hairline running behind his neck to the jagged edge where it has been torn away. The god's head has been removed from its body.

"*Auwē*," I cry, despair filling me. "What have they done?"

"We went to the ships to get back what they took." Keahi holds the idol tight against his middle as we continue walking. "This is the only one we could find before they were upon us with their wood-and-metal weapons in our faces. We didn't even have a chance to offer them the remains of their captain before they chased us away."

"They thought we were stealing," Puna says. "How could we steal what is rightfully ours?" He shakes his head, confused. "Once the weapons of thunder and smoke started, we turned and ran."

"Did you all survive?" I look around the group, though it's impossible for me to know if anyone is missing.

"We did," one says, stepping forward. "They couldn't find their targets, though one almost got me." He shows me the side of his upper arm where blood runs down from a fresh wound, but it doesn't seem to bother him. "The gods were protecting us."

I say a silent prayer of thanks that nothing more serious happened. "You must stay away," I say. "Don't go back, not until the chief returns."

They nod slowly, though they probably didn't need the admonition. I doubt they'll head back to the white sailors and their killing weapons any time soon.

"And what of the idols?" Keahi asks.

Sadness overwhelms me when I look at the broken statue, making it hard to answer. "Take this one to the *kahuna*," I say. A holy man will know how to fix it. "Tell him what has happened, but that he is not to return without my father, either."

I don't know what the sailors will do if any of our people, holy man or not, come to the field where the white men are repairing their ship. Not only do they trespass on our home, they dishonor that which is most precious. They've no consideration for anything important to us—why would they treat our religious leaders any differently? We can't put anyone else at risk with these barbarians.

We walk the rest of the way to our village in silence. There's a sadness that hangs between us, the same despair and regret I have felt since the day of the battle. These men shouldn't have gone there, not this soon. But their intentions were honorable. And they didn't even get a chance to give the white men the offering that could have healed some of their pain.

"What will we do with Cook's remains?" Puna turns the basket in his hands.

I swallow hard. I don't want the responsibility, despite what I told my brother earlier. I don't want to be accountable for what happens next, but I promised John I would try to find out what happened to his captain.

"I will take care of it," I say, reluctantly taking the basket from him. "I know what to do."

The men leave to find a holy man to give him the sobering news of the *heiau* and destroyed idols while I head to my hut to think. Because despite my guise of confidence in front of my own people, I have no idea what I should do.

John Harbottle's Journal
22 February 1779

The natives worship a number of deities, with a multitude of lesser gods and an abundance of idols. But the four main gods are Kāne, Kanaloa, Kū, and Lono.

Kāne seems to be the highest of the gods, the creator and the giver of life associated with the dawn, the sun, and the sky.

Kanaloa is the god of the underworld and rules over the spirits. Though it sounds grim, he actually serves more as a balancing force for Kāne rather than as a being who delights in morbidness.

Kū is the god of war and politics. It seems even those who the world would consider uneducated savages know the two are inseparable.

And Lono is the god of peace. I don't understand why the natives called the captain by this name, except that he possibly fulfilled a prophecy in which this legendary white god would return to their shores. I once took the designation as a good sign. After all, what could go wrong when the god of peace is involved?

But if the Hawai'ians once considered the captain to be a god, they certainly don't anymore. I wonder what changed their minds. Was it something James Cook did, something he said? Did he break some rule none of us were aware existed? I'm not sure if we'll ever know the reason, and that frustrates me the most. Not the fact that they don't consider him deity anymore—he never was—but even when we do our best to respect the indigenous civilization, minimize our cultural influence on the natives, it's impossible to know the extent of our impact, however innocent we think our actions might be. We could inadvertently cause a significant interference, lives could be lost on a much greater scale than one battle on the beach.

While the search for a passage to the Atlantic is an undertaking vital to England, is it worth the risk of destroying a people while doing it, whether intentional or not?

ʻumi

Chapter Ten

I take the path leading south. I stop to rest several times along the way, not because the basket I carry is heavy, but because I don't know what I'll say to John when I get there and I want to delay our meeting. My emotions fluctuate from anger at what his men have done to a desire for peace while it's still within reach.

In the end, I decide I won't tell him what happened at the temple today. There's nothing he can do about it, and I don't want to give him an excuse to escape sooner than his health should allow. And not before I've had the chance to determine what advantage he could be to our people in future relations with the sailors.

I finally make it to the clearing and take the basket to John's hut, but I hesitate in the doorway. He's standing at the table, hovering over something on the surface. I can't tell what he's doing, but he's intently focused. I lower my basket to the floor and step closer. The moment he sees me, he jumps back in surprise. He didn't hear me enter.

"What are you doing?" I nod toward the table. A square of bound cloth is open, reminding me of the one I buried in the forest. Only this one is much smaller. John must have had it hidden somewhere in his coat when I brought him here. An image of a girl with long dark hair falling to her waist fills one of the thin cloths. She is outlined in black, as though he's taken ash and used it to ink a design like a tattoo. Except his ink is thin and fine. I don't know how he could have achieved such detail with ash.

As quickly as he jumped back, John moves forward and closes the bound cloths, hiding the image he made. He slips the square object into his coat, confirming my theory about where it came from.

"It's nothing," he says, wiping a line of sweat from his brow. "I was bored."

He pulls his hand away from his forehead, and I hold back a laugh at the line of black left behind. He looks like a child caught playing in the wetlands with mud streaked across his face. Whatever he used to make his design, whether ash or another kind of ink, has stained his hands and now his face. He catches me grinning and realizes what happened, and then he tries to scrub it off with still-dirty fingers.

"I'll get more water for you to wash up," I say, grabbing the gourd before heading out the door.

At the spring, I fill the container and hear the familiar whistle of a golden finch. It reminds me of my dream, the one about the bird I couldn't keep for myself. Though I can't see him, I whistle to the finch, nudging him to reply to me, to tell me his chant, sing me his song, the way I did the other day for John. But the finch either stops his song or flies away; I'm not sure which. I wish I could have at least seen him.

I carry the gourd back to the clearing, and John hurries out, his expression a combination of confusion and . . . revulsion? He steps away from the hut, backing up to the nearest coconut tree and bringing his hand to his mouth. When he sees me, he motions to the door of the hut, a new line of black ink streaking his face.

"What is that?" he asks.

Not knowing what he's talking about, I drop the gourd and hurry inside. The only things in here are the mats and the table and . . . oh. Just inside the doorway is the woven basket of bones. I lift it and walk outside, holding it as carefully as I can.

"What is it?" he asks again.

"It's . . ." I pause, worried this might have been a terrible idea. Will he wonder why so little is left? I realize I have no idea what his people traditionally do with their dead, and the only explanation I have is the truth. "It's James Cook. What remains of his body."

A look of horror crosses John's face. "What . . . what have you done to him?"

I begin to explain about the removal of hair and bones to preserve the captain's power, but John interrupts me. I don't even think he hears what I'm saying.

"Why did you bring that here? Have you any sense at all?" Anger fills his features. I've seen his desperation, fear, sorrow—but never anger. He seems like another person.

I stand straight and press my shoulders back. I will not let him belittle our traditions when I was trying to do him a favor.

"I brought this for you," I say.

"There's no way I—"

"Let me finish." I wait until he presses his lips together, then I continue. "When Ikaika died, his family took his hair and bones to preserve them—to preserve *him*. So they could pass his *mana* among the rest of his family. They did this because they love him and wanted to honor his memory."

John shifts his weight, but I know despite his impatience he'll let me finish.

"Your captain was treated the same way as Ikaika." I will my voice not to shake, but I still feel tears gather in my eyes. I wipe at my face, hating that John sees me being so emotional, especially when he's the one who did this to me. But I don't know how else to explain in a way he'll understand.

"He was treated no different than the men we respect and love," I say. I pause and let that thought penetrate him. He needs to know that Cook was treated the same way as someone so important to me.

He stops shifting his stance and gives me his full attention, not taking his eyes off me. John was there when they knocked Cook on the back of his head, stabbed him in his back, and dragged him away from the beach. He knows his captain was our enemy, but now he knows he was a respected one.

"And I . . ." I take a deep breath. "I thought you might want a chance to access his *mana*. A chance to say goodbye." I look down at my feet, my confidence sucked out of me. John had been asking about his captain, and when I learned Cook had been like a father to him, I thought he would appreciate this. But obviously I didn't know anything at all—not about his feelings or the traditions of his England. I'm like a child learning how to speak, to walk, to understand. And I feel like a fool.

John clears his throat, and I look up. His face has softened; the anger is gone. He looks at the basket in my arms and swallows hard. Yet he says nothing.

"Would you like to make something with the bones?" I ask. "I could help you carve a relic or—"

"No, no." John's eyes go wide. "I wouldn't . . . I don't think that will be necessary." He brushes his hair away from his face and stands tall like I had a moment ago. Maybe he's trying to find his own courage.

He takes a deep breath. "What do your people usually do with your dead, besides . . . ?" He motions to the basket.

"We bury them at sea," I say. "Or in caves. That is, if the body isn't burned."

John swallows again, and his face whitens. "I don't think I can make it down to the water yet."

We both look at his chest, where the bandage covering his wound has started to fray.

"Perhaps we could bury him in the ground?" he says. "That's usually what my people do. Somewhere near here?"

I nod.

"Yes," he says, forcing a smile as though trying to convince himself. "I would like that. Thank you, Maile."

I ignore his words of gratitude; he doesn't mean them. I know now he didn't want me to actually bring the captain's remains here. But we're strangers trying to do our best with each other's odd traditions and views, so I conceal the regret and frustration this entire encounter has stirred in me and help John find a suitable burial site. After scolding him three times for trying to help me dig amidst his groans of pain, I tell him to clean his hands and face of ink while I finish digging a hole deep enough with a hollow coconut shell.

He insists on placing the remains inside, though, and I let him.

"Do you want to say something?" I ask, holding the digging shell against my waist.

John nods. "Here lies James Cook, captain in the Royal British Navy, on"—he pauses, counting on his fingers—"the twenty-second of February, in the year of our Lord, 1779. He was a qualified sailor, a valiant leader, and an enthusiastic explorer. He will be remembered as one who made what may be the greatest discoveries of the eighteenth century, and revered as one of the most accomplished men to walk the earth."

John pauses. I think he has run out of words, and I'm about to shovel in the dirt to cover the basket when he begins to weep. He lowers his head into his hands, his shoulders shaking. I can barely hear the sound of his grief, so different than the loud wailing of my people when they mourn for their dead. But I feel his sadness as much as if he were crying out his pain—perhaps more. Because this is sorrow meant only for him, a grief that he holds inside of himself. That he's not willing to completely release.

I kneel next to him and run my hand down his hair. It's barely long enough to be tied back from his face, not like my sister's when I comfort her. But it doesn't matter. I smooth my fingers down his scalp and hair in an effort to calm him, to help him release his pain.

When John's cries have died, he lifts his head and glances at me. His face is red and splotchy, more vulnerable than I've seen it in these past few days. Even when he lay helpless and bleeding or shaking from a fever. Here, now, is a John more broken—his emotional pain taking harder a toll than his physical pain.

"He was a father to me," he says.

I don't know if his words are still part of his speech or if he just wants me to hear them. "I know he was."

John looks at the grave. "Some saw a hardened man, stubborn and even depressed at times, but to me he was determined. He always looked to the horizon in search of what was out there, not satisfied with what he'd already achieved. Ambitious, yes. Callous, no. He was a God-fearing man."

"And you loved him," I say, pulling my hand from his head

and looking down at the grave as well, trying to see Cook as John saw him. It's not difficult. It's strange how once you get to know someone, even your enemy, you can't help but care for them. Even if their ways are foreign, even if they've harmed you. I can see those qualities in Cook because I see them in John, too.

"Will you chant for him?" John asks.

I don't know enough about James Cook to do it properly, but I nod anyway, standing over the grave as I sing of what I do know. I sing about Cook and his ships and everything John said about his explorations. About how he was a good leader and an honored man filled with power. But mostly I sing about John's love for him, and I plead with the gods to watch over him, for John's sake.

When I'm done, John whispers, "Thank you, Maile."

I nod and let him thank me, then pass him the coconut shell so he can shove some of the dirt into the grave. He grits his teeth and does it until the hole is completely filled, and then he sits back, panting from the effort.

"Is there something we can use to mark the grave?" he asks. "At least until I find a more permanent headstone?"

I don't know what a headstone is, but I understand what he's asking. I gather several fallen coconuts and form them into a rainbow on the dirt the same way I did with the items that were stolen. John will easily find this spot again.

"This is perfect," John says, and then he winces in pain, holding his side. But the exertion was good for him, I think. It helped him have control over something that he must have felt spiraling away. It brought his captain back to him. Helped John own his death.

And it helped me, too. I'm glad he gave me a chance to do something for him, something meaningful. A chance to not only heal the wound across his chest, but heal his heart, too. More

John Harbottle's Journal
23 February 1779

I've been worrying so much about how British and Hawai'ian people differ that I never considered what we might have in common.

We both mourn for our dead. We feel sadness when we lose someone we cared for, someone we loved. We show respect for the bodies their spirits left behind. We might show that respect in different ways, but it's there all the same.

We cry, we fight, we make mistakes. We are patient, and we are angry. We both want peace but don't always know how to find it. I'm surprised how willing Maile is to find that peace, even after all my men have done—after all I did. She is truly royal, looking beyond herself for what is best for her people.

We both appreciate beauty in the things around us. I've been so moved by the beauty of this island, this Eden reincarnated, that I know I will never be the same again. But the natives don't take it for granted, either. Though this is all they've known, they understand that this place is special. In fact, they may have mastered the appreciation of beauty more than we ever will; I've learned ten Hawai'ian words for "beautiful" in my short time here:

Nani: *the grandest sort of beautiful*
U'i: *a youthful and lively countenance*
Maika'i: *pleasant to look at*
Makalapua: *beauty that has blossomed*
Pōlani: *clean and pure*
Nonohe: *attractive*
Hiluhilu: *exuding elegance or grace*
Luhiehu: *honored beauty*
Mikihilina: *ornate*
Pa'anehe: *a subtle beauty*

There is one difficulty with having so many ways to describe something beautiful, however. When you find someone who exhibits all of the above, how do you decide which word to use?

ʻumikūmākahi

Chapter Eleven

"It looks good," I say, removing the bandage. After two weeks, the wound has closed up, and there are no signs of infection, just the faint redness of a scar that will likely fade to match John's natural skin color. "And you're probably desperate for a bath."

John startles for a moment, then his shoulders relax. "That would be wonderful. We can go for months without a bath on the ship."

"Months?" I ask, astonished. I scrunch my nose at the idea of going so long without a proper cleaning.

"Yes," he says. "Months. Years. It's not as glamorous as it sounds."

I can't tell if he's teasing or not. "But how do you eat?" I ask. "Drink?" I've seen how many men they fit on a ship. Even if they had the space to store the food they needed for such a long journey, it would spoil before they could eat it.

"We make supply stops when possible," he says. "Like on the islands in the Pacific. But most of our food is salted or dried—flat cakes and meat as tough as leather."

I don't understand many of his words and metaphors, and he frowns, detecting my confusion.

"It's not the most nutritious diet," he says. "Cook has never had any of his men die from any dietary deficiencies, though. We make do."

Considering how large the world is and what John showed me about the vast seas, I suppose even a canoe could take months or years traveling through them.

"And all of it is worth finding this Northwest Passage?" I sound the phrase out slowly, not sure I'm remembering it correctly.

"The Crown seems to think so." He shakes his head. "It's not too terrible. I have time to study maps and compile what I've learned about the Pacific languages. I like to write in my journal—record where we've been and the things I've seen."

I know we're different, so different, but he keeps talking about things I can't understand, and a part of me feels like a child who can't grasp a basic concept like tying a knot.

John's shoulders fall. "I'm sorry. I didn't mean to talk so much."

Though confusing at times, I like learning about his culture. But I don't admit it.

"Bath?" I ask again.

"Yes." He exhales, as though glad for a subject change.

"There's a spring not too far from here." I gather his ripped blue coat and stained shirt along with the water gourd. "Do you think you can walk for a bit? It's not as far as the hike to the beach."

His face lights up, and he nods.

We walk at a slow pace, me holding his things and him gazing at every leaf, branch, and bird around us as though he's never seen this kind of plant or animal life before. A flood of guilt rises in me for keeping him here. He's likely well enough to go back to his ship, but I'm still not willing to give up the possible leverage he is to my people.

When we reach the spring, I hand him the water gourd. "It isn't as good as a waterfall," I say. "And there's not a large enough pool to submerge in, but the water is clean and will do the job."

"It's perfect," John says. "Thank you." He carefully removes the small square of bound cloth from a pocket in his clothing, placing it a safe distance away from the water on a nearby stone. Then he fills the gourd with water and pours it over his head, groaning from the pleasure of it.

I kneel at the base of the spring and scrub his bloodstained clothes against a rock. The water turns pink, and I think of my own bloodied clothes. It will be good for John to have this gone too, I think. It's his own blood—not his enemy's, not Ikaika's—but it's still a reminder of past pain and the tragic circumstance that put him in his current position. Removing the blood will help me feel better as well.

"Do you want me to wash that, too?" I point to the cloth that surrounds his waist and runs down both his legs. I don't know what to call it—a loin-and-leg cloth?

"I . . . uh . . ." John hesitates. "Yes." He turns away before pulling the cloth down and off his ankles. He has another layer beneath—this one just to his knees, though. How many layers do these men wear?

He hands me the off-white cloth. "Breeches," he says.

"Breeches," I repeat. His language is hard and abrupt. Explosive on the tongue and cutting off short.

I point to the layer remaining on him, wet and clinging to his pale and hairy legs. "What about that one?"

He slips on a slick rock but recovers quickly—not without a hand flying to his chest in pain, though. "Oh, no," he says. "I'll . . . I'll be fine with this one on."

I shrug and continue to scrub his clothes until they are clean. Then I lay them across dry rocks to air out in the sun. I find another large rock and perch on it while he finishes washing.

The water has smoothed all the curl from his hair, and I'm surprised to see it reaches his shoulders. His hair looks as dark as mine when wet. His face has a layer of scruff that wasn't there the day of the battle. I'd offer him a knife to shave, but I'm still not confident he won't turn it on me. Well, I'm fairly certain he wouldn't hurt me, but offering an enemy a weapon doesn't seem like the wisest action.

After scrubbing at his face with his hands, he pours one last gourd full of water over his head before resting on a nearby rock to dry out in the sun like his clothes. Water runs down the rock beneath him, the wet coloring the rock darker in little rivers that slide along the surface. John runs his hands through his hair to squeeze out the extra moisture, then his eyes land on me.

Embarrassed to have been caught staring at him, I quickly look down. I pull out the bone needle I brought and begin mending his shirt. It hasn't dried yet, but I prefer to have something to keep me occupied other than awkward glances at John.

Though he seems curious about what I'm doing, he says nothing. He lies back on the flat surface of the rock and closes his eyes against the sun. I finish closing the gash in his shirt. The thread is a bleached strand of coconut fiber, not quite the color of the cloth, and I keep the stiches as small as possible. Though a line is noticeable, the shirt will be functional and stay on him with ease. I lay the cloth back out to dry and reach for his navy blue coat. This cloth is much thicker—more like the wraps woven from *hala* leaves than bark pounded thin and soft. It takes longer for me to run the bone needle through the fabric, but the mend should hold.

"Tell me about the designs on your clothing," John says.

I glance up to see him still lying on the rock, eyes closed. I look down at my wrap, a beige-colored cloth secured with a fiber belt. A diagonal line down the front separates two areas of designs. The bottom half has large triangles stamped from a wooden beater. Each triangle is made up of smaller ones with a combination of red and brown dye. The top half is more detailed, curving patterns of small shapes made from a bamboo stamp in a yellow-orange dye.

"Do they mean anything?" he asks.

I smooth the cloth against me and see the sharp teeth of a shark, the spine-like bones of a fish, the delicate curve of a feather . . . all mimicked in the arching, repetitive patterns. "They are things we see around us. Our world."

"What about the colors?"

I glance again at the red and brown, the yellow-orange. "What about them?"

John sits up, and his eyes roam down my clothes. Not in an inappropriate way, but it still makes me feel self-conscious. I focus on threading my needle through his blue coat again.

"On the other islands we've visited in the South Pacific, there are mainly black and brown designs, some red. But here there is yellow and blue, purple and green. I think I've seen every color of the rainbow on your clothing."

I don't know how to respond. "We make our dye from many sources: root bark, coral, berries. More applications mean a deeper color. It takes time, but it's not complicated." I push the needle through a particularly thick portion of blue fabric. "It's nothing like this." I hold up his coat so we can both see the deep rich color, a blue so saturated it absorbs all sunlight and reflects none of it back. "How do you achieve such an even and heavy tint?"

John shrugs. "I don't know. They're made in factories, and I'm not familiar with fabric-making at all."

"Is this what everyone wears in England?" I hold it against me, the fabric stiff and still damp. It's too big for me, and the cloth is scratchy. I can't imagine wearing such a thing for long. I would itch and suffer from heat exhaustion, not to mention there can't be much room for easy motion. How could you toss a fishing net into the water properly?

John chuckles, seemingly unable to imagine me wearing it, either. "Coats like these are worn by men only."

My eyebrows rise. "What do your women wear?"

"Dresses."

I wait for him to explain.

"Much like your cloth, except"—he stands and motions toward the ground—"the skirt runs long to the floor." He moves his hand from his neck down one arm. "And the fabric rises on her neck, and the sleeves reach her wrists."

My mouth falls open. "Isn't she hot?"

"I suppose." He sits back on his rock. "But the winter is far colder than it is here, with lots of snow."

We have snow on the highest peaks of nearby islands, but I've never seen it in person. "How does she move with such a long skirt? Doesn't she trip over it when she runs?"

He laughs again. "Our women don't run."

Again, I feel like a child, questioning everything as though what I do is lesser, immature.

"It's not nearly as comfortable as your own clothing," he reassures me. "You aren't missing out on anything. Trust me."

I prick my finger with the bone needle and hold my finger against my mouth, though it's not bleeding. "And do they wear under layers like you?" I ask around my finger.

John's face turns red. "Yes. And corsets or jumps." He holds up a hand to stall my question, knowing he needs to explain. "It's a wrap of fabric lined with whale bones women wear to cinch in their waist and make it smaller."

Whale bone? Smaller waist? "Why would they want to do that?" I thought dresses sounded uncomfortable, but that is ridiculous.

"Good question," John says. He must think it's ridiculous, too.

I pinch the side of my waist, pressing in and wondering what I would look like with a whalebone wrap. If a woman on our island tried to make herself look thinner, she'd be considered crazy and sent to the holy man for help. The heavier you are, the more beautiful you are. It means you have to work less, have a higher position in the village. Even my own father has teased me for not having enough flesh on my bones. But now I wonder if John thinks I'm not thin enough for a proper woman.

"Like I said"—John clears his throat—"you aren't missing out on anything. You . . . you look fine the way you are."

That makes me think about John appraising me again, so I focus on finishing his blue coat, and the next several minutes pass by in silence. John eventually pulls his breeches on, followed by his boots and white shirt.

"Thank you for this," he whispers, fingering the small stitches across the front of his shirt.

There's still a slight stain from the blood, but the cloth is much cleaner than I expected. I offer John his coat, but he winces while attempting to get it on, the soreness of his injury still bothering him. So I help him slip his arms into the sleeves, then lift the bulk of the coat onto his shoulders, pulling it taut in front of him. He reaches up to fasten it together, but I want to see if I remember how the contraptions work, so I swat his hands away.

It takes me a few attempts, but soon his coat is fastened all the way to his neck, a small tuft of the white shirt sticking up beneath his chin. He touches the stitching I made on the coat, and a small grin forms on his mouth. There's a strange puckering on one end of the repair, and the coconut fibers stand out against the dark fabric. It looks like a child mended it.

"I'm sorry," I say. "Let me pull out the thread and try again."

"No." He stills my hand as I try to undo one of the buttons. "It's perfect just like this."

My hand falls, and I step back to look at him in his uniform. He almost looks like the man I saw standing in the boat next to Cook, speaking my language and staring at me. I didn't like that man; maybe it was because I didn't know him yet. But something's still missing.

"Should I retrieve the white hair thing from the hut?" I ask.

"No, no." He runs his hand through his hair, brushing it back from his eyes. "That's just for formal occasions. I don't care for it, actually."

I nod and pick up a piece of thread before stepping on a rock in front of him, bringing me to his height. I run my hands through his hair, pulling it back, and then tying it in place at the nape of his neck. It seems to be how he prefers it. At least he won't have to brush it out of his face anymore.

"There." My hands rest on his shoulders for the briefest of seconds, until I realize how close we are, his face right in front of mine. I move my hands behind me, grasping my wrist to keep still.

"Thank you, Maile," John whispers so softly I don't know if he said it or just mouthed it, his eyes never leaving mine.

I used to hate him expressing gratitude to me—hated knowing I'd done something to please him. To help him. I didn't want him to thank me for anything. I don't know when that hate turned into not minding. When him saying those words didn't bother me anymore. But now, there's a strange feeling inside me that not only doesn't mind when he says it, but longs to hear him say it again. And that . . . that's not good.

I step down from the rock and back away, taking a good look at him with his hair tied back. "You look . . ."

He rubs his thumb and forefinger on either side of his chin, perhaps self-conscious about needing to shave. I want to say he looks fine the way he is, the same words he spoke to me earlier. But then I imagine him thanking me again, and the feeling inside me that longs to hear it rises like the tide. I need to get away from that shore before it covers me.

"I . . . I have to go."

I don't ask him if he can find his way back to the hut. I don't answer him when he calls after me. I don't even look back to make sure he's fine before I'm out of view. I just run toward my homestead. Away from my enemy. From my prisoner. From John.

John Harbottle's Journal
28 February 1779

Sometimes I think I am making progress with Maile. I can almost see the barriers she holds tight around her fall away, piece by piece, letting me see glimpses of her. Other times she remains guarded, protecting herself from what she doesn't understand. But the worst times are when, without warning, she completely changes her countenance, making a decision I never would have guessed was approaching. Such as running away after daring to come nearer to me than she ever had before.

Is it the nature of her gender to vacillate so? I admit to having little experience with the fairer sex, so I'm uncertain if it's a universal trait or something that is rooted in her culture. Or could it just be Maile herself, coming and going as often as the surge of water on the beach, never letting you get comfortable with knowing when she will rise again?

It is forbidden for a commoner to speak to or look at a member of the royal family without permission. Cook, as Lono, was of course granted special privileges. But I don't think Maile, as daughter of the chief, would have interacted much with others outside of her family. She's not accustomed to open conversation with someone in a lower station than herself. Perhaps by conversing with her so freely, I've inadvertently caused her strain.

But her inquisitive nature compels me to share what I know, to answer her questions gladly. Maile frustrates me abundantly, but she intrigues me in equal measure. My curiosity lies in wondering how she feels about me.

Other things that are forbidden:
Trespassing on marked, sacred lands
Eating of particular foods, especially by the women
The logging of specific trees
Intermarriage between the castes
Wearing someone else's clothing
Fishing for certain fish or in specific areas outside of the
    allotted seasons
Uninvited contact with the chief and his residence

ʻumikūmālua

Chapter Twelve

As I run through the forest away from John, one thought pushes to the front of all others. If I were a woman in England, I would've tripped and fallen in my dress by now, unable to breathe in my corset and sweating profusely under endless clothes. I laugh out loud, remembering how John thinks their attire is ridiculous, too, and that I'm fine the way I am. His preoccupation with my own clothes makes me think of the squabbling women in the *kapa* huts. I try to picture him as a goose among them, like I envision those women, with feathers sticking out of his head. Then I remember his ornament of white hair and realize he's a peacock already. I laugh even harder and then stop myself short.

I halt and lean against a tree, catching my breath. It's the first time I've really laughed since Ikaika died, and the fact that it's connected to John disturbs me more than the feeling of wanting to hear him thank me and say my name does. He is not my friend. He's a means to an end, though I'm not sure what that end is. One thing is certain. Every day I spend with John leaves me more confused—confused about what's going to happen to him, about these white men and what their presence here means for my people. My head hurts, and I wish things could go back to before Cook. Before his ships. Before the Lono celebrations.

Before Ikaika died.

Instead of mourning Ikaika's absence like I should, I am spending time with the man who killed him. I am smiling and laughing and dishonoring Ikaika's memory just weeks after he was killed. I have no right to feel any kind of joy.

Maybe my father was right. Maybe I am not fit to lead or do anything worthwhile for the village. My priorities are in disarray. Once again I question the gods and why they let these men come into our bay. Why is this happening to me?

I pick up my pace again, thinking only of my family. Of my parents and sister and what they are sacrificing to keep us safe. Enemy threats are on the horizon, and the last thing I should be thinking about are clothes and baths and a man I don't even know.

As I get closer to the homestead, I hear the distinct sound of a conch shell being blown. It is loud and long, signaling the arrival of royalty. When I come into view of the clearing, I see a crowd of people hurrying to the beach. I follow behind them, pausing when I reach the berm that divides the grass from the sandy shore beyond. The familiar red-and-gold feathers of the *kāhili* standards rise above the double-hulled canoe that took my family to Wai'ole not long ago.

It's too soon. Too soon for them to be back. What happened?

I pace along the small hill and wait for them to come ashore. Even with the paddlers dipping long wooden oars into the water to guide the canoe to land, it takes far too long for them to get here. Others from our village wade into the water, anticipating the news like I am. But the moment I recognize the faces on the royal canoe, my shoulders slump. The holy man, the guards, the chief, my mother. And . . . my sister. Haukea.

It could mean nothing. Maybe they've scheduled the wedding for a later time. Maybe everything went so well there was nothing much to bargain, and they will have the wedding here in a few days. Or perhaps Father was able to negotiate peace without needing to give my sister away in marriage.

But once they disembark, I see it on their faces. Disappointment. Worry. Defeat. Haukea is the first to meet me. I reach for her, but she sloughs away and hurries to her hut, likely wanting to be alone. My parents follow behind, slowly.

"What happened?" I ask.

"What do you think happened?" my father barks.

After giving him a scolding look, my mother says, "They would not accept. They're determined to attack." She sighs. "They kept the dowry we brought in exchange for our freedom, for letting us go unharmed. There will be no wedding."

I fold my arms across my waist. "So what do we do?"

"Your father is going to talk to his advisors right now. Make plans to fight."

"But we'll be killed."

"What other choice do we have?"

I hurry and catch up with my father near the council hut. His warrior advisors are already gathered. He sees me when I slip in the back, but he doesn't send me out. He's too preoccupied with more pressing matters than making sure his daughter follows proper procedures.

"We're short on men," he tells the others. "We will need the younger boys for the battle as well. Train them right away. Our men must be able to take on several warriors at once. We must be stronger. Faster. Braver." He looks at each of his leaders one by one. "We can't afford for anyone to be a weak factor."

"Why not let the women fight?" I say. "I could wield a knife or spear as well as—"

"Maile!" Father's patience cracks. "It was bad enough you joined the battle against Cook's sailors. There's no place for you in this. I will not tempt the gods any further. They've obviously been offended, and we can't give them an excuse to wipe us out altogether. We will do this the traditional way." He looks at his men again. "More warriors. More training. More weapons."

After making assignments about who is to organize what, the chief dismisses his men.

"There has to be something else we can do," I say.

Father rubs his head, but he doesn't scold me again like I expect. "And what would you suggest?" His voice is more tired than angry. Frustrated, mostly. He's too defeated to argue right now, and he doesn't really want my advice, but I answer him anyway.

"Perhaps we attack first," I say. "Go to their island on our terms, when we deem the time is right. Catch them by surprise. They will not expect it, and we will have the advantage. We have iron weapons now." I swallow hard, thinking of the metal daggers and hatchets we traded for. "We could defeat them."

"You didn't see it, Maile." Father's eyes glaze over. "They have *thousands* of men, all large and strong. I've never seen anything like it before. Their weapon stores takes an entire wing of their homestead, not just one hut." He sighs. "Our iron blades won't matter. If we were to go there, fight on land they're familiar with, I'm afraid our chances of winning would be even smaller. It's as though they've prepared for this battle for generations. They have spies on the beaches and mountain ridges. Guards on duty throughout the night. We'll stand a better chance on our own soil."

"But our homes are here," I say. "Our families. Children. It's too much to protect and defend. We should take the offensive."

Father stands slowly and begins walking toward his hut. "I'm hoping the presence of homes and families will spur our warriors to fight even harder when they see that what they're fighting for is in imminent danger."

I keep pace with him and wave my hands in frustration. "Well, what about other islands? If 'Eleu intends to capture our island, what's to stop him from taking over other nearby islands? If we can form an alliance with them, perhaps they'll agree to fight alongside us."

"Fight in a cause not their own?"

"Fight to make 'Eleu think twice about trying this same tactic against them. Fight with a guarantee that if threats fall upon others, we will be there to fight for them as well."

Father stops and flares his nostrils. "And reveal to the other islands how weak we really are?" His voice lifts, and several nearby villagers stop to stare at us. "Confess to them that we allowed white foreigners to come upon our land, that we worshipped them then let them kill our warriors? I will not admit to a loss of *mana*. It will only invite others to take advantage of us as well. If this battle doesn't destroy us, another one will. I won't take that risk."

My father can be a great leader, but he can also be blinded by his pride. And he's more stubborn than anyone I've met. Sometimes there's no reasoning with him. I huff and storm away, determined to find Haukea and see if she can give me more information about Wai'ole.

As I get close to the hut, I hear a loud yelling coming from the south, from the forest beyond the dry taro patches. I squint and shield my eyes, trying to see what else has gone wrong this day. A line of our people, both men and women, march from the forest. They continue to yell, but not at each other. At something . . . No, at *someone*. Two men in the center of the crowd drag a man between them. A man with fair skin and a British naval officer's uniform.

Oh, no.

I hurry toward the crowd along with others in the village. The mob stops in front of the chief's hut, not realizing he isn't there. After tossing John to the ground, the villagers form a circle around him. A few curse at him; one hurtles a small rock his way.

"*Pau*," I say, stepping out from the circle. "Stop."

When everyone turns to look at me, it's not out of respect for the chief's daughter, but confusion over why I am speaking out against them hurting an obvious enemy.

"The chief isn't h-here," I stammer, trying to stall. "He's the only one fit to pass judgment or declare a punishment. How do you know this man has done anything wrong?"

John looks up at me. He's on his hands and knees but leans back on his heels, facing me. His eyes hold a mixture of relief and understanding. Relief that I'm here, that he has somewhat of an ally among his enemies, and understanding that no one knew I was keeping him prisoner in the clearing. That I didn't tell anyone about him.

"Done anything wrong?" one of the villagers asks. "He is one of Cook's sailors. He killed our people, tried to kidnap your father. He may have even killed your beloved."

I startle at that. I didn't think anyone saw what happened to Ikaika on the beach, but the truth pierces me, and I wonder why I don't just let my people finish him off. John deserves it, doesn't he? I'm the one who's been confused and disoriented about what all this means. I'm the one with muddled priorities. So perhaps I'm not the one who should be passing judgment, either.

I look at John. I have so many questions I want to ask him, but they all turn through my head, unanswered. How did you get here? Did you follow me? Why did you come? Are you hurt? Along with a selfish plea for him to not tell anyone what I did, what we've been doing, how I hid him in the forest. I see the awkward stitching on the front of his blue coat, and I hope no one else notices. If they do, surely they would suspect one of their own has been at his aid.

Father pushes his way through the crowd and into the open circle next to me.

"What is this?" he asks. When his eyes land on John, anger rushes over his face, and I think he might step forward and kill John with his bare hands. Knowing his frustrations of not being able to appease 'Eleu, and the weakened state of our warriors caused by the foreigners, I wouldn't blame my father for wanting to take his revenge on one of Cook's men.

"We found him in the forest," one of the villagers says. "Just beyond the tree line. He was hiding, out of breath, as though he'd been running here."

He likely wasn't running, but even at a slow pace, he'd be exhausted from the pain of his injury. The injury I inflicted. Why did he follow me? What did he think would happen?

"I apologize," John says with his slight accent. His head is high, shoulders back, trying to exude as much confidence as one could while kneeling on the ground in front of an enemy. "I have no ill intentions toward any of your people." He looks at me, then away quickly. I don't think he wants to bring suspicion on me or single me out. Once again, he's trying to protect me, the same way he did on the beach from one of his own soldiers.

The crowd becomes so silent, I almost think I can hear the quick beating of my heart in my chest.

My father is in awe that John speaks our language, and after a moment, understanding crosses his face. I don't think he remembered until then who John was. That he was Cook's translator—that he could understand and speak our tongue. Perhaps he didn't recognize him without his false head of white hair. Father waits before speaking, realizing he needs to choose his words carefully.

"What explanation do you give, then, for coming into our village?" Father asks.

"I . . . I've been on the island since the day of the battle," John says. "I only want to return to my men. To my ship."

"Since the battle?" Father looks him over. "That's impossible. That was weeks ago. How have you not been discovered until now?" He curls his hand into a fist. "You're a spy."

"No." John holds up a hand defensively, trying to appease the chief. "I'm not a spy. I—"

This time John looks at me and holds my gaze, possibly thinking of a story that will satisfy my father. I shake my head almost imperceptibly, begging him not to reveal what I've done. I don't know how I could explain it to Father, not after all this time.

"I was injured in the battle," John admits. "I managed to hide in the forest, but I couldn't get far while I healed." He clutches the front of his coat, as though ready to reveal evidence of his injury to corroborate his story. "I haven't been able to move much until now." His eyes return to my father. "Please. I mean no harm. I just want to return to my men."

"You're not returning anywhere." The chief orders one of his men to get a knife. "And you've already done a lot of harm."

"What will you do with him?" I ask my father, panic building inside me. I'm glad I haven't told him about the desecrated temple near the ships. If he knew what the sailors did while he was gone, he might not wait for his knife to deliver John's punishment.

The chief growls. "He's the reason we're in this position right now. Why we don't have the means to fight against our enemy."

John's head perks up at that. He doesn't know anything about the neighboring island and their threat of war.

Father notices John's interest, too, and he lowers his voice to a whisper, angling his face toward mine so no one else can hear. "He must pay for his crimes. To not punish him would further anger the gods. Further make my people lose faith in me as their leader."

"Is that what you're worried about?" I whisper. "You think you've brought this on your people? That you failed them some-how?"

"I *have* failed."

It all makes sense now. It's more than his pride that's been hurt. He feels like he's failed as a leader, and he will do whatever it takes to fix it.

"No, you haven't." I motion toward John. "You didn't know where these foreigners came from or what their intentions were. No one on the surrounding islands has ever had to face this cir-cumstance before. Ever. It's impossible to do the wrong thing when you don't know what the right thing is."

"It doesn't matter. I still failed." Father grabs a knife from his guard and makes his way toward John.

John doesn't move. Doesn't flinch. He looks resigned. It re-minds me of that day on the beach, when I came at him with my own knife. He refused to fight against me or protect himself. I thought it was because I was a woman, but maybe it was because he already felt defeated. His captain had just been killed and stolen away, and the other sailors were escaping to their ship. Perhaps he felt there wasn't anything worth fighting for. He has the same look of defeat on his face now, as though if this is what his end will be, he's fine with it.

But I'm not fine with it.

I run past my father and stop just short of John, spinning around to protect him from the chief. "You can't kill him."

Father's eyes go wide. "Maile." He looks so angry I wouldn't be surprised if he decided to use his knife on me instead. But I stay in place.

"Think about it," I say loud enough for the crowd to hear me. "Cook's ships haven't left yet, though they've had ample time to make repairs. Why not? Maybe they're not done with us. Maybe they're making plans to attack us, preparing for another battle as we speak. To seek revenge for the death of their captain, perhaps."

I don't dare look down at John. It's much easier to keep my thoughts straight without seeing his face, without trying to decipher what he's thinking.

"We can't afford to lose any more men," I say. "Not with a battle against Wai'ole imminent."

Father is fuming, but he waits for me to finish.

"We should keep him alive," I say. "He obviously ranks high among his men." I motion toward his uniform. "We saw him standing next to the captain when they came ashore. If they threaten to attack, we have John as a ransom. A bargaining piece to protect us. We can't take any chances, not when we need every man for another fight."

Father pauses, then says, "How do you know his name?"

I can't believe I let that slip. I move my hands to my waist and think fast. "He told us his name that day on the beach. He introduced himself as Cook's translator."

Father seems satisfied with my answer, and I breathe out a sigh of relief.

"We can tie him up," I say, hating that I'm yet again making John a prisoner. But I can't think of an alternative. "Assign someone to watch him. If he is injured like he said, he won't be able to escape our restraints. Besides, his men attempted to kidnap you to get what they wanted. Why not do the same with him?"

Several people in the crowd nod, and I see it in the chief's eyes. He agrees this is a better plan than killing John right away to appease his anger.

"Take him to the prisoner hut," my father orders.

Several men pull John from the ground and lead him away. I don't get a chance to see his face before they do, so I don't know if he's grateful or upset or relieved. Whatever he feels, it doesn't really matter. Because now I have no idea how, or if, he'll ever get back to his ship again.

John Harbottle's Journal

28 February 1779

I once saw a woman killed on the island. It was near the end of our stay the first time we were here. I don't think any of the other sailors saw it happen, but I did. From what I could interpret, she'd been caught pinning yellow feathers in her hair in the privacy of her hut. The red and yellow colors are reserved for the chief and his family, and those not of royal blood caught wearing them are sentenced to death.

That memory is all I can think of as I sit in this prisoner hut. The sun has gone down, but a single torch lights the room enough for me to write by. The guards have left, though I heard them whispering about getting the chief's permission to punish me. I can only guess that's where they've gone—to get his approval to do something to me befitting my crime.

Thanks to Maile, I don't think they will kill me, at least not intentionally. I'm grateful for her quick thinking on my behalf. I once thought she wanted any excuse to see me dead, short of having to kill me herself, but our time together has done more than allow my wound to heal. I think we've both learned the benefit of being patient with each other and our unfamiliar traditions. So much so that we can see the potential that exists for our people to do the same.

She might not have cared whether I lived or died today, but she recognizes the advantage that sparing my life gives us both. I only hope my following her into the village didn't ruin that advantage. In my haste to find her, and, admittedly, in my impatience to return to my men, I put at risk the peace we both want.

But if a woman was killed for wearing the wrong-colored feathers, I know whatever punishment awaits me will be no less severe. England's policies on the treatment of thieves and other criminals haven't always been the most humane, either. Still, it is strange to see a culture like this one that is motivated by so much love and generosity resort to such violence. There is still so much I don't know about them. I only hope I live long enough to learn more.

'umikūmākolu

Chapter Thirteen

I intercept the girl heading to the prisoner hut. She has a banana leaf in her hands, topped with a chunk of taro and dried fish. Food for the prisoner.

"I'll take it," I say, reaching for the food.

"But—"

"It's fine." I make my expression go cold. "I want to look into the face of the man responsible for Ikaika's death."

She narrows her eyes, thinking of what the sailors have done to so many of our beloved. "Of course. Here." She places the food in my hands.

"Thank you," I say.

She doesn't know John literally killed Ikaika, but he admitted to the crowd he was there on the beach, injured in the battle. It's a good reminder for my people of the tragedy that happened not long ago. And it's a good reminder for me that the man in the hut is not my friend. Not really. I need to remember the line dividing us is not a moveable one.

I enter the hut. It's dark, and a guard who had been standing against the far wall takes several large steps toward me, his spear at the ready.

"Food," I say, showing him what's in my hands.

He spits to the side and grunts before taking his place back against the far wall.

I approach John, who is on the ground, his legs extended, and his arms held behind him, tied with coconut fiber rope. I expected him to be tied up, but I didn't expect the rest. His lip has a fresh cut, and his left eye is swelling. His hair has been pulled out of its tie and has become tangled, framing his face. Though we'd washed his clothes just yesterday, his white breeches are covered in dirt and blood. His coat is torn open and split at one sleeve. Whoever ripped it didn't take the time to undo each fastening the way John showed me. Pieces of metal are missing, likely stolen by the guards, and there are more tears, though none as large as the one I mended.

I kneel in front of John, and he lifts his head toward me, opening his mouth as though to say something. I quickly glance toward the guard; it's my way of telling John it's not safe for him to speak. He closes his mouth and offers me a small smile instead. I don't know what he has to be happy about, not after how my people have treated him, but it lifts my mood to know he's not completely broken.

"Is he to eat while bound?" I ask the guard.

"Those were your father's orders," he says. "Do you want me to call one of the servants to feed him?" He begins walking toward the door.

"No, it's fine," I say.

He gives me a look of disgust as though he would never consider helping this man, not even to feed him, then he takes his place again.

I break off a piece of taro and hold it to John's mouth. The root is tender and has been soaked in coconut milk, just how I like it. He gratefully takes it in his mouth and chews, swallowing with difficulty. A flash of pain crosses his eyes, and I fume inside that they've punished him to the point that he can't eat without hurting.

"I'm fine to watch him," I say to the guard. "The men have prepared food. You should go eat while it's still hot."

"I can't leave the chief's daughter in the hands of our enemy."

I laugh out loud. "I think you're thinking of the wrong daughter." He knows my reputation like everyone else. I'm better at playing predator than prey. I pull a small knife from the back of my belt. "I can handle myself fine."

He hesitates, unsure.

"I've already eaten," I add. "I don't think it's fair that the prisoner eats before one of the chief's warriors, do you? I hope there's enough left back in the food hut."

That one works. The guard glares at John and heads to the door. "I'll be back soon."

When the guard is gone, I settle more comfortably next to John and give him another piece of taro. "I'd untie you if I could," I say, "but he might return any moment, and I don't want to bring suspicion on either of us."

"I understand," he says. "Thank you."

"Don't thank me. Stop thanking me." It's the first time I've commented to him about those words.

A look of confusion fills his face. "I'm sorry."

I sigh. "And don't apologize, either."

John opens his mouth, but snaps it shut again, perhaps afraid he'll say something else I don't want him to.

"Say something mean to me," I suggest.

"Excuse me?"

"You are too kind for your own good." I let a small smile escape so he knows I'm teasing. "Stop thanking me for every little thing I do and tell me something you hate about me."

His face reddens, and I offer him another piece of taro to chew while he thinks of a proper insult.

"You're a terrible seamstress," he finally says. "Just look at my coat."

I follow his gaze down toward his chest.

"Yesterday morning there was a simple tear through the fabric," he explains. "But since you've had your hands on it, it's become unrecognizable. The sleeve is torn. The fabric is stained. And I think you might have lost a few of my buttons."

I give him a small laugh, and he smiles in reply.

"You also need a lesson on how to tie a piece of string properly." John blows a puff of air toward his forehead to try to move a wisp of hair out of his face. "My hair didn't stay tied back for long, thanks to your meager skills."

I reach for the lock falling into his eyes and sweep it back. I wish I could run my fingers through his hair to untangle it, tie a fresh cord to keep it secured. But the guard would notice any change, and I don't think I could explain why I was touching the prisoner, let alone being kind to him.

Instead I brush my finger against the side of his swelling eye and whisper, "I'm sorry." Sorry for the way he's been treated. Sorry I can't do more for him.

"No apologizing, remember?" One side of his mouth rises, the side without the cut. "Your turn."

"My turn for what?"

"Say something mean about me."

I snort, as though I could come up with a thousand things.

But then my face falls, thinking of John killing Ikaika. If there were ever something I should hate John for, it's that. And I do. I did. How could I not?

He seems to sense the shift in my mood and begins to apologize, but I quickly stuff another taro piece into his mouth before he can finish.

"You're slow," I say. "You can't keep up with me, and you walk funny." I roll my eyes. "I have to do everything for you. Heal you, clean you, feed you." I motion to the food in my hand. "And I'm still trying to forget how disgusting it is that you go months without bathing."

After a moment, we both laugh out loud, and I cover my mouth to silence the sound, worried people outside the hut may have heard us. John's laugh softens as well, but he crouches over in pain as it does.

"Don't make me laugh," he whispers. "It hurts too much."

"I'm sorry."

My apology starts us giggling again, so I press my mouth closed so no more words can escape. Instead, I offer John a piece of dried fish. This one's harder to chew than the taro.

"It's no sea snail," he jokes.

I sigh and ask, "Why did you follow me? Why did you come here?"

"I was tired of waiting," he says. "I told you I needed to get back to my men."

"And I told you I'd take you when you were healed."

He raises one eyebrow. "We both know that was a shallow promise."

I don't deny it. I had planned on taking him back, but I was never sure under what circumstances. I'm surprised by my disappointment that John wants to leave so desperately.

"What was your father saying before—about fighting another enemy?"

I look down, not wanting to talk about the weak position we're in. I don't believe John would hurt us on purpose, but I've seen what he's willing to do to get what he wants. And I know what his sailors are capable of. If John knows about the threat we are facing, and if word got back to his men, would they somehow use it against us?

"And how you don't have enough men or the means to fight against them?" he nudges.

I finally look up at him, but say nothing.

"Maile." There he goes, saying my name again like it means something to him. Like he can convince me he cares about me and isn't just trying to save his own life.

"It has nothing to do with you," I say.

"Is there someone your people are afraid to face? Another army?" He pauses, choosing words I'll understand. "You have an enemy but not enough men to fight them off, because of us?" He pulls against his hand restraints, and I imagine him pointing to his chest if he could. Admitting his soldiers have rendered us powerless against our enemy. A different enemy, that is.

"It doesn't matter," I say. "Like I said, it has nothing to do with you." The damage is done. It's not like he can give us our men back or pretend he and his foreign ships had never landed here in the first place. "What you need to worry about is how to prevent my father from executing you. Think of a way to bargain for your life, your freedom."

"That's just it," he says. "There might be a way for us to solve both problems at the same time."

"What do you mean?" I ask.

John's eyes shoot to the door before he lowers his head in a submissive position.

I glance behind me as the guard walks back into the hut. The rest of our conversation will have to wait. I finish feeding John his meal in silence.

"Fetch me some water," I tell the guard, making it a command rather than a question. I don't want to give him an opportunity to argue. If I were anyone but the chief's daughter, he likely would. But he merely grunts and leaves the hut again, giving John and me a brief moment of privacy.

John leans forward. "I must speak to your father. I have a proposal."

"What is it?" I ask.

He lowers his voice. "In exchange for—" But then he cuts off his words and leans away from me.

"No talking," barks a voice from behind me. The guard has returned too soon. He drops a coconut shell half full of water into my lap before kicking the side of John's extended legs.

The impact knocks John to his side, his face pressing into the dirt. It takes everything in me not to yell at the guard and help John as he positions himself upright again without the use of his arms.

While lifting the water to his mouth, I try to brush away the dirt from his face without attracting attention. When he's done drinking, I run out of excuses to stay and gather the food supplies before standing slowly. I hate having to leave John alone with the guard, afraid of what the guard will do in my absence, but I don't have a choice. The only thing I can do now is convince my father to speak with John before it's too late.

Late in the night, while the guards slept and the fire had long gone out, a figure entered the prisoner hut. At first I thought it was Maile. This woman's silhouette was so similar, but she moved differently. A little more refined, a little less rushed. She approached me carefully, kneeling a small distance away. Her proximity allowed me to finally make out her features. It wasn't Maile, but I suspected who she was before she spoke.

"My sister sent me," she said, lifting a small bowl filled with liquid and a clean cloth. "I'm here to help." Her voice held hesitation, as though she was not certain if she could trust me.

But she trusted her sister. She trusted Maile.

I didn't know what Maile had told her about us. I wasn't sure if she knew Maile injured me, held me captive, healed me. I didn't know if she knew I killed Ikaika. Maile could have merely told her it was safe for her to come. It was impossible to know what was safe to say, so I said nothing. I didn't even ask her name, just nodded when she asked if she could administer to me.

She unfastened the restraints on my wrists and quickly cleaned my injuries, at least the ones on my face and arms. Then she applied an ointment on the open cuts that was both foul-smelling and soothing at the same time. After giving me a few leaves of a plant I didn't recognize, she waited until I chewed and swallowed.

"Thank you," I said as she left. I smiled, imagining the scolding I would have received from Maile for saying that if she were here in her sister's place.

Now it's early morning, and I can't sleep. Whatever medicine Maile's sister gave me softened the pain of my bruises, but it made my stomach queasy. Still, I'm in awe of the lengths Maile has gone to help me. Except for the initial assault with her knife across my chest, she's made every effort to ensure my well-being, even down to asking her kin to come to my aid.

It's obvious her sister is more skilled in the healing arts. Her bedside manner is more practiced, and at least she attempted to speak to me. I remember those first days with Maile—the rough and reluctant way she administered to my wound, her brusque responses, her disgusted looks. I smile, a part of me preferring Maile's stubborn disinclination over her sister's adept and leveled manner.

If anyone could convince the chief to speak with me, establish a plan that could benefit everyone, it would be Maile.

I hear voices approaching.
I think the chief is here.

ʻumikūmāhā

Chapter Fourteen

I pace outside the prisoner hut, waiting as my father talks to John inside. It's morning, two days after John's capture, but too dark inside the hut to see anything through the doorway. And except for an occasional shout from my father, I can't hear anything, either. I worry the chief's temper will overtake his patience before he can hear what John has to say. Whatever that is. He never got the chance to explain it to me. I have to trust he knows what he's getting himself into.

Finally, one of Father's guards leaves the hut, followed by the chief himself, and then . . . John. His hands are untied, and he's walking of his own volition, though with a slight limp, favoring one side. His torn clothing has been smoothed and tucked the best it can be under the circumstances. One of his arms hangs as though injured. I can't tell if it's a remnant from the battle or a new injury from the guards.

I hope Haukea was able to ease his suffering last night, even a little. She's a natural healer, and I'm grateful for her help and discretion. I think she knew there was something I wasn't telling her, something besides a fleeting concern I had for the beaten soldier, but if so, she kept it to herself.

Either way, it's strange to see John walking on his own. The guards' weapons aren't even drawn. Whatever John and my father are doing, they're doing it together. Another guard follows John, the one who had been watching him two days ago.

"Alika," Father says to his man waiting outside the hut. "Find La'akea and two more warriors. The four of you will join us on the beach. Bring your weapons."

Their weapons? What do they need their weapons for?

"Right away," Alika says, and he hurries to find my brother.

John sees me and frowns, regret in his eyes. I wish I knew what was going on. I wish we could speak to each other freely. And I wish his smile would return. This new expression has me worried.

I hurry to my father's side as the men head for the beach to await reinforcements.

"What's happening?" I ask, nervously glancing at John walking behind us.

The chief exhales with impatience. "Not now, Maile. This is urgent."

"What is urgent?" I ask.

"Matters that don't involve you."

I flare my nostrils. I'm the one who got him to talk to John in the first place. I hate that he involves me with important matters when it's convenient for him, but dismisses me when he tires of me. I wish he'd trust me. He has to know by now I'm more than just a girl who's good for nothing except to marry off. I'm his daughter. And I want to help.

We pause at the beach while my father orders the royal canoe ready.

"Where are you going?" I'm so confused about what's happening.

Father ignores me and boards the canoe, followed by John and the guards. John gives me another frown from the canoe, and I keep silent though it kills me. Where could they possibly be going? Will my father drown his prisoner at sea? Or is he returning him to his ship? If so, why does my father need to accompany him?

It's obvious John is leaving of his own free will—our men aren't afraid of him escaping or attacking the chief. Almost as though he's an equal. What did John say to my father? If John's men took some of ours hostage, then perhaps he's brokered a trade: our men to be released in exchange for returning him to his ship. It would gain more warriors for my father, so I understand why the chief would agree to it. But does that mean this is the last time I'll see John? Is he leaving with his men, never to return?

As the canoe heads out to sea and those gathered on the beach dissipate, I sit in the sand and shade my eyes, watching as the vessel retreats farther into the ocean. I tell myself it's good if the foreigners leave. That it's what I've wanted this entire time. For them to leave and never return. There shouldn't be this unsettling feeling inside me—the feeling that something is missing, that something which should have happened, didn't. Of words that should have been said but were never spoken.

When the canoe reaches the *Resolution*, I can barely see the sails set against the dark wood of Cook's large ship. I don't know how long it stays there. Perhaps hours, for my stomach begins to growl, but I don't move. I just sit and wait. The day is extra windy, and the breeze coming off the water sends my hair into a frenzy behind me. It's sure to become a tangled-salty-sandy mess that will be laborious to brush through later, and my face may even redden from the burn of the wind, but I don't care. I only watch for the movement of the ship or the canoe. I feel as though I'm not on a beach but on the edge of a cliff, ready to fall. Into what I'm not sure. Something I'm not certain I want.

So when I see the small sails of the canoe begin to grow, approaching shore, I feel some relief that my father is safe at least. He's likely returning on that canoe. But is John with him, or is he on the *Resolution*, ready to set sail for England? Or perhaps to the Northwest Passage he talked so much about. Will I ever see him again?

The large white sails on the *Resolution* are raised, and my heart sinks. This is it. They are leaving. John is leaving. The part of their ship they'd been repairing appears to be whole again. I stand and walk to the water's edge but I don't stop. I walk into the waves until the water level reaches my chest and I am no longer fighting the push and pull of each incoming and receding wave, just keeping my balance above each crest that comes. A part of me longs to swim out and try to reach the ship, while another ties imaginary stones to my feet to keep me in the place where I belong and where they—he—does not.

But it isn't long before I see movement in the distance and realize the *Resolution* and its companion ship aren't setting out to the open ocean, but are moving closer. They sail toward the shore, as though following my father's canoe.

What is happening?

The royal canoe approaches, then skims past me, and I count the men, noticing one is missing. John is no longer with them. I watch as they disembark on shore and head inland, as though nothing was amiss. Several of them carry the large wooden idols that were stolen from our *heiau*. Have the sailors given them back?

I return my attention to the *Resolution*. It pauses in its approach, and I watch as the crew lowers an anchor to the ocean floor, just outside the reef where the water is still deep enough for their giant ship. It's the same spot where they stayed during their month-long visit before. Do they intend to remain, then? And is my father letting them come to our shore, or are they preparing for another attack?

I stay in the water and watch Cook's ship. It no longer has its captain, yet somehow that gives me no comfort. I debate leaving to ask my father what John said to him and why the ships have moved closer, but a part of me feels if I turn my back on the ship, it will either catch me unawares or disappear forever. So I wait, letting the water push and pull me, camouflaging the push and pull of my own emotions, as I try to make sense of something I can't understand.

Finally, a small boat is lowered into the water, and a handful of sailors board it before paddling to shore. I look back at the beach, but no one is there. Either my father doesn't realize they're coming, or he's expecting them. After all, something was discussed during his hours on the foreign ship. If he's expecting them, then . . .

I make my way to the shore at the same time the small boat reaches it, and I notice one of the men wears a navy blue coat while the others wear red. His hair is tied back neatly, away from his face so that from this distance I can see his bruised eye, his cut lip. But his uniform is mended again. No, it is a different uniform. A second one he must have had stored on his ship. He doesn't wear his false white hair, but his face is freshly shaven, and it's clear as he steps onto the sand that he moves with purpose, no longer with a limp. His men follow close behind him and toward our homestead beyond.

John pauses once and glances my way. There's no one else on the beach; it's not difficult to see me. Still, he looks surprised, maybe a little cautious. He says nothing, just angles his head inland so slightly, I'm not sure his soldiers saw him do it. But his message to me is clear: he wants me to follow them. And it's also clear my father is expecting him.

It's not as though anything would keep me away—perhaps I'll finally get the answers I seek. But something seems different about John, not just his clothes and freshly groomed face. He's hesitant. Like he's not sure I'm going to like what I'm about to learn. Still, I feel a strange sense of relief to see him again. To know he hasn't left—at least not yet. That feeling is enough to make me just as hesitant, and I fall in to step behind the soldiers as they lead me to the council hut where my father is waiting.

The chief motions for me to stand on the platform beside him and my brother, which is unusual. John and his company are in the open-air hut with us, along with several of my father's guards. I can't help but notice many of our people gathered outside, though they are not officially invited to this council. The chief obviously doesn't intend to keep these matters private.

"John Harbottle"—my father says the name slowly and carefully to get it right—"and I have spent the last several hours discussing terms."

Terms for what? John's freedom?

"Because he was one of James Cook's trusted officers, I gave him the honor of voicing his proposal to me. After learning of our situation with the enemy threat of Waiʻole in the south, John offered us the use of his sailors' weapons."

What?

"With these guns—" Father looks at John to see if he got the word right. "With these guns, we'll have the clear advantage over our enemy and will defeat them with ease."

The scene around me disappears, and all I see is Ikaika in the shallow water of our beach. The wound in his chest. The smoke dissipating from John's weapon . . . his gun. The thing that caused so much despair for our people. And now we're to welcome it like some sanction from the gods? I narrow my eyes, not believing my father has actually agreed to this.

I look at John. He glances away the moment I do. He must have been watching for my reaction. And for good reason. He knew I wouldn't like this. How could he do this to my people? To me?

"These weapons are complicated," the chief continues. "So in addition to letting us use the guns, the sailors will train our warriors in their use." He looks around the room carefully to make sure he has everyone's attention. "I have given permission to John and his men to come ashore for the purpose of teaching us how to use the weapons and to instruct us in additional methods of combat."

My mouth falls open, and I quickly shut it again. He's right—there's no way 'Eleu could defeat us under such circumstances. Guns? Advanced training? But this is a lot to ask of John and his crew. So much so that I'm afraid of what we have agreed to give up in exchange.

I turn to the chief. "What did you promise in return for these . . . guns?" The word is hard to say, and I don't think it has to do with their hard and abrupt language, but rather the meaning behind the word.

"On the day of the battle, the foreigners attempted to retrieve items they claim our men had stolen from their ship. Navigational equipment and supplies. John asked only that we return those items so he and his men can continue on their voyage after the battle is over."

I swallow hard. If only I'd given John the equipment the day I found it. Convinced him to keep quiet about where it came from and made him leave right away with his men. I wouldn't be here in this moment, facing the horror of seeing guns in the hands of my people. But it's too late. My father will never abandon this opportunity now.

Father continues, "I told him we don't have the things he spoke of. And to my knowledge, we never did." He pauses, remembering something. "Maile, you told me that on the day of the battle you escaped the beach on one of their small boats. Was it the one we tried to return to his men? Perhaps there were items in the vessel with you."

I can't help but look at John again. None of my people know I took him hostage on that boat. I told John the skiff was gone the next day, which was almost the truth. But the way he's looking at me now, with the reminder that I've been dishonest to my own people, does he suspect I lied to him, too?

"Maile?" my father prompts.

"No," I say. "I mean yes. Yes, it was their boat. The one they came for. But no, there was no navigational equipment in it." I take a deep breath and continue to look at John as I speak, trying to convince him along with my father. "At least I don't think there was. When I returned to the beach the next morning, the boat was gone." I swallow and look back at my father. "If the supplies were there, I'm afraid they were lost at sea."

The lies don't come easily, but I remind myself I have no choice. I have to protect my father's honor, defend his position as high chief. If I admit our people stole the equipment without his knowledge, he will lose the respect of the sailors and the respect of his people. It will leave him vulnerable to those who would fight for his rank. The secret needs to stay buried in the high forest.

The chief looks back and forth between John and me. Though I know it's impossible, I worry he knows what transpired between the lieutenant and myself these last weeks. But then he nods. Surprisingly, my father doesn't seem upset by the news. I would have thought the loss of those items might negate the deal, but . . .

"I knew the equipment wouldn't be found among us," Father says. "And so I proposed another offer to John."

I wait, trying to think what the foreigners would want so desperately that they'd lend us their guns and sacrifice their time to train us.

"The purpose of the navigational equipment is to help John and his men return home." The chief sits taller in his seat. "Luckily, they've landed among a people quite skilled in the practice of navigation. I proposed we teach them our knowledge of wayfinding—the method of reading the stars and oceans and weather to plot a course. They can use that knowledge to return to their England."

"But . . ." I start to say. But England is far away, on the other side of the world. But their ships are different than ours. But it takes years of training to become familiar with our practices on the ocean. But wayfinding and gaining an intimate knowledge of the sea isn't something you can teach, it's something you feel.

"But," the chief says to John, finishing my sentence for me, "Ikaika is no longer with us. As my prime navigator, he would have been the best candidate for the job. However, my daughter is just as skilled in the ways of navigation and will be more than willing to teach you our ways. Enough that you'll be able to return home when the time comes."

He can only mean me, since Haukea knows nothing of

navigation; her life has been much more sheltered and austere than mine. His statement brings up a slew of emotions within me. Did he really say I'm as skilled as Ikaika in wayfinding? It's a generous compliment, and I'm humbled and grateful that he regards me in such a way. It's something I never would have thought he would admit to in public, always treating me as lesser, as merely a girl.

But there are other navigators—other men—who could teach the sailors, which makes me think this is a masked insult from my father. To offer a woman to teach them marks the sailors as inferior. A show of disrespect toward the sailors makes more sense than the chief honoring my ability as a navigator. I don't know if those from England view women as less than men, so I'm not sure John would recognize this as an insult. He's treated me with nothing but respect, from the battle on the beach to our time together in the southern clearing. He's too kind, and I think my gender only makes him more so toward me.

"Maile," my father says. "You will teach John over the next several weeks."

"John?" I say, surprised. I figured I'd be teaching one of his sailors, perhaps an officer assigned to navigation. I thought John was a language expert, not necessarily skilled in the details of sailing.

I glance at John, wondering if he had requested me for this duty. If he had volunteered himself over others. I admit we've established a sort of hesitant friendship. Maybe he felt as jumbled as I did about the possibility of his leaving. Though I'm far from happy about this arrangement for the guns, I'm surprised to realize I'm not opposed to spending more time with him. Perhaps it's the relief of not needing to hide our acquaintance with each other anymore.

"Of course you will teach John," my father says. "He's the only one who speaks our language." He laughs. "How could you teach any of the other men?"

I feel like a fool. He's right—John's the only one who could learn, at least with the timetable we've been given. How absurd of me to think John volunteered to learn from me of his own volition.

"The sailors will stay on their ship and come ashore for training. We will help to feed them, but for the most part they will not be a further burden than they have been."

He means we aren't to lavish them with goods the way we did before. We aren't to worship them, praise them, honor them. They are not gods. They are equals. Allies.

"John Harbottle will be staying in one of my huts," the chief says.

"What?" I snap my mouth closed the moment I realize I said it aloud.

Father ignores my outburst. "After settling his men and arranging the training schedule, he will begin working with Maile. As soon as possible."

John frowns. I still can't tell what he thinks of all this. He likely knew this was the arrangement when he left the prisoner hut this morning, most definitely when he came ashore and saw me. I understand his hesitation now. He didn't know what I would think, if I'd be upset or confused or angry. I'm a little of each, but I'm mostly unsettled and unsure about this plan, especially since it involves weapons that have caused us so much pain. Items I never wanted to see again.

I could dig up the navigational equipment. Plant the items where someone else could stumble upon them. Even sneak them onto one of their ships. John could be on his way. But now that my father has his weapons, there's no way he'll give them up. The deal has been made. Even if I did produce the equipment, John would likely stay to fulfill his end of the bargain with the guns. Because he is a good man. A man of honor.

I look back at my father. His eyebrows are raised, waiting for my answer though he never asked a question. Still, he needs to know I will do what he has asked. That I will teach John how to navigate using our methods so he can take his men home.

I nod once.

Father dismisses those both inside and outside the hut, but I can't make myself move. There's been another shift in the wind, but it comes at me from so many different angles, I'm not sure which way it wants me to go. So I stay, trying to understand it. Make sense of it.

John also waits while the others around him leave. Perhaps waiting for me. Or gauging what he should do next as well. But when my father reaches him, they both turn and head back together toward the chief's huts, perhaps to discuss training plans or John's new sleeping quarters. As they disappear from view, I'm left alone, wondering how our circumstances have shifted so quickly.

John Harbottle's Journal
2 March 1779

There is a story the children like to tell about the waterfalls that flow down the mountainside on this side of the island. During a time of drought, a woman gave birth to a child with the power to shape-shift into a pig. She kept him away from the village, afraid the chief would put her child to death if his unnatural ability was discovered.

The child's appetite was unrivaled, and he was not satisfied with his mother's meager harvest of dry root vegetables. So he ventured into the village each night and stole a chicken for his meal. When the chief's prize rooster went missing, he waited with his army in the dark to catch the thief unawares. They captured the child with ease and tied him up in the prisoner hut. But when he shifted into his pig form, he burst through his constraints and expanded beyond the seams of the structure, for his ravenous appetite had made him grow to a monstrous size.

With the chief and his warriors in pursuit, the boy-pig ran toward the mountains and climbed to the other side to escape, but not before carving long grooves into the mountainside with his sets of hooves. The gouges were deep enough to reach hidden springs of water that sent a rush of waterfalls flowing down to the valley, washing away the chief and his men. The boy-pig made it to the other side, never to be heard of again, though he is remembered as a hero, bringing much-needed water to his people.

I think the children enjoy the story because it is about one of their own not only getting away with mischief, but being praised for it. However, I like the way it takes something seemingly bad and damaging and turns it into a blessing in disguise.

I've struck a deal with the chief. I've offered him the use of our guns, though it took me hours to convince the crew it's for our best interest, especially the sailor who saw me taken captive. Now I must return to the island. The chief is going to tell his daughter she must spend these next few weeks teaching me to navigate.

I feel like that boy-pig, causing problems no matter what I do. My men have wrought turmoil in the lives of the Hawai'ians the moment we returned, and I don't know how to begin trying to fix what's been broken. So though we might not have the ability to erase all that has happened, perhaps we can give them something beneficial in the aftermath. But none of it will be worth it if I disappoint her. Not after everything she's done for me.

My stomach twists not knowing how she will react.

'umikūmālima

Chapter Fifteen

I walk along the beach where the water meets the sand. My feet sink into the dampness, marking my path. It gives way easily, evidence of where I've been. Of where I am. I look behind me to measure how far I can see my footsteps. I frown at how few remain, how easily the waves have washed them away. I frown again when I see John following my path, heading toward me. I avoided him yesterday after my father's announcement in the council hut, but I know I can't put off our training any longer now that he's found me.

I stop walking and stay still, waiting for him to catch up and letting my feet sink deeper and deeper into the sand with each wave. I shade my eyes at the rising sun, peeking its rays behind the wooden planks of the *Resolution*. It's still a strange sight to see Cook's massive ships in our bay, something I'm not sure I'll ever get used to.

"You're angry." John stands beside me and looks out at the horizon as well.

It's not a question, but I answer him anyway. "Yes."

"If there were another sailor who could speak your language,

I would appoint him instead. I apologize the circumstances require you to be with me."

I huff. "I'm not angry about having to be with you." I turn and speak to him directly. "And I'm not angry about having to teach you how to navigate, either."

If anything, teaching him more of our traditions and practices will help him understand us better. Knowing our language is one thing, but understanding a culture, its people, goes a lot further. Perhaps it will help him fathom the harm he's doing by throwing his weapons into our hands. It can't end well.

Relief washes over his face, and he asks, "Then what is it?"

I raise an eyebrow. "Isn't it obvious? Those guns of yours. I want nothing to do with them. I don't want my people to have any part of them, either."

He nods, understanding. "I can't promise you that all of your men will survive the fight. I can't promise you something won't go wrong, that the guns won't cause harm to people you care about. I can't even guarantee you a victory against your enemy." He reaches a hand to my shoulder and squeezes it. "I know you don't want this."

I glance at his hand on my skin. Is he referring to the guns or . . . or having to be with him?

He drops his hand and stands taller. "But we ruined your chance at a victory when we fought against you and diminished your ranks." He pauses, searching my eyes. "Let us help you get it back."

I glance behind him at the sand. The two paths of footsteps we created are no longer there, washed away by the water. If only the impression the sailors made on my people were so easily erased. Here one moment, gone the next, leaving no evidence they even existed. No lasting mark. Easily forgotten.

"Maile?"

I look back at John. He wants me to tell him it's all right. He wants me to forgive him. There are so many things I need to forgive, but I'm not ready yet. I'm not sure if I'll ever be.

I sigh, eager to change the subject. "Take off your clothes," I say.

John trips over his feet though he hadn't been moving, stumbling in the sand.

"What's wrong?" I ask.

He clears his throat and dusts off his uniform though there's nothing to clean. "I . . . I'm sorry. Did you say what I thought you said?"

There he goes with his concerns about modesty again. "You can keep your . . . under layers on if you like." I reach for the fasteners on his jacket to help him remove it. I feel like I've become an expert at it. "But I don't want you to ruin another set of clothing now that you're looking . . . nice again."

John blushes but helps me remove his coat before pulling his white shirt over his head. "Why do I need to undress to learn about navigation?"

"Because you're getting in the water." I help him place his clothing a safe distance from the tide then motion for him to follow me down the beach. "The first step in learning how to find your way across the sea is to get to know the sea herself. Feel her. Let her feel you. Become one together."

John blushes again and stays silent until we've reached a length of rock surrounding a pool of water close to the beach. The rocks essentially block the incoming waves, creating a quiet, shallow pool just deep enough to wade in safely. It's where we bring the little ones before they've learned to swim. It's the perfect way to get to know the water without harm.

I motion to the pool. "Your job today is to stay in the water. Sit, lie, wade, whatever you like. But I want you to get all the way in. Immerse yourself."

"You want me to sit in a pool of water all day?" His words hold confusion rather than frustration. "What will that teach me?"

"Did you not hear me a moment ago?" I roll my eyes as though I'm talking to a child. "You need to get to know the ocean. Feel her."

"Yes, I remember all that, but . . ." He pauses. "I grew up near a shipyard. I've spent years at sea. I've seen more of the ocean than most people ever have. This is pointless."

"Years on a ship," I say. "Twelve meters up in a floating mountain doesn't count. How often did you actually get in the water?"

He presses his lips together. "I don't see what that has to do with navigating a ship."

"And that's precisely why you need to do this," I say. "So you *can* see what it has to do with navigating a ship." I pause. "You aren't going to be stubborn about this, are you? My father trusted me to teach you. I need you to trust me, too."

"I trust you," he mumbles before stepping into the water.

"All the way in," I say, tilting my head as he tiptoes slowly.

John walks to the center of the pool, the deepest part, and the water reaches just below his waist. "I'm all the way in."

I sigh and walk in after him. These next few weeks will test my patience if he keeps being reluctant, forcing me to explain every little detail.

"No," I say, pushing down on his shoulders. "All the way in."

He sinks into the water until nothing but his head is above the surface.

I lower myself into the water as well, but fully immerse myself, wetting my hair and face before breaking the surface again to breathe. I float on my back and close my eyes. Every part of me is touching the water. Not the sand. Not the rocks. Not the man beside me. Just the water.

"All the way in," I whisper again.

I hear the sound of John submerging into the water and the silence that follows as he floats on his back like me. I let the gentle stillness of the secluded pond seep into me, making me impossibly still. I don't drift; the only movement my body makes is the slow lift of my lungs as I breathe in and out. I angle my head back so the water covers my closed eyelids, but not so far that I can't breathe. The water even closes up my ears, and I can hear the subtle yawn of the sea as she awakens for the day.

I shift my body to a vertical position slowly, letting my feet find the sand, and I wipe the water from my eyes. John is still floating a small distance from me, but his body is taut, tense. His arms shift back and forth as he struggles to keep his body afloat, and his eyes are scrunched closed, tiny wrinkles forming at the sides as he fights against this exercise.

Determined to find the source of his resistance, I ask, "What do you feel?"

"Cold," he says.

I groan inwardly. "What else?"

"Wet."

He's not going to learn anything about navigating the seas if he doesn't learn to trust the water. If he doesn't trust the winds or the clouds or the sky and all the things the world is trying to tell him. I think about what he does trust, hoping to use it as a starting point. James Cook? His ship? His sailors?

Me?

I wade through the water towards him and position myself near the top of his head, carefully reaching out with my hands to cradle it. His eyes shoot open, and his body jolts at my touch, but the moment his eyes meet mine, he relaxes again.

"Shh," I whisper. I spread my fingers along his scalp, rubbing gently to coax him to trust me. Trust that I won't let anything happen to him. That he can release his will to me.

John closes his eyes again, the muscles along his neck relaxing as he lowers his head into my hands. The rest of his body follows, easing into a stillness that involves releasing himself to the water, not fighting against it. It's only me and the ocean holding him up now, not him. There is no current in the pool, but his body sways back and forth anyway, creating a calm rhythm that I think must be a conversation he's having with the sea.

I tilt his head back slightly to let the water rise above his ears and over his eyes. He doesn't resist or try to break free. Instead, he releases a breath in slight surprise at the sensation. He really does trust me. And that's a good thing. I'll need to place him in more precarious situations than this if he is to learn to navigate properly. I don't know that I could have established such trust with any of his sailors in so short a time. John, who was once my hostage, is now a friend. Perhaps that's still too generous a word, but I've nothing else to describe the relationship between us.

I raise his head just enough so he can hear me when I ask him again, "What do you feel?"

He takes a moment to answer. "Cold," he repeats.

I frown, frustrated he's not putting as much effort into this as I thought. But then he continues.

"She's cold from the absence of the sun. Of hours spent in the dark. Alone. Without his warmth. But he greets her on the horizon, a sunrise kiss." He pauses. "She's reluctant at first, still cold, still lonely. But he persists, and she can't help but greet him with an embrace, letting his warmth seep into her. Slowly, but steadily."

He opens his eyes and looks at me. "Eventually she will be filled with such warmth, she'll forget he's to abandon her again. It's a dance that repeats itself again and again, but for a moment, she allows herself to be with him as though time were something you could pause forever. And she dreams of never being cold again."

His words are beautiful and stir something inside me. "I think you would make a good chanter," I say. "I would have mistaken those words for a song. How can someone who's just recently learned our language use it so effectively?"

John shifts upright, finds his feet, and turns to me. "It's not hard when you have the right inspiration."

It's my turn to blush. I run my hand along the surface of the water. "She's amazing, isn't she?"

"Yes, she is." John clears his throat. "The water. The ocean. She makes quite an impression."

"I'm glad you like her. But I was serious about you spending the day in here. Immerse yourself." I begin to walk toward the beach.

"Where are you going?"

"To give you time alone with her," I say, as though teasing him about his lover. "I'm afraid I'm too much of a distraction for you. She's liable to become jealous." But a part of me thinks it's really *him* who's too much of a distraction for *me*.

He doesn't respond, as though he agrees with me, and it's no use to fight it. He moves onto his back to float in the water again.

I escape my chores periodically to spy on John, pleased to see he's still in the water each time I check on him. Splashing the surface with his cupped hands, blowing air along the surface to create bubbles, exploring the surface of the rock's face both above and below the waterline. And floating on his back again and again, adjusting as the tide rises and the movement of water within the pond becomes more pronounced.

At midday, I bring him a basket of roasted breadfruit and raw fish. It's much softer than the taro and dried fish I fed him the other night and hopefully easier for him to chew as his injuries continue to heal. I motion for John to join me on shore, and he sits in the sand next to me, the basket of food between us.

"Thank you," he says, picking up a chunk of golden breadfruit, the bumpy rough skin still attached on one end. "I'm so hungry."

"Careful," I scold, shoving his shoulder away. "You'll drip salt water over everything."

He responds by shaking his head back and forth like an animal, spraying me and our lunch at the same time. My mouth falls open, but John just laughs, his mouth full of half-chewed breadfruit.

"One morning spent without your uniform and you've turned into a boar," I say, teasing. I lay a strip of fish on a length of breadfruit and take a small bite.

"My apologies for my ravenous behavior," he says. "I never imagined spending hours doing nothing but sitting or floating in a child's pool would weaken me so." He points toward the water.

"You're exposed," I say.

John glances down at himself to make sure he still has some clothing on.

"No." I point to the sky. "I mean the sun, the wind, the water. You're not used to being outside, fully exposed to the elements, for so long. It's natural for the world to steal your energy in the process."

John nods and takes another bite. "I'll probably burn, too."

"You're accustomed to exposure as a sailor on a ship. Often for months at a time," I add, remembering what he told me about his sailing experience. "The sea may beat you up a bit at first. Until you really get to know her well." I glance at him, his disheveled hair, the water dripping off his back, the pink hue to his cheeks and shoulders that wasn't there this morning. "So what have you learned?"

"She's a beast," he says. "Unassuming. Surprisingly agile. But she can come at you with unexpected ferocity. She's a force that isn't to be tamed, only allowed to be understood one secret at a time. And only when she gives her permission."

"That's good," I say. "And all this came to you while you were playing in a child's pool?"

"You know this place is more than that."

I wait for him to explain.

"The tide came in slowly. The water rose, and with it, its movement, its response to her swell. It wasn't long before the rock wall itself couldn't keep her back, and the waves washed over the top of it and into the little lagoon."

I glance out to the rocks where John points, the tide still high, the waves still pushing past the barrier into the pool.

"And not calming flows of water over the ridge," he continues. "But a meeting with a clash and a roar and a burst of white. Water entangling with the air to create a visual chaos before falling with equal violence on the other side." He slaps his palm to his knee, remembering what it was like to be in the water. "No longer still. No longer calm. She wasn't whispering to me anymore. This was a woman shouting, refusing to be ignored. Unafraid to remind me of how insignificant I was. Pushing me against the rocks. Making me work harder and harder to keep my balance."

"Perhaps she is angry with you," I say.

John looks at me. "No, not angry. She's testing me. I think she wants me to learn." He keeps a straight face, making sure I know he's serious and not teasing with his words. "She wants me to know her. But I have to earn it."

"Then perhaps this is her way of making you stronger," I say. "After all, isn't it through obstacles and adversity that we are able to learn best? Having gone through the trial, we become more knowledgeable, stronger than we had once been."

"Yes," John says, looking back out to the water. "I think you're right."

"Of course I'm right," I say, a note of teasing in my voice. "I'm the teacher. I'm always right."

John laughs before taking another bite of breadfruit.

"And I look forward to seeing what she wants to teach you after lunch," I add. "Hurry and eat."

He smiles and then salutes me, the way I've seen some of the sailors do to him. "Yes, ma'am."

We eat the rest of the meal in silence, and I think teaching him to navigate might not be as difficult as I thought.

John Harbottle's Journal

3 March 1779

I'm embarrassed to admit that the amount of time I spent in the water today is likely more than the total amount of time I've spent in the water on all three voyages with Cook combined. Though at first reluctant, I eased in to a familiarity with the sea that both taught me how little I knew of her as well as how much I looked forward to experiencing more.

I also hadn't realized until now how intimate Maile was with the ocean. She's spoken of navigating by the stars and observing nature before, but the news that she was an expert came as a surprise. I can see it in her eyes, though. And the way she carries herself. She's different when she's in the water. More alive, somehow. It's a wonder to see her in her element.

Ikaika was the chief's prime navigator, so it makes sense that he taught Maile all he knew. They were engaged. Of course they were close. I wonder how she feels about having to pass Ikaika's teachings on to me now—the man who killed him. She said she didn't mind being with me or even teaching me about wayfinding, but a part of me thinks I should tell the chief what I did. That I was the one who killed his navigator, and that Maile saw it happen. Then maybe he wouldn't force her to work with me. It's not fair that she has to spend all her time with the man she should despise most.

But I'm selfish. And I'm afraid of what her father would do to me after learning of my part in the battle. And I'm too greedy for Maile's companionship. She knows me better than anyone on the island, possibly better than most of my men. I trust her completely. She's had numerous opportunities to turn on me, to give me up. But she hasn't, and I'm grateful for her mercy. I thrive on it.

Besides, no one can make me feel the way she makes me feel. In some ways, she is to me as the ocean is to her. Maile makes me feel different. She makes me feel more alive.

ʻumikūmāono

Chapter Sixteen

The next morning I call for John outside his hut, but he's not there. I ask a few of my father's men if they've seen the lieutenant, but they all lower their heads and say they haven't. It isn't until I walk past the canoe hut that I hear the contorted sounds of a nose flute played incorrectly followed by my sister's familiar laugh.

I enter the triangle-framed hut, the smooth pebbles lining the ground are cool against my bare feet. The canoe currently under construction in the shelter is a medium-sized outrigger. It's meant to be manned by six or seven adults for a short trip with paddles, no sails. The *koa* wood is still being shaped, the basic contour of the canoe in place with rough edges and corners.

I hear Haukea laugh again, and I make my way to the far side of the hut, where she and John sit on the ground just past the head of the vessel. I step back, not expecting to see him here. The faintest flutter of jealousy enters my middle at seeing the two of them together. Laughing. Smiling. But the feeling is gone as quickly as it came, and I'm left curious about what they're doing.

John holds a bamboo flute in his hands. The node on one end has been removed, though the other side is intact. The instrument is about the length of his forearm. Both a breath hole and several finger holes have been burned through the top.

John places the breath hole beneath his mouth and blows a puff of air, creating a sound that resembles some kind of dying animal.

"You defile it," Haukea says before another round of giggles comes out of her.

"I think he destroyed it," I say.

They both turn to me in surprise.

"Maile!" Haukea stands and walks to me, a smile on her face. "I didn't mean to keep him from his training. I just came to check on his wounds." She motions to John on the ground. "He's found himself a new toy."

"I see that."

John stands, brushing imaginary dust off the instrument. "One of the children gave it to me. I tried to find a private spot to practice playing, but I guess I didn't try hard enough. You both found me."

Haukea laughs. "I think the entire village could find you with that outrageous sound."

John's face reddens. "I suppose music isn't my specialty." He doesn't seem upset, just a little embarrassed.

"We can't all have Maile's gift with song," Haukea says. "Promise me you'll stick with learning navigation from now on."

John chuckles.

Haukea moves closer to me, pressing her nose against mine. We each take a breath, and then she leans toward my ear. "Be careful with this one," she whispers. Then she exits the hut, leaving John and me alone. I don't know what she means.

"I apologize," John says, stepping closer. "I lost track of how long I'd been here. I know we were supposed to meet this morning at my hut."

I shrug. "It's fine." After a moment of awkward silence, I reach out and take the flute from John's hands. "This is meant to be a romantic instrument. Did you know that?"

He shakes his head.

"When a young man wants to woo a lover, he takes a length of bamboo and cuts it, sanding it like so." I run my fingers along the smooth, even surface. "Each instrument is different, creating a sound unique to him. He plays it for the one he wants to attract. It's not meant for a large gathering or celebration, but rather a more private audience."

John glances to where Haukea just left, a nervous expression on his face. "I didn't know. I didn't mean to—"

"Don't worry," I assure him. "You aren't attracting any potential lovers with the song you made."

His face reddens again. "She said I defiled it."

"You did," I say. "But only because you were playing it wrong. It's a nose flute."

"Nose?"

I nod. "Our mouths are capable of saying beautiful things, but they also curse and speak evil too often. The air that comes out of them is not clean. But the breath from our nose is pure. Undefiled. That is the kind of air you want to use to impress someone."

I hold the flute to my nose, press a finger against the side of one nostril to close it, and gently exhale so that air flows across the opening. A long, smooth sound emerges from the flute. There's a clarity to it so distinct, though the sound might not be loud, you know it can be heard from far away.

I finish with my single note and hand the flute back to John.

He mimics my actions, placing the flute under his nose and closing one nostril before exhaling. An unpleasant howl sounds.

I withhold a wince. "Not so hard," I say, encouraging him to try again.

John does, and this time a beautiful note sounds and holds steady for as long as he has air to feed it. His eyes light up in victory, and he plays it again, this time the fingers of his other hand finding a place over the sound holes. He forms a simple melody with his notes, his fingers lifting up and down to alter the pitch.

"Very good," I say. "The women are probably lining up to meet you at this moment," I tease.

He lowers the flute, contemplating. "But you said he can play it for one in particular? The woman he desires?"

"Yes," I say. "Then perhaps she will form her own flute and compose a response. You can recognize your lover this way. It is said a chief, in a time long past, played his flute from the top of the mountain, and his woman heard his call from the shore and played her response. Their songs created a harmony so beautiful, even the gods were envious of their love."

"I like that." John runs his thumb over the breath hole of the flute. "Is the idea to mimic birds—like a mating call? Is that why the song is meant only for a romantic interest?"

"Not quite. When we kiss . . ." I pause, trying to think through an explanation.

"When *we* kiss?" John asks, his eyes wide.

"No, no." I give a nervous laugh. "I meant when someone kisses another person, they press nose to nose, *honi*, exchanging their breath of life. The pure breath." This is the type of *honi* my sister just gave me. "But when you kiss your *ipo*, your sweetheart, it's more intimate. You move closer and touch noses side to side, then shift to do it again on the other side. You inhale each other's aroma, their life force. In that closeness, your breathing becomes one." I press my finger to the side of my nose. "It is this action that is mimicked when playing the flute. It's a display of affection, alluding to the kiss you hope to share with your sweetheart."

John lifts the flute to his nose again, playing a single note, long and clear. It's as though he wants to be certain he remembers how.

"You should be cautious with that thing." I turn toward the exit of the hut and motion for him to follow me. "You don't want to cause a heart to break the day you finally leave this island."

If he understands my joke, he doesn't let on. He tucks the flute into a pocket in his breeches and quickens his pace until he's beside me. We head toward the beach in silence, and a part of me wishes he would take out the flute and play as we walk. Thanks to my sister and me, though, I think he's been teased enough about the instrument to prevent him from using it in front of others anytime soon.

When we reach the south end of the fishing ponds near the shore, an explosion sounds in the distance—from near the ships?

BOOM.

John and I both fall to the ground, an instinct to protect ourselves from whatever ignited the blast.

It's not the sharp thunder sound of the sailors' smoking weapons, not unless a thousand of them went off at once. But the noise is so penetrating, it's like an invisible wave passing through the air, a rush of wind fleeing the site of danger, and it rattles every part of me.

"What was that?" I ask.

John rises carefully, shielding his eyes as he gazes to where the sound came from. There, just off the beach where the *Resolution* and *Discovery* are anchored, is a fire. It's one of my people's huts, one of our homes. Violent flames rise above the structure, releasing black smoke into the otherwise clear sky.

We break into a run, John falling in behind me as I lead him along the trail in the direction of the temple that was destroyed by his sailors. Has their thirst for destruction not been satiated? Have they decided to destroy more of our things, more of our property, even after the deal was made between John and my father?

An equal mix of anger and worry propels me to move faster. John can barely keep up, his fresh wounds layered over the old, causing him to run at a slower pace. When we finally reach the scene of the fire, the high temperature of the flames winds around me in a whirlpool of heat, making me flinch. It's so hot. A small group of people, both John's men and mine, are working to put out the fire, or at least keep it contained.

Not waiting to be told, I hurry to the nearest hut and grab a couple of gourds, then run to the beach to fill them with water. After getting as close to the flames as I dare, I pour the water on the fire. I repeat the action again and again. Others, like John, dump baskets of sand over the fire to smother it. We do whatever we can to suffocate the inferno, and it takes a good hour of exertion to finally put it out.

The fire hasn't been extinguished for long before quarreling begins among my people and the foreigners. They yell hateful words toward each other, but neither group can understand what the other says. Not that they would listen. The arguments turn physical, and soon rocks and fists are exchanged as well as threats.

"*Ho'opau*," I yell, stepping into the middle of the fight. "Stop!"

John rushes to my side and spins in a circle, protecting me, as though gauging who might make me their next target. He yells something in the language of his England to the sailors then waits for me to continue.

"Why are you fighting?" I ask everyone.

John speaks to his men, and I realize he's repeating what I say, translating for the foreigners.

"Haven't we lost enough?" I wipe the sweat from my forehead, ash and salt staining the palm of my hand. "So many men have died—from both sides. When will it be enough?" I wait for John to finish translating then continue. "Have we become a blood-craving people, abandoning our laws to gratify an inhuman appetite?"

"They destroyed our home," someone yells.

"It was a mistake," says another. "Their weapon misfired."

I wait for the sailors to finish explaining to John their interpretation of what happened.

"They're right," he finally tells me. "The gunpowder . . ." He pauses and tries to think of a way to explain it to me. "The substance that allows our weapons to create thunder and smoke was stored near the hut. We use this much"—he holds his thumb and forefinger close together—"to make our guns smoke. But there was this much"—he moves his hands far apart—"near the hut. When the weapon fired by mistake, it created that much more thunder. That much more smoke. It started the fire, but it was an accident."

I had been right—it was like a thousand of their guns firing at the same time. But I can't let on that I hate those weapons. Not when the chief has declared their use for our benefit. I have to find a way for everyone to get past this or they'll never be able to work together.

I look around the crowd of weary people. "No one has died," I say. "No one was harmed. The only damage done was to a hut that can be rebuilt." I point to the ashes. "And look—we banded together to fix what was broken. We mended something that could have easily spiraled out of control."

John translates my words then looks at me. He nods, encouraging me to finish.

"Yes, we lost something," I say, my voice shaking, thinking of more than just the hut. "But we also saved so much more. Together. And we can do it again."

I exhale, trying to convince myself that my words are true. If they aren't, then at least I hope it's enough to motivate our people to work together.

John Harbottle's Journal
4 March 1779

Similar to other Pacific Islanders, the natives here kiss by pressing nose to nose, sometimes forehead to forehead. This honi is accompanied by the exchanging of breath, or hā. I find it curious the word for that breath is included in the name of their home: Hawai'i.

The honi is used in greeting, similar to a formal handshake. The obvious difference is it's a much more intimate gesture, and as a result, is regarded with more reverence.

I witnessed the captain receive this greeting no fewer than twenty times a day during our first stay here, the people not wanting to pass up a chance to access his mana, his power, by the brief interaction. Familiar with the custom from the other places we'd visited, he didn't seem to mind it.

But today I learned there are nuances when it comes to honi, especially as it applies to romantic encounters. I've yet to take part in the traditional greeting, sans romance, even with all the islands I've visited that were filled with people who participate in the practice. I don't seek female companionship like many of the other sailors, and I've never had the confidence to initiate the innocent greeting with any of the natives. I'm not even sure I would like it.

From what I can tell, the western practice of pressing lips together as a show of affection, both for casual friends and family or familiar lovers, has yet to be introduced.

Postscript:

Maile can speak words with so much blaze behind them, I think she could be the fire goddess Pele herself.

ʻumikūmāhiku

Chapter Seventeen

Over the next several days, I take John out to the reef, then to the water that surrounds the small atoll off the coast, and then to even deeper water in the bay, though all still within swimming distance of the shore. His skin has darkened and his hair has lightened, both having been touched by the sun for hours on end. There's a new resilience to him as well. I never would have described John as delicate—he's a sailor, after all—but he's more patient now. With me, with the ocean. It's as though he's no longer eager to leave as soon as possible, but is willing to learn and grow during his time here.

A week after we begin our training, I wake a couple hours before dawn and get dressed before heading to John's hut. It's not far from mine, as he's staying in one of my father's huts, but I haven't been inside before. I wait outside the doorway, a part of me wishing he'd sense my presence and wake on his own, but all I hear is the sound of deep, even breathing.

I walk inside, and the moonlight that trickles in is enough for me to see well enough. When I reach his bed, I extend my arm to shake his shoulder but hesitate. I don't know why—it's not like I'm pushing any boundaries by being here alone. We've even spent the night in the same hut before, sleeping on opposite sides of the room the day of the battle.

But somehow this is different. He's not sick or injured. He doesn't need my help to get around or heal. Is there a reason why I am sneaking into his hut in the middle of the night that doesn't seem scandalous? Yes. I'm doing this to teach him how to find his way home. This is part of his navigation training. I also don't have a choice. My father, the chief, commanded it. I let my hand fall to John's shoulder, and he blinks his eyes open.

Turning onto his back and seeing me next to him, he says, "Am I dreaming?"

I'm not sure if he's trying to be funny, but I laugh anyway. "Please don't tell me your dreams involve being woken up in the middle of the night by random women." I widen my eyes as though the idea is shocking.

John rubs his eyes, a new awareness settling on him, as though he's now fully awake and aware of his surroundings. "Shipwrecked on an island paradise. Held prisoner by a native woman. I've dreamed it before, remember?"

"Held prisoner by a *beautiful* native woman," I amend, remembering our long-ago conversation. "But a dream is not the same as a hallucination, and you're not hallucinating anymore."

"I never was." He holds my gaze a moment before changing the subject. "What can possibly be so important that you had to wake me this early?" He scrunches his eyes and looks outside through a window flap that had been propped open, trying to determine what time it is.

"Get dressed and follow me. Your lesson for the day starts now."

He groans but rises to his feet. He's already wearing his

breeches, but he pulls on a loose shirt before following me outside.

When we reach a small outrigger canoe, I toss in two paddles and get John to help me push it into the water. With him in front, we paddle past the break and keep going. The canoe is small but swift, and soon we're so far from shore I can no longer see our island by the faint light of the moon. Once the sun rises, we'll see it easily, but for a moment I feel as though I'm floating in a black abyss, not knowing where I am or where I came from. And definitely not knowing where I'm going. I lift my oar from the water and rest it beside me, then instruct John to do the same.

He looks back toward me. "What are we doing out here?"

"Just watch," I say, smiling at the small sliver of purple that appears on the horizon—the sun blinking open his eyes. I think of John and his grogginess this morning, wondering if the sun resists waking up as well, longing to stay in the safety of his dreams. I also think of what John said about the sun kissing the ocean as he rises, then feel grateful for the darkness that hides my blush.

We sit in silence, the light of the sun spreading through the sky before he has even made an appearance. And as he peeks his head past the horizon where sky meets sea, I watch John's profile. I'm sure he's seen any number of sunrises on the ocean during his long voyages. But he's never seen it with me, on this canoe, in this moment. Each one is special, different. And I don't think I'll ever forget this sunrise.

"It's beautiful," John says simply.

"It's the most important time of day," I say. I don't want to break his obvious peace and serenity, but we're here for a lesson. "You use the sun as he rises to determine the weather of the day, or even future days."

I lift my paddle and dip it into the water, positioning our

canoe parallel to the horizon. We each shift in our seats to face the rising sun, side by side. John can see me easier now that I am beside him rather than behind.

"If the sun is hazy," I say, "it means there is wind coming. The colors are important, too. If there is a bluish-yellow hue to the rising sun, there will be moisture."

"I didn't know that," he whispers.

"In the early morning, we look at the water and its swells. We look at the clouds, the moon, and the receding stars. They don't just help us to navigate in the moment, they tell us what the weather will be for the day." After a beat, I say, "To be a good navigator, you have to be a good observer of nature. You have to understand it. Use the resources it gives you. Be sensitive to the things the world is telling you."

"So it's not just the sea I need to know." John dips his hand in the water in front of us then slides his fingers along the rim of the canoe. "It's the moon and the stars and the wind. It's everything."

"Yes. And navigation is not the only reason to know them. The moon has thirty phases, and each one tells us when to fish, what to farm, which god to worship. It affects us by the tides, by its light or lack of light. It causes changes in the weather, and it even raises or lowers our underground water sources. You don't just navigate by nature, you live your entire life by it."

"You're amazing, you know that?"

I glance at John to see if he's teasing.

"Your people. Your traditions. It really is amazing." His words are sincere and a heartfelt compliment. "The people of the world will be in awe of you, I know it."

I don't want to think about the countless people in the world right now. I don't want to think about the changes that wait for us ahead and what that could mean for our home. I just want to get through the current challenges we're facing.

"It's time for the next part of today's lesson." I tilt my head toward the side of the canoe. "Into the water you go."

His eyes widen. "But we're so far from shore."

We both look back to see the island in the distance. The sun has risen entirely into the sky, revealing the sloping green mountains.

"Yes," I say. "So far, in fact, you won't be able to swim back."

John swallows but removes his shirt anyway. I know he will do what I ask, no matter how difficult.

"What about sharks?" he asks, looking around us. "We're no longer within the safety of the reef and shallower waters."

I point to the sky. "The sun has risen. Sharks hunt closer to the surface at low light, but there's enough light now that they've probably retreated to lower depths for a time."

"Probably?" There is the slightest tremor in his voice. "And what of jellyfish?"

"Sharks and jellyfish are nothing compared to a giant octopus."

His arms shoot out to grab the rims of the canoe on either side of him, his knuckles turning white.

"I'm kidding," I say. "You'll be fine. I promise."

"And . . . and will you be getting in the water, too? Or at least stationed nearby? Just in case."

I point to myself. "Too much of a distraction, remember?" When he shows no signs of calming down, I say, "The sea is calm, and there are no signs of danger. Though you won't be able to see me, I won't be far. I will leave you here for an hour."

John closes his eyes and takes a deep breath.

"Do you trust me?" I ask.

He opens his eyes again and holds my gaze. "I do," he says, quiet but firm.

"Let the ocean decide if you deserve to know her or not."

I remember Ikaika doing this same thing to me, though I was much younger than John is, not a mature adult. I was afraid too, not having the option to escape or save myself. But I also remember it being the moment I fully gave up my will to the sea. That day my spirit somehow became entwined with hers. It was one of the most moving experiences of my life, one I will never forget, and I refuse to deny John a similar experience just because he's afraid.

John slips into the water with barely a splash, then releases the side of the canoe, letting me paddle away from him farther out to sea. I don't have to go far to be out of his sight. With him so low in the water, I can position myself so I can see him when I look for him, but he can't see me. I don't want him caught up in a current and pulled so far from me I lose track of where he is.

Time moves slowly, but I am patient and wait. I spot a pod of dolphins in the distance, gently gliding through the water with a speed I could only dream of. The clouds drift slowly in little puffs; the winds are calm. And the sun . . . He is happy today, spreading his warmth to everything he touches. I wonder what the sun feels like in England. If their clouds and skies and seas are similar to ours. I know nothing of the world beyond our shores, and for a moment, I feel silly teaching a man about observing nature when he's observed more things in his life than our people could ever imagine.

Still, he seems in awe of the things I teach him, so maybe he hasn't seen as much as I think he has. Or maybe he hasn't had the time or patience or circumstances to really feel what he's observing. Perhaps he's never stayed in one place long enough to know the people like he has here. To hurt them and help them and trust them. That is a sort of intimacy that cannot come from surface explorations.

After an hour has passed, I paddle back to where John is treading water. When he spins around and sees me, his eyes light up, and I think it's more than mere relief that I've returned. Something has happened to him here. As I help him back into the canoe, he can barely contain his excitement.

"Maile, it was amazing." He struggles to catch his breath after exerting himself for so long. "I'm exhausted, but the power and the peace I felt while keeping afloat out here . . . I have no words to describe the feeling."

I think of his bound cloths and wonder if he will find adequate words later to record about today.

"I fought it at first, not willing to let my worries and anxiety go. But then the most incredible thing happened." John holds his hands up as though forming pictures of what took place. "I felt something rub along one side of my leg, and I panicked, thinking it was a shark or—thanks to you—some kind of mammoth octopus creature. But then the head of a giant beast breached the surface and blew out a puff of air. Loud and wet and powerful."

"It was a whale," I whisper, leaning forward, wanting to hear more. "What kind was it?"

"A humpback whale. And it wasn't alone. There were several more, swimming around me, surfacing right where I could see them. I even reached out my hand to touch one of them. I've never felt so small yet significant at the same time." John smiles. "They didn't stay on the surface long, their dark, giant bodies submerging below me, but I knew they were there. Beneath me. Protecting me somehow."

Something twists in my stomach, and I lean away, settling into the base of the canoe hull to steady myself.

"I knew in that moment," he continues, "she brought them to me. The ocean brought them. It was her way of saying that though the sea is vast, and though millions of creatures reside within her, she knew me. She knew I was there, and she acknowledged me."

I hadn't seen the whales, not even their sprays, though they were so close. "They usually travel north during this season," I say, confused. "It's rare to spot them, especially an entire pod, this time of year."

"Is something wrong?" John asks.

I look up at him, at his brows wrinkled with concern.

"Are you upset?"

"No. Just . . ." What am I feeling? I'm not upset I missed seeing them, or jealous that John did. He just doesn't understand the significance of humpback whales to my family. To me.

"Just what?" He shifts closer to me, wiping his wet hair away from his face.

"The humpback whale is my family's ʻaumākua," I finally say. "Our family god. Ancestors who protect and guide us." Why my ʻaumākua appeared to John, I don't know. Why the sea allowed it to happen . . .

There's something significant here I don't understand. Perhaps John Harbottle has more to do with me and my family than I thought. Perhaps his life is somehow intertwined with ours in a way I can't comprehend yet.

I reach for his hand and squeeze it. "The whales are a good sign," I say. "They are voyagers, like you. Even if they're somewhere they never intended to be, they will always find their way back home."

John nods, understanding. "This place is where they return again and again. To have their babies. To protect your family. To guide you." He pauses. "This is their home."

But this is not John's home. What does he have to do with the whales' presence here? It seems the only thing his men have managed is war and death and mourning. Yet the ocean and my ancestors have softened their hearts enough to accept him. To protect him. It makes me wonder if a person's home can change, or if all of this is to get him back to England where he belongs.

I plaster a smile on my face the best I can. "And this is where they decided to welcome you, John Harbottle, whatever their motives. You are under their protection. It is a good thing."

He mirrors my smile, but his is genuine. "Thank you, Maile," he says reverently. "Thank you for bringing me out here. Thank you for sharing this with me."

There's a swelling in my chest, and I try to bury it with every force within me. I only nod once and instruct him to paddle back to shore. Though it's still morning, this is enough of a lesson for today. For both of us.

John Harbottle's Journal
11 March 1779

I've seen thousands of sunrises in my lifetime, and they've all been beautiful. Hawai'ian sunrises are my favorite, so I didn't mind waking early to witness one this morning. Its beauty was unrivaled, but it wasn't its pleasing appearance that impressed me most. It was the nature with which I viewed it. It was like the boundaries of my own personal light spectrum had expanded on both ends, allowing me to see things I never knew were visible.

That's what Maile does. She tells me things I least expect and teaches me things I never even considered. She expands my limitations, allowing me to learn so much more than I thought possible. It makes me feel naïve, amazed, and blessed all at the same time.

She asked me if I trusted her, and I told her I did.

I lied.

In truth I was terrified, and I wasn't sure what would happen to me out there in the water. But I did what she asked. Yet after my time alone in the water, alone with my thoughts and fears, I was reborn. Made into something new that couldn't have been there before, but is very much there now. Did she know that would happen to me? Had it happened to her?

I want her to ask me again. I want her to ask me if I trust her so I can say it honestly this time—yes. Yes, I trust you, Maile.

ʻumikūmāwalu

Chapter Eighteen

As we paddle up to the beach, I see a crowd of men on the sand, both English sailors and our warriors. John helps me bring the canoe onto shore, and then grabs my hand. He pulls me with him as we walk toward the men who are gathered for what is obviously weapons training.

The first man I recognize is my father, and he has one of the white men's weapons in his arms. My knees give out, and I begin to crumble toward the sand, but John's hand in mine keeps me from completely dropping.

"What's wrong?" he asks, helping me back up.

"I . . . I don't want to be here." My eyes scan the scene, the same bout of weakness overcoming me every time I see one of my people holding a gun. It's so unnatural, so foreign, so . . . wrong. Despite everything I told the men after the fire, my mind can't mesh the two together into something I can accept.

John must sense my apprehension because he turns to me and lifts my chin so I'm looking straight at him. He's all I can see; nothing else is in my vision.

"Do you remember this morning out on the water? When I

was afraid?" He drops his fingers from my chin. "I didn't want to do it, but I trusted you. And because I did, the sea and your ancestors trusted me in return. You said so yourself."

A flare of anger rises in my chest. I don't like that he's using my 'aumākua against me, even if he's right.

"I'm asking you to trust me in return." He pauses. "Trust that I won't let anything happen to you. Trust that this is what's best for your people at this time. That we'll ensure everything is made right."

I've forced him to surrender his will to me over and over. During the battle on the beach, in the boat, in the clearing, even during these past days of navigational training. And though he's questioned and pushed back, he still yields to me every time. He deserves my attempt to do the same. But if I'm to fully trust him, there's one thing I need to know. One thing that has created an invisible barrier between us since the day we met. I'm ready to erase that line and give him my trust.

"Did you kill him on purpose?"

"What?" John lowers his head as though he didn't hear me, though I know he's just confused about my question.

I take a steadying breath. "Ikaika. That day on the beach. Did you mean to aim your gun at him? Did you use it with the intent to end his life?"

"Oh, Maile." John grips both of my arms. "I didn't want anyone to get hurt that day. I tried to avoid it at all costs."

"You didn't answer my question." I press my lips together to still their trembling, then I add softly, "I have to know."

John drops his hands and nods, taking a small step back. He waits before answering, and I can see the dilemma in his eyes, as he gauges how he should answer.

Finally, he says, "Ikaika raised his spear and aimed it at my captain. Before he had a chance to throw it, I shot him. I . . . I did it to protect my leader. I did it with the intent to stop him from harming one of my own. And yes"—he pauses—"I knew the shot would likely kill him, and I did it anyway."

I pull at the bark cloth near my neck, suddenly unable to get enough air into my lungs. John reaches forward, but then changes his mind and drops his hand, taking another step away from me as he does.

"I'm sorry, Maile. I'm so sorry."

"You killed him on purpose," I say, confirming his admission. My voice is raspy, struggling. "I tried to convince myself that maybe it was an accident. Maybe your weapon fired without you realizing it. Maybe you weren't aiming for him and he got in the way. Maybe you only meant to injure him, not send him to the afterlife."

John waits. There are no more words, no more explanation. Because things are what they are, and if he were given another chance, he'd likely do it all over again. He'd do it to save Cook, to protect the man who was like a father to him. I don't want to hold this against John. In war, you do what you must to win. To survive.

But why did it have to be Ikaika? Why did it have to be John? And why did it have to be me?

I curse the gods for putting me in this position. If they want John and me to work together, if my ancestors approve of him being here, with me, why did they cause such a rift between us to begin with? It would have been so much easier to have started as friends, not enemies.

John could have told me it was an accident. That he didn't intend to kill my betrothed. But he didn't hide from the truth. He decided to reveal every part of it, even if it meant losing my trust.

Even if it meant losing . . . whatever this is between us. If he was willing to risk all of that, I know he would never lie to me. He's a good man—a man I can trust.

"I'm sorry," he says again and again. "I'm sorry I hurt you."

I step forward and wrap my arms around him, tucking my head beneath his chin. He returns the embrace, holding me together. Tears gather in my eyes, and I let them fall, releasing my hurt and my anger along with them.

"I believe you," I say. "And I trust you." I pull away and wipe at my face. When I look up at him, there's a new emotion in his eyes. Relief? Hope?

He gives me a small smile, and we head toward the group of men again.

I take a seat next to Haukea on the berm while John joins the other sailors in their training. She's weaving something with the long thin leaves of a *hala* tree.

"How long have you been here?" I ask.

"Not long. They were making so much noise I decided to come and see what they were doing."

"What are you making?"

"A hat, I think." She holds it up and rotates it to view each angle. She laughs and says, "We'll see."

It has a large, uneven brim with corners that remind me of the hat John wore the day he stood on the deck of the *Resolution*, staring down at me. So much has happened since then, it feels like another life.

I quietly observe the men training, learning a lot about the weapons in a short time. The ones they're practicing with aren't loaded, so they need to install small metal objects—bullets—within specific chambers that are then catapulted through the long pipe by the gunpowder John spoke of when the fire happened. The pipe is attached to a firing mechanism and a trig-ger. Our warriors will practice with ammunition at a later time, once they've mastered the use of the guns themselves.

They look heavy and awkward, especially in our men's hands, but everyone is determined to keep working at it. The warriors re-peat maneuvers, learn how to clean the weapon, and even practice formations as they work through different battle scenarios.

"He's kind of handsome," Haukea says, startling me. It's the first time she's spoken in about an hour.

"What? Who?" I look over the crowd of men, wondering which one has caught her eye.

"Your John, of course." She says it like it's the most obvious thing.

Oh.

"He's not *my* John," I say. "He's not a possession."

Haukea raises an eyebrow. "He certainly follows you around like he belongs to you."

"Not by my choice," I say. "Father's the one who assigned me to teach him."

She focuses on her weaving pattern. "Well, if he doesn't be-long to you, perhaps I will ask Father to arrange for me to marry him."

Something catches in my throat, and I cough. I turn to see if she's kidding. The corner of her mouth has lifted, but I can't tell if she's delighted at the thought of marrying John or just amused by my reaction to her saying so.

"Marry him?" I ask, my voice cracking.

"Why not? I'm obviously not marrying anyone in 'Eleu's court anymore." Her face falls slightly, likely remembering the arrangement Father tried to make with our enemy. But then she grins again. "I'm meant to marry either an enemy or an ally. John is a little of both—it's perfect." She gives me a small laugh, and then I'm certain she's having fun at my expense.

I indulge her. "So you would travel to England? To the other side of the world?"

"It would be the grandest of adventures."

"Months, years, on one of Cook's ships?"

She makes a face then nudges me with her elbow. "Perhaps I could teach those sailors how to improve their behavior, how to show etiquette and respect when dealing with those of other cultures. I could show them how to become refined."

It's my turn to laugh. "You will need the gods to intervene if you expect to accomplish that." I'm sure their peoples' definition of etiquette and refinement is much different than ours, considering all the ways we contrast.

"I don't know." Haukea lays the hat in her lap and looks out at the men in training. "John seems gracious, and he has an even way about him. There may still be hope for his men."

It's true. John does have a smoothness to his demeanor, a kindness and control that makes him a natural leader. He has that in common with my sister, and I think maybe they would be a good match.

Haukea picks up her hat again. "Besides, what makes you think he wouldn't stay here?"

"Stay in Hawai'i?" I ask. "Not return to England at all?"

She looks at me out of the corner of her eye. "If he had a strong motivation to stay, something he cared about enough, then . . . yes. I think he would stay." She focuses on her weaving, our conversation over.

I watch the men and think about what Haukea said. I don't think she is serious about wanting to marry John, but I'd never thought about him, or any of the other white men, choosing to stay on our island. It should seem impossible, but the more I think about it, the more inevitable it sounds.

John and his men will surely leave this place after the battle, but what about the others John spoke of? Those who would come after him once news of our home spread, even months or years from now. Will some of them arrive and decide to stay? Is that what our future holds? And if so, will there be room enough for all of us?

The chief lowers his weapon. "This will not work."

Everyone on the beach pauses and waits for him to continue, some with surprised looks on their faces. Has he changed his mind about using the foreigner's weapons against our enemy?

"These lines," he explains. "You would have us stand together, side by side, fully exposed to our enemy. It's like inviting them to wield their spears and clubs at us as we present ourselves for slaughter." He motions to his warriors. "We must be free to engage at will. Stealth and the ability to skirt in and out of danger is the only way to guarantee survival and victory."

John steps forward. "But there must be some kind of order, a commander to take charge. Communication. Strategy. If there is no plan, if you are not working together as a single unit, there will be chaos. That's what will bring slaughter."

"What about both?" I ask loud enough for them to hear.

Everyone turns to me. I leave my sister on the berm and walk toward John and my father.

"It's evident these guns don't work well in close quarters with an enemy since they take time to reload." I rest one hand on my hip. "That makes you vulnerable. Use our traditional methods up close: knives, clubs, spears. Use guns at a farther distance, in waves or teams. Stealth and order. Flexibility and strategy. There's no reason we must abandon one for the other."

The chief nods. "They would not expect it."

John looks at me approvingly then turns to the chief. "It would also help if you could back them into a corner where they could not retreat. This is your island, not theirs. You know the landscape, the layout."

"They'll come from the south," Father says. "If we can push them toward the southern cliffs, they'll be trapped. Forced to fight us or fall to their death."

My stomach drops. "You could be putting our own men in danger, too. What happens if they find a way to back *us* into the cliffs? There will be no escape for us, either. It's a dangerous location."

My father shakes his head. "We will use both guns and our native weapons, plus two forms of combat. At the ideal location of our choosing. It will be impossible for us to lose."

I picture my father falling over the cliff, his feathered helmet and cape along with him. It would be a terrible way to die. I wouldn't wish it upon anyone.

"Your father's right," John says. "A victory is practically guaranteed." He looks at his sailors then back to me. "But there is one more thing that would seal a win for your people. Something even you can't argue with, Maile. Allow my men to fight alongside yours."

I pause, surprised. "You would do that?"

John shrugs. "You need the numbers. Let us help you."

"I don't know."

John grins wide. "Trust me, Maile."

I suppress a similar smile and turn to my father. "What do you think?"

"You've already been generous with your weapons," the chief

says to John. "But I would be a fool not to accept your soldiers as well. We would be grateful for the added numbers."

John nods in submission to the chief. "It's decided, then."

I return to my spot next to my sister. There's a new atmosphere hovering around the men. A new sense of faith and confidence. An amity of sorts, the kind that exists between trusted allies. Even Haukea feels it, having abandoned her weaving project, becoming fully immersed in watching the men train on the beach.

John Harbottle has not only managed to earn my trust, he's brought together two unlikely groups. They are no longer sailors and natives. I daresay those who once sought to destroy one another might actually become friends. Friends who may even forgive each other for the hurt they've caused.

It's happened before.

John Harbottle's Journal
11 March 1779

When we first arrived on the island, it was during a season of cel-ebration, or makahiki. *In addition to the food, dancing, and general merrymaking one would expect, there was a tournament of games akin to that of the ancient Greeks. Events included foot races, spear throw-ing, rope pulling, wrestling, and a variety of competitions of strength.*

There were also strategy games. Kōnane was played on a grid with figures of white coral and black lava stone. Similar to check-ers, the players took turns capturing each other's pieces in orthogonal moves until one side couldn't make a capture.

Like other islands in the Pacific, boxing was also popular. Each man took a turn punching his opponent barehanded, back and forth, until one of them either relented or passed out. It was quite brutal.

The common thing I noticed about all of these sports, whether they were physically demanding or a challenge for the mind, is that they focused on the offensive. There were no evasive tactics, no defen-sive moves. These people are bold and strong. Audacious.

It wasn't until today during our weapons training that I real-ized such competitions weren't merely games meant for entertainment. They were training exercises, meant to teach the people how to fight, how to win should a real battle ensue. In fact, the native warriors are so advanced in their combat skills, I'm surprised my own men weren't obliterated that day on the beach.

With the combination of their proficiency and our weapons, I feel confident of a victory. Of course, there is never a guarantee when it comes to war, but I can't think of a more advantageous situation than we have right now. I know if I were ever to come against these two groups of men—no, this singular group of men—I would make certain I'd made peace with my family and with my God.

ʻumikūmāiwa

Chapter Nineteen

I recruit a group of men to help me and John launch a canoe rigged with sails into the water and past the white break. After the men return to the homestead, leaving John and me alone on the canoe, I take out a piece of cloth. When John realizes I intend to blindfold him, he takes the cloth and slides it through his fingers.

"This canoe is bigger than the last one," he says simply.

"Yes."

"We're going farther out."

"Yes."

"And you can sail it by yourself?"

I raise one eyebrow. He knows I can. He's stalling. "Yes."

After a moment, he offers the fabric back to me and nods.

I tie it around his eyes and position him in a comfortable seat before raising the sails. I maneuver them to send us out to the sea, away from the island. After a while, I change direction, and long after that I do it again, intent on confusing John should he be trying to determine our position.

We travel for a couple of hours, but John doesn't complain once. I finally lower the sails. Though I know where we are, I can no longer see land in any direction, be it our island or a neighboring one. And I definitely can't see the tall masts of Cook's ships in the distance. The sun is high in the sky. We could be anywhere in the middle of the ocean. It's perfect.

I untie the fabric from around John's eyes and give him a moment to adjust to the noonday light.

"Where are we?" he asks.

"I don't know," I say. "I guess you'll have to figure it out."

"You aren't going to dump me in the water this time, are you?" His expression tells me he only half thinks I wouldn't do it.

I laugh. "No. Not this time."

He stands and walks along one side of the canoe before crossing the beams that connect the hulls. He spins in a circle slowly, studying the horizon in every direction to decipher any clues. After shading his eyes and looking up at the sun, he returns and sits beside me.

"I have no idea."

"You know a lot more than you think," I assure him. "Let's start with something easy: birds."

"Birds?" he asks.

I nod. We both wait, watching the sky for any sign of them. It doesn't take long for one to appear and land on the top of our mast for a moment before continuing its flight, giving us enough time to examine it briefly. Its black plumage and red gular pouch are hard to miss.

"It's a frigate bird," he says.

"Good. Frigates refuse to land on water. Their feathers become waterlogged, making it impossible to fly."

"So if one is spotted," he says, "land is near."

"Exactly."

"What else?" he asks, his voice filled with awe.

"Did you see food in its mouth? A fish, perhaps?"

John shakes his head. "I don't think so."

"That could indicate which direction it's heading—to a nest to feed its chicks or out to sea to hunt. If it's holding food in its beak, it's probably not looking for more food."

"It's such simple logic. I just never thought of it before."

"Observing nature takes time," I say. "But it will reveal everything you need to know."

"So with a frigate, we are near land. But no food in its mouth means it could be coming or going, so its flight direction isn't necessarily an indicator of where that land is."

"Correct. Most birds will fly out to the fishing grounds in the morning. At night, they'll rise high in the sky to spot land before heading home. So utilizing birds those times of the day is easier."

"A perfect way to set your course at dawn or sunset."

"Yes," I say. "What else do you observe?"

He points to the sky. "Clouds. Now that's easy. I can watch their movement to determine both wind direction and speed. With that information, I can set my sails. The winds change during different times of the year, too."

"Good. What else about clouds?"

"If they are small and puffy, there is no wind. Long and stretched means there's a soft breeze. Cut up and spotty means there's a lot. No clouds, then the sky is dry." He looks at me to see if he's on the right track. "And I know they gather near an island. If they hit the mountains there, they will release their moisture and rise higher before moving on. That is what determines the wet and dry side of each island. Only a shift in the wind will alter their pattern."

I appraise him, impressed he already knows so much. "And the color of the clouds?"

"Stormy gray. Pleasant white. All the shades between."

"There are more than just shades of white and gray in the clouds." I angle my head up to observe the wisps above us and the tinge of blue they reflect.

He thinks for a moment. "You can see the colors of the sunrise and sunset in them, like the morning we watched the sun rise." After another pause, he takes in a breath with sudden realization. "And blue. The clouds are blue, reflecting the ocean."

I stay silent and wait, hoping he comes to the next conclusion on his own.

He squints hard at all the clouds in the sky, both those near us and those far away. He frowns and points to a cluster of clouds in the distance. "Those clouds," he says. "They are a lighter shade of blue than the others. Is the angle from which we're viewing them causing that?"

I shake my head and continue to wait as he puzzles it out.

"The water there is shallower," he finally whispers with wonder. "The clouds are reflecting a lighter water, shallower water. Like that of a reef surrounding an island."

Like the color of your eyes, I almost say. Instead, I smile approvingly. "Very good." I'm surprised at how adept he is at observing things around us. He's patient and eager to learn, and of course that helps, but he's naturally gifted, too. Intelligent, determined. It explains why he was able to study languages and adjust to the idiosyncrasies of ours so quickly. Even in these past weeks, his accent has become less noticeable, and his vocabulary has increased.

"Now," I say, returning us to the lesson. "What do you feel from the water?"

He looks out to the sea in every direction, observing the current, the wave crests, the color. All those are good, but . . .

"No." I touch his eyelids to encourage him to close them. "What do you *feel*?"

After a minute, he opens his eyes. "I feel nothing," he admits with some frustration. "Nothing but the rocking of the canoe." He holds up a hand. "And that is not an invitation for you to throw me over the side."

"Come here." I motion for him to lie on his back along the length of the hull. "You can feel her better against the wood. Lower yourself into her a bit."

He lies down, but after a while, he sighs. "More rocking, only the movement feels stronger, the sound of the water crashing against the hull is louder. It makes my stomach turn and my head throb."

He's ready to give up, his frustration overpowering his patience.

"Move over," I say, shoving him to one side. I stretch the length of my body beside his, so we're both lying against the base of the hull on our backs, side-by-side. "Press your back into the wood, feel the weight of your legs sink down, your shoulders relaxing into the canoe." I feel him shift beside me, trying to do as I say. I press myself into the wood as well, following my own instructions. "Spread your fingers and feel her beneath you."

I widen my hands and press my palms against the hull on either side of me. John does the same and a few of his fingers land on mine, the space between us not as wide as I'd thought. My first instinct is to pull away, but John acts first, squeezing my hand slightly before sliding his hand off mine and finding a spot next to it. When he tries to spread his fingers again, though, the length of his little finger presses against the length of mine, and . . . he doesn't pull away again. I don't dare move, shocked into stillness, hyperaware of my small sliver of skin in contact with his.

It's not like we've never touched before. He laid across me during our escape from the beach; he leaned on me as we made our way to the hidden hut. I've administered to his wounds, helped him dress. We've even held hands at times, leading each other where we needed to go.

But this . . . this is different. It feels different. It feels significant, somehow. And when his small finger moves ever so slightly to cover mine, my heart starts to beat so violently the sound seems to ricochet through the hollow of the hull, echoing so loudly he's bound to hear it, too. I want to pull away and I don't want to pull away. I have no idea what it means. I try to ignore that he's touching me on purpose, but my attempts are futile, so instead I pretend.

"N-now imagine yourself in the w-water," I stutter, cursing how much I've let him rattle me. "Like the first day of your training, when you were in the pool, floating on your back, feeling every part of her." I swallow hard, thinking about how I touched him that day. I'd held his head to help him relax, tilting it back, all while he looked right into my eyes. I take a quick breath. "Relax into her like you did that day. Let her keep you afloat. There's no longer a canoe beneath you, it's just you and the ocean, getting to know each other again. Try to feel her."

Feeling the ocean is the last thing on my mind, because all I can feel is John beside me, his finger on mine, burning into me. There will be a mark there later, not from pain or pressure, but because I doubt my hand will ever feel the same after this.

I wish I could leave my body, suspend myself from its tether for a moment, so I can peek at him and see what expression is on his face. Seep into his mind to determine what he is thinking. What he is feeling. Does he realize he's affecting me so? Does he care?

"I can feel it," he says. There's a rawness to his voice, and I don't know if he's talking about the sea or . . . or something else. His hand shifts again, and this time he slides another finger over mine, so that two of them are threaded with two of my own. The sensation of his skin sliding against mine makes me light-headed.

I think of Ikaika. Of the times he brought me out on his canoe and had me lie against the hull like this. The times he taught me how to feel the water beyond the *koa* wood. My hands were spread just like this.

No, not like this.

Not with John's touch so intimate with mine. I can't even use the memory of Ikaika—the man John killed, the man I loved—to erase the stir of emotions I'm feeling in this moment. All because John is touching my hand.

"Maile," he whispers sometime later. "Do you feel that?"

My hand begins to shake, and John senses it. He moves his entire hand over mine, his long fingers engulfing mine.

"Something has changed," he says.

Does he sense it too?

"The water has shifted," he continues. "Do you feel it?"

Wait . . . is he talking about us or—

He presses his hand against mine, as though forcing me to feel the water beneath us and decipher what he already has. I curse my weakness in letting his presence distract me from what we're doing out here. After focusing on the water—like I should have been the entire time—I finally sense what he's talking about.

"I feel it, too," I say before sitting up, reluctantly pulling my hand from beneath his as I do. "There's a storm coming."

John sits up. "But the sky is clear."

I point northeast to the horizon. There's barely a hint of gray low in the sky. It is hazy and blurry, hard to determine where the water ends and the clouds begin.

"I see it," he says.

"We have to hurry," I say, ready to raise the sails. "It will take us a while to get back, and we don't want to get caught in the storm while we're on the water."

He stands to take over the rigging from me, pulling at the ropes to raise the fabric quickly. "Will the storm come that fast?" he asks. "It seems so far away right now."

I rub the length of my small finger, the spot that had been touching his only moments ago. I'll never forget the sensation—he's definitely left a mark there.

"Yes," I say. "The storm can come quickly. When you least expect it. When you're not ready for it."

John Harbottle's Journal
23 March 1779

Observation is an art—Maile has taught me this over the last weeks. You can't simply look around at your surroundings and expect to know all there is to know about where you are. You must slow down, pause, let the signs of the world come to you. You can't force it. And it takes practice, a lot of practice. But if you're patient, the world will reveal all its secrets. You can use that information to chart your course, to plan your journey.

But when I try to observe Maile herself, none of the rules of nature seem to apply.

When I do something she doesn't approve of, her brows come together and the skin between them wrinkles. I fight the urge to run my finger along that space and smooth it out. Instead, I try to determine what I've done wrong so I can fix it, but often before I do, her demeanor changes and her face relaxes. Unless I can figure out a way to look into her mind and interpret her thoughts, I'll never know if I did something wrong in the first place. She's possibly just exercising patience with my ineptitude.

And I never know how she will react to my company. Some days she will smile when I approach, other days she remains contemplative, as though trying to puzzle something out. And just when I think we've developed the familiarity of trusted friends, she will tense and pull away emotionally, severing the invisible connection I thought could withstand more than a few obstacles.

Her alterations are so inexplicable, in fact, that sometimes I don't think she even knows what she's feeling and is at a loss of how to interpret her own actions. How can I ever hope to comprehend her if she can't?

The only thing my observations of Maile have determined is that

I can't determine anything at all, at least not with any degree of certainty. This makes my study of her both frustrating and fascinating. I don't know that I will ever predict what she will say or do in any given moment, but I enjoy the challenge of trying to all the same.

iwakālua

Chapter Twenty

By the time we see the island, the storm winds have already reached us, causing the water to rock erratically, our sails shifting this way and that as we fight to keep control. The sharp, snapping sound of the sails as it catches each gust of wind is piercing and unsettling. We have just gotten the canoe as far onto shore as we can when huge drops of rain begin falling on us, making loud smacking sounds with each drop. The sand is spattered with large dark circles, but within seconds, the rain increases to a pour, and the drops are no longer discernible from each other. The smacking sound is replaced with an onslaught of a constant whooshing.

As we hurry to my homestead, we see several people scurrying to their own huts for shelter, surprised by the sudden storm. The rain is falling so fast the ground hasn't had enough time to soak it up, and a layer of water sloshes around our feet. When we reach the chief's hut, we hurry inside. A pair of arms wrap around me.

"Maile!" my mother shouts, straining to be heard above the roar of the rainfall. "We were so worried about you."

"I'm fine," I say, squeezing water out of my skirt. "*We're* fine."

She looks behind me to John, then back at me. "Your father

is missing," she says. "We knew you were out on a canoe, but we couldn't find Haukea. He went looking for her at the northern fishponds—"

Haukea interrupts us, a solemn and guilty look on her face. "It's my fault he's missing. If I hadn't strayed so far from—"

"It's not your fault," Mother says, then she turns to me again. "Your sister has obviously returned, but your father is still out there. If he hasn't found shelter from this hurricane, he may not last the night."

"I will find him," I say, turning to head back outside.

"But Maile—" My mother's voice cuts off the moment I step out of the hut. I ignore her and keep going. She knows as well as I do he will not stop looking until he has found his daughter. He'll stay out all night if he has to. We can't afford to lose our chief. I can't afford to lose my father.

The wet wind slams against my face, and I feel as though I've been slapped. I duck my head and push through the weather toward the fishponds. It isn't long before I realize someone is following me. I can barely see anything in the chaos of the storm, but still, I can tell it is John. I halt, turning to yell at him to go back.

He can't hear me, but he knows what I'm saying. He shakes his head as though I'm being ridiculous and of course he's coming with me. I don't have time to argue, so I push forward, holding my arms around my head to fend off flying branches and leaves, shielding my face from the stinging winds. I can barely keep my eyes open.

When we reach the south side of the fishponds, I duck behind the nearest stone wall that protects the pond against the prevailing winds. I try to get a glimpse of anyone, anything, but it's impossible to see more than a meter in front of me. John kneels next to me, removing his coat and raising it over our heads to block the storm from our faces the best he can. It creates a small hollow so we can speak and hear each other.

"Should we split up?" I ask. "You take the east ponds, and I'll take the west. We will need to cover a lot of ground if we hope to find him."

"I don't think we should separate," he says. "What if one of us becomes lost or hurt?" He looks into my eyes, a worry there I've never seen before. "And if the chief is injured, it will take both of us to get him back to the huts. I don't want to leave you." His voice cracks on those last words.

I nod. "All right. Together, then."

John puts on his coat again and grabs my hand, threading each of his fingers with mine and holding tight. It's the worst possible time to be thinking it, but I like the way his hand feels in mine. Different than it did before. Solid. Safe.

The fishponds are laid out in a rectangular grid, and we weave through each path to cover every part of them. The ground is wet and muddy, and we both slip several times, leaning on the other to stay upright.

We reach the last pond, and I realize my father is nowhere to be found.

Now what?

A large snapping noise sounds, louder than the storm, and I look up in time to see a large coconut branch falling toward us. I feel the impact when it hits the ground, and I lose my grip, releasing John's hand as we both collapse. I fumble about my body, trying to see where I've been hit. I find nothing, though my limbs still shake from the near miss.

I look at John and see a long, deep, bloody cut along his forehead. He raises his hand to his head, and blood mixed with rain runs down his hand and soaks into the fabric of his shirt and coat. For a moment, I'm back in the battle on the beach, after I made my first kill, watching the combination of blood and water running down my arm. I pray to the gods that John's injury looks worse than it actually is.

I untie my fabric belt and wrap it around John's head. "We need to get back."

"It's fine," he yells. "I'm fine. We need to get to your father."

"Can you stand?"

He nods and rises from the ground, but he's unable to steady his feet and has to lean on me for support. "This feels familiar," he says. "We have to stop doing this."

Despite everything, I laugh aloud. John injured and bleeding, me supporting his weight as we head to shelter—it's definitely familiar. Though this time I don't think his life is in danger. But given his dizziness, I don't know that he'll be much help finding my father right now, either.

"I'm more worried about your clothes," I joke. "We can't let any bloodstains set. This is your only good set of clothing."

He smiles. "I'm willing to risk it to find the chief."

"He's not at the fishponds. Perhaps he headed home."

John agrees. We make our way back toward the huts. When we come within a few hundred meters, we practically trip over someone crouched in flooding waters.

"Father!" I lift his face to look at me; his expression is worry mixed with pain.

"I'm fine," he says, grasping my hand. "Just twisted my ankle. But your sister—"

"Haukea is home," I say. "She's safe."

Relief replaces the worry on his face, and John and I pull him upright, each of us taking an arm and helping him walk. When we get to the hut, my family takes over with his care, elevating his foot and wrapping blankets around him, making sure he stays warm and dry.

John looks terrible with streaks of blood running down his face, but there's a steadiness in his eyes that tells me he'll be fine. He's no longer dizzy and was stable enough to help my father.

"Thank you," I say.

The fabric I'd wrapped around his head is completely soaked through from the rain. "No, thank *you*."

I'm ready to make a joke about him being prone to injury and how he's lucky I'm always there to save him, but Haukea cuts me off.

"Maile," she says, noticing John's injury. "Why are you just standing there? This man is wounded. Were you going to tell anyone?" She leads him to the side of the room to administer to him.

"Let me do that," I say, following them.

"Don't be ridiculous. You're soaking and shivering, and your hair is so tangled I think there are more leaves than hair in the mess."

I reach up and feel my hair. She's exaggerating, but not by much. I'm shivering and need to dry off. I find a couple of blankets and bring them to John, and Haukea plucks them from my arms.

"Don't worry," she whispers to me. "I'll make sure he's all right." She wraps the blankets around his shoulders before cleaning his wound.

A pang of jealousy runs through my chest as I remember our conversation the other day when Haukea said she wanted to marry him. It was meaningless banter, but she said she thought he was handsome. I wonder if he thinks my sister is beautiful. Most men do.

I brush the jealousy away, embarrassed to have let it in.

Haukea is better at administering to the sick than I am. In fact, she's the one who taught me how to use *nahele* weeds to ward off infection. He's in better care with her than he would be with me. Still, I've grown so used to taking care of John these last weeks it feels strange to see someone else do it.

I squeeze my hair to release as much water as I can and then wrap another blanket around my wet body to warm up. Some of the *kukui* nut oil lanterns in the room have gone out, so I light dried pine needles from the still-flaming lamps to reignite the others. The room soon reflects an eerie brightness, erratic shadows waving against the wall as the winds continue to blow against our home.

Finding a spot out of the way, I lower myself to the ground and watch the walls of the hut sway back and forth, squeaking at the seams as they do. It's an unnatural sound, and I would press my hands against my ears to shut it out if I didn't think I would frighten the children huddled inside with us. I hope the others in our village have found shelter in their huts, and that their homes will withstand this hurricane, no matter how long it lasts.

The movement of so many shadows against the brightly lit walls is hypnotic and makes me drowsy, but the storm won't let me sleep. The sounds grow louder. The wind screeches as it blows at incredible speeds. A constant thunderous vibration shakes the ground. For a moment, I wonder what has angered the gods to warrant such a fierce tempest.

The thought makes me look at John. Did the gods send him here? If not, they're certainly allowing him to stay. My ancestors made that clear. His presence here means something. As it is, we need him.

John's head is bandaged now, and he's watching me from his corner while Haukea rattles off words to him I can't hear. I smile, letting him know I'm well and that I'm glad he is, too. He smiles in return, his eyes full of gratitude, before saying something to Haukea.

John is a good man. Kind. Self-sacrificing. I've come to look forward to our days together training in navigation. The truth is, I will be sad when his training is done, and I no longer have an excuse to be by his side every day. Worse will be the time when the battle is over, and he will return with his men to England. A part of me doesn't want him to leave. The thought is ridiculous, but I can't deny it. He's become such an integral part of my life, I'm not sure it will ever be the same without him.

John Harbottle's Journal
24 March 1779

I was injured in the storm. This time it was a gash along my head. The chief's eldest daughter administered to the wound, and she says it should heal quickly. It doesn't hurt much, at least the physical pain doesn't, but my pride has taken a beating. Between this, the slice from Maile's knife, and the thrashing I received from the chief's guards, I've spent most of my time on this island as an invalid.

It's arrogant, I know, but I wish for a moment I could be the one helping, saving, serving. I abhor being such a burden to Maile—can't I aid her, for once? It's not that I want her to come to harm, of course. But I've caused her so much pain, brought her so much despair, I long to be a source of relief instead. I think I cause her more distress than any one person deserves.

At the very least, I yearn to do something that might impress her. I don't know what that would look like, though. Maile is so adept at everything she does, it'd be difficult to best her in anything.

Still, I'm the one who always needs to be taught, tended to, or supported. What must she think of me? I am broken and inadequate when I want to be valiant and bold. Perhaps it's because of these unworthy desires that the universe has humbled me so. Is it every man's wish, I wonder, to be a hero?

I don't want any fanfare; I've no desire for an audience. I only ask to be the person she needs, just once. There is value in that, is there not?

iwakāluakūmākahi

Chapter Twenty-One

The next morning I wake in the hut, still damp but warm, huddled in my corner. I carefully step over the bodies sprawled on the ground, people sleeping wherever they could find space. John isn't here.

When I step outside, I turn in a circle to gauge the damage. It isn't as bad as I feared. There are fallen trees, and leaves and debris are scattered over every meter of the landscape, but most of the huts appear to be intact. Portions of some roofs have been ripped away, but all damage seems fixable. The ground is muddy from the onslaught of water, and the wet taro patches and fishponds have likely flooded over. It could have been much worse. I hope no one was hurt out in the storm last night besides John and the chief.

Just as I have the thought, John steps out of his hut and sees me. After a pause, he makes his way over. His hair is combed and tied back, his face freshly shaven. The uniform looks as clean and crisp as the first day I saw him, and his bandage has been removed, leaving a small line of red where his wound is healing.

"It doesn't look so bad," I say as he approaches, pointing to his forehead.

"It's not," he admits. "It bled a lot, as most head injuries do. I'm afraid we all thought the injury was more serious than it was. I'm going to be fine."

I nod, thinking of his dizzy spell, grateful the momentary light-headedness was all the knock on his head managed.

"Your father has ordered combat training to be halted for a few days so everyone can work on repairs."

"Likely he just doesn't want to be left out of the training," I say, one side of my mouth rising. "He wouldn't put up with his warriors practicing with those guns of yours while he nursed a sore ankle."

"Perhaps." John laughs. "But his ankle isn't too bad, either. He'll be on it in a day or so." He pauses, looking to the ground between us, sliding his boot in the mud. "I suppose we should halt our training as well? To help with the recovery efforts?"

Oh. Right. He posed it as a question, so I suppose I should answer. "Yes," I finally say. "Of course." It's selfish of me to wish I could steal away with John on the water and abandon everyone on land, but halting our training means I'll lose time spent with just the two of us. Disappointment settles in me, and I'm disgusted with myself for being so weak.

"And I should probably go check on my sailors on the ships," he says. "Make sure things are well after the storm."

He's not even planning to stay on the island? "Yes," I say. "You should." I can't hide the frustration in my voice. I've never been good at masking my emotions.

After another long pause, John looks up from the ground. "Do you want to come with me?"

"To the ships?" I ask, my eyes widening.

"Yes, to the *Resolution*. You don't have to, of course." He bites his lip. "I just thought you might be interested in seeing how we live, maybe take a walk around the boat and get a glimpse into the way we do things. If you like."

"I would love to," I say. I brush my hair away from my face, and a small leaf falls from my fingers. "Just . . . just let me clean up first."

"I'll wait for you at the beach."

"Thank you." I hurry to my hut and curse myself for not realizing I probably look like a wild boar twisted in the brush right now. I untangle my hair and pull it up into a bun, securing it in place with a turtle-shell comb. After cleaning my face, I put on a fresh set of clothing and run out to the shore where John has already dragged one of his smaller boats to the water.

He waits for me to get in before pushing it farther out and boarding it himself. The water is a murky brown for several hundred meters out, evidence of the muddy water that ran down from the mountains and into the ocean during last night's storm. The dirt will settle within a couple of days, but it's a vivid reminder that we were lucky to survive the storm relatively unscathed.

When we reach his ship, he anchors the boat to the side and helps me ascend a rope ladder. Once I'm over the side of the ship, I turn and grasp the railing, surprised at how high we are. I've climbed a number of coconut trees in my life, and this light-headed sensation feels similar.

"So high," I say as John climbs over the side and stands next to me. "How can you feel the water way up here? How do you know what she's saying?"

"It's different," he admits. "But trust me, she speaks quite loudly." He smiles and says, "Come on."

I follow him along the deck of the ship. Men are scattered

everywhere, some repairing sails and rigging, others lugging boxes of inventory. One man is even scrubbing the wooden floor we walk on, surrounded by buckets full of murky water.

I shield my eyes from the sun and look up at the masts and the endless cords of rope hanging from them. I reach for a length of one, surprised at how thick it is. It's not made of any fibers I'm familiar with, but it's obviously strong and able to withstand a lot of wear. The rigging for the sails seems quite complicated, not like the simple system we use for our canoes. And though the sails are down, they're still gigantic, dwarfing those of us who stand below them.

As we walk the perimeter of the deck, I'm surprised by the sounds as well. Clinking of wood and iron, the stretching groans of rope, men mumbling and talking among themselves. On our canoes, all sounds are eclipsed by the sound of the water, but up here, it's like being in a giant structure on land, not on the sea at all. I wonder if that sensation is the same when the boat is moving on the water, if the men ever forget they're on a sailing vessel in the first place.

There is obvious damage from the hurricane, but like our village, most of it appears minor, easily mended. The sailors give us ample space as we tour the boat, and though a couple of them stare at me, most keep their eyes averted. There's a mysterious feeling hanging around us, as though the humidity has been sucked out of the air, leaving the world quiet and dry. I'm sure it's just that I've never been on a ship like this before. Everything is new and strange.

John tells me about the different names for each side of the ship, all words I've never heard before and will likely forget. He shows me the steering station and tells me how many men it takes to work the sails. Then he points out large wooden containers piled on top of each other on one end of the ship.

"These are barrels of gunpowder," he says. "The thing we use to fire our guns."

"The thing that burned the hut?" I swallow hard, watching as one of the men tries to mend a cracked barrel. A layer of fine black soot covers him and the floor surrounding him, the powder having spilled out during the storm.

"Yes," John says.

"Is it dangerous?" I step back, as though it could catch fire if I get too close.

"Only near a spark," he says. "James Cook forbade smoking of any kind on his ships. There are too many things that could catch fire on a ship made of wood."

John offers his hand to lead me below the deck. What once felt so open is now cramped and crowded. A few men give me unpleasant looks as we walk past, but John doesn't seem to notice. Instead, he tells me about the kitchen galley, the pantry, and the sleeping quarters.

John is a tall man, and in some rooms he has to crouch to keep from hitting his head on the ceiling. I try to remember Cook's height; I think he was even taller than John. It's strange that the captain wouldn't quite fit in his own ship.

The passageways are so dark, I can barely see the things John points out, even when my eyes have adjusted to the dimness. I don't think I'd be able to find my way around down here without a torch.

"How many men are on the ship?" I ask.

"About a hundred."

My people's huts aren't the most spacious, but there's a lot more headroom, and we spend most of our lives outdoors—fishing and hunting and farming and eating. Despite the massive size of this ship, I'm surprised there's enough room for all of the men. Months spent here would make me lose all reason.

"And here are my chambers," John says, propping open a door. "Most of the men share quarters, but the officers are allotted a bit more privacy." He lights a lamp sitting on a corner table, and the walls brighten, reminding me of last night during the storm in the chief's hut.

There isn't much room to walk around, so I stand in the center and spin to take it all in, my arms crossed in front of me. Rolls of thin bark are piled in a corner, and I wonder if they are the maps he tried to describe to me using rocks and ash. I want to ask if he uses them to navigate, but I don't want to remind him of the items stolen from his ship—the items I hid.

I reach for the hardbound cloths sitting on a table. This bundle is similar to the small square version he carries everywhere. I flip it open. John reaches out his hand to stop me, but then pulls back, likely remembering I can't read what any of it says.

"You wrote in this one?" I ask.

He nods, watching as I flip each cloth carefully. *Paper*, I think he once called it.

"Your journal?"

"An old one," he says.

I flip to the back to find every cloth has been filled with his ink characters.

"Who will read it?" I ask.

He shrugs. "I don't know. Perhaps no one but me."

"If no one will read it, then why write it?"

"Habit, I suppose." He sits on the edge of his mattress, situated much higher off the floor than the mats we sleep on in the village. "James Cook was an avid journal keeper, and I adopted the practice. It helps me sort out my thoughts, helps me make sense of things I'm confused about. Sometimes I like to read about events that happened to me in the past that I may have forgotten. It helps me be grateful for all the opportunities I've had."

I wonder if he will read his journal years from now and remember his time here. If he will remember me. I run my fingers across the symbols on the paper.

"Do you write about me?" I ask. I don't dare look up at him in case he thinks the idea is ridiculous.

He stands from his bed and takes the journal, flipping the papers to one in particular. He scans the words and says, "I met the daughter of the chief today. She is stubborn and conceited and doesn't answer any of my questions. But mostly she gets angry at me for saying thank you. I think I will continue to thank her every day just to see if she will one day break into a tantrum like a small child."

"It does not say that!" I take it back from him and scan through the scribbles, wishing I could read the words.

He laughs. "I couldn't help it. I am sorry."

"Hmm." I flip through the papers, wondering if he's made any images with fine ink like he did in his other journal. The edge of one of the papers slides down my finger, stinging my skin. "*Auwē.*" I pull my hand away, a line of blood beading where it was cut.

"Are you hurt?" John rushes to me, taking my hand and examining the damage.

"It's nothing," I say. "Barely a scratch."

He pulls a small cloth out of his coat and wraps it around my finger. "Let me find you a bandage."

"You don't have to do that," I say. "It's fine. Really."

After glancing quickly around his room, he strides to the

door and says, "Stay here. I'll be right back." And then he's gone, disappearing into the dark hallway.

I admit it's sweet how excited he seemed to be at the idea of helping me. Perhaps he's grown tired of always being the one getting hurt. I smile and sit on his bed, a soft creak sounding as I do. I peek beneath the cloth on my finger; the cut has almost stopped bleeding. After adjusting the cloth against my finger again, I hear a soft knock outside the room.

"That was fast," I say.

But it isn't John who angles his head in through the doorway. It's one of the sailors. There's a line of grease on one of his cheeks as though he'd been cleaning something soiled. He says something to me in his language, but I don't understand. He sounds angry.

Where is John?

The man steps inside the room, and I instinctively reach to my belt cloth, but there's no knife there. I didn't think I'd need to arm myself for an excursion to John's ship. I can't stay here, trapped. I scan the room for something to defend myself with, and I end up reaching for the lamp on the side table. I'll need it to help me see in the dark hallways.

I move past the sailor, and he gives me leave. Once I'm in the hallway, though, he steps out and makes to follow me. I don't know where I'm going, but I can't stay here. With each turn I make, I pray that the gods will lead me to John. A second man joins the first, and I pick up my pace to get away from them, finally breathing relief when I see a beam of light coming from a doorway that I hope leads to the top of the ship.

Once on the deck, I blink my eyes, trying to adjust to the light of the sun. I place the lamp on the floor and shade my eyes, looking for John, but he's nowhere. A man covered in soot steps in front of me, barking words I can't understand. He's the one I saw working on the barrels earlier.

I feel something tug on the back of my head, and my turtle-shell comb shatters on the ground, my hair falling from its bun and tumbling down the length of my back. When I spin around, the two men who followed me from below block my way and shout at me.

Don't they realize I can't understand what they're saying? I don't know if they intend to hurt me, but they're angry. So angry. My heart races with the uncertainty of what they will do to me.

The soot-covered man shoves me, and I trip on something at my feet—the lamp. I hear the glass crack as I stumble. The man kicks it away, grabbing hold of my arm and yelling at me some more.

"John," I cry out. Where is he?

Out of the corner of my eye, I see the broken lamp, the oil escaping the cracked enclosure. The tiny flame grows, igniting something next to it—the small cloth John gave me for my bleeding finger. I must have dropped it in the commotion. And behind it, I see the stacked wooden barrels of John's gunpowder. The layer of black is way too close to the flames.

"Look out!" I try to point toward the danger, but the soot-covered man just squeezes my arm tighter, and the other men around us are focused on me, not the fire.

In an instant, someone crashes into us, his shoulder pushing through the crowd, effectively knocking everyone to the ground. It's John, and he's not just angry, he's seething. Some of the men hold their arms up to fight back, others continue to yell, aiming their complaints at John instead of me now that he's here.

But John ignores them all and heads straight for the broken lamp. He slips out of his coat and tosses it over the flames. He tries to stomp it out before any sparks can reach the gunpowder, but his coat catches fire instead. Without hesitating, he picks up his flaming coat, along with the remnants of the lamp, moments before the fire would have reached the gunpowder spilled across the deck. He tosses the burning bundle overboard, saving us from another accidental explosion.

The moment the men realize what John was doing, their shouts cease. John wasn't trying to hurt them or punish them for harassing me, he was trying to save them. Even in the midst of his anger for how they were treating me, he risked himself to save his men.

A sudden flash of flames ignites the soot-covered man's breeches, near his ankle. The cloth must have caught fire when he kicked the lamp away. I scramble for a nearby bucket of water and pour it over his leg, dousing the fire. After the steam has dissipated, he looks up at me, in shock that I came to his aid.

John, still a few meters away, holds up his hand as though to ask me to stay where I am. Then he speaks to his men, a crowd gathering around our little group to listen in. I don't know what he says, but based on the heat of his words and the authority behind them, it's more than just a reprimand; it's a threat—a warning. Those who had been harassing me mumble words in my direction that I think are meant as an apology. They listen to John with such awe in their expressions, you'd think they were listening to James Cook himself.

John's tone changes from anger to something stern yet encouraging. I would say he sounds royal, and if I didn't know better, I would have said he was a chief from a powerful nation.

The men stand and the crowd dissipates, returning to their chores with a renewed sense of duty. John strides to me and grips my waist, guiding me below deck without saying anything. His fist curls around the fabric of my wrap, and I worry he's angry with me, too. But as soon as we're alone, he spins me around.

"Are you hurt?" he asks gently, his eyes roaming over me in the low light, searching for any sort of injury.

"I'm fine," I say. Besides a bruised arm, I came out of the conflict unscathed.

"Are you sure?" He lifts my hand and looks closely. "Is your finger all right?"

"My finger?" I give him a small laugh. "You're worried about my finger?"

He finally looks me in the eyes, a flood of relief filling his.

"Oh, Maile." He pulls me close, wrapping his arms around me and holding me tight against him. He's shaking. "I thought I was going to lose you. I thought—"

I hug him back, thinking about how you can't lose something unless it was yours in the first place. "You didn't," I say, my voice cracking. "I'm still here."

He exhales against the top of my head. "My men are tired, and hungry, and homesick. The storm sent them over the edge of their patience. Their behavior . . ." John loses his words. "There's no excuse for what they did to you, what they said. I am so sorry you had to suffer through that."

"I'm fine," I say again, trying to reassure him. "You . . . you were amazing up there."

He pulls away slightly to look at my face. "They won't be difficult anymore. They've vowed to follow my commands from now on. No more pushing back."

I nod. "I trust you." Despite everything that has transpired today, I can't think of a safer place to be than with John. I know he will protect me when I need it most. He will put my well-being before all others. "There's only one problem," I add.

He brushes a strand of hair away from my face. "What's that?"

"I don't think I can mend your coat after that."

John bursts into laughter, and I can't help but join him, feeling a much-needed release of anxiety as I do.

John Harbottle's Journal
24 March 1779

We departed from the port in Plymouth on the twelfth of July 1776, nearly three years ago. It was my third voyage with James Cook, so I didn't share the same excitement some of the new sailors did. I remember them crowding the decks, waving goodbye to friends and family as the ship was released from the dock, and then celebrating into the night in drunken stupor, eager for the adventure ahead.

They didn't know then that our trip would be more work than anything. That they would become homesick for the people and country they left—even homesick for the food and comforts they'd grown accustomed to. They didn't know that their skin would burn and peel, their stomachs would rot, and the flesh of their palms would rub raw. But now they have stories to tell their children, and their children's children, that can't be rivaled.

That day, with no one to say farewell to, I remained in my quarters as we set sail, cataloging my inventory of maps and linguistic texts. I've never experienced the ache of missing England or its people and places. I've never felt a pull for that which was familiar. Not like the others did, even Cook himself. It's always made me wonder if England was intended to be my home, or if I was meant to be somewhere else. Somewhere I hadn't yet found. Or perhaps home was someone I hadn't yet met.

iwakāluakūmālua

Chapter Twenty-Two

We sit in the sand, the sun having just set below the mountains. The water has subsided into long, slow waves that run in and out of reach, the perfect conditions for surfing by moonlight. John's men take turns standing on a long wooden board in an attempt to learn the sport. John and I laugh as they fall off, one after the other.

"I don't think I've ever found surfing to be so comical," I say. "Even when young children are learning how to do it, they don't look so ridiculous."

"My men are jesters," John says. "Clowns trying to keep steady on a tightrope."

I don't know his references, but I smile anyway. "I think my people are getting frustrated. They may abandon your men soon. Surfing lessons aren't meant to be a joke."

"Their combat training is almost done," he says. "They deserve some time to relax. Both your men and mine."

"I suppose." I gather my knees to my chest and wrap my arms around them. "At least *I'm* enjoying it."

John laughs again as one of his men slips off the board and

into the white water. "And what about my training?" he asks. "Are we almost done with that too?"

"Soon," I say, resting my chin on the top of my knee.

"That's what you told me when you held me captive." He looks at me with a grin. "You said I would be healthy enough to return to my men *soon*, but you were never going to let me go, were you?"

My heart speeds up, and I pull my knees in tighter. I know he's teasing, but the truth of his words cuts deep. I don't want him to leave, but I'm too afraid to say so. I think about the stolen items I hid in the forest. There are so many reasons I tell myself about why I haven't given them back. If I tell him, he'll know I've been lying, hiding them from him this whole time, and then he might leave with his men before fulfilling his end of the bargain with my father. But the truth is, I don't want him to leave at all. And I'm not willing to hand over the means for him to do so.

I try to match his lightened mood. "Maybe you'll never be ready. Maybe I'll keep you as my prisoner forever."

"I knew it." Though John smiles, my stomach still churns with an ache, a fear, that I will lose him soon.

"Besides," I say, "we've yet to go out at night."

"Ah, yes. But I know the stars."

I raise an eyebrow. "I doubt you know them like I do."

"I'll prove it." He motions for me to sit in front of him.

I move so that my back is to him, and he leans forward with his arm over my shoulder. He points to the sky in front of us, his mouth at my ear.

"The cluster of seven little stars there," he says. "Those are the Pleiades—the Seven Sisters. They are named for the daughters of Atlas, who holds up the sky, and Pleione, the protector of sailing."

"Hmm. I like that," I muse. "We call them the little eyes."

"And there," he continues, "is Orion the hunter. The two pairs of stars on each end are his shoulders and knees, the row of three stars is his belt."

I turn my head sideways, trying to see the picture he describes before laughing. "So your hunter is our *hei hei*?"

"*Hei hei*? I don't know what that means."

I think for a moment of how to describe it, but finally decide to show him instead. "Speaking of belts . . ." I untie the thin coconut fiber belt from around my waist. I knot the ends together to form a loop, and then thread each side between my fingers, holding my hands apart, palms facing each other. "It's a child's game," I say. "You pull at the strings with your fingers, back and forth, manipulating the string to form different pictures and shapes."

I alternately pick at the strings from one hand to the next, remembering playing the game with my sister when we were children. When the string forms the picture I want, I hold it up in front of us with my thumbs and forefingers in each corner of the pattern, superimposed over his hunter in the sky.

"*Hei hei*," I say.

"*Hei hei*." He slides his fingers next to mine to help me hold it up. "That's amazing. It looks just like it. Teach me," he says, scooting closer so his legs are on either side of me, his chest pressed against my back as he leans over my shoulder.

I slide the string onto his hands, thread it around his fingers. "Keep it tight." I tell him which finger to use to pull which string and in which order. I scold him twice for letting the string go slack, and in the end, when it's time to push his thumbs and forefingers through and twist it away from him to reveal the pattern, one side slips, and the string knots, tangling in his fingers.

"You and your men are hopeless," I tease. "I thought falling off a surfboard was bad, but you can't even play a child's game without failing horribly."

John grunts in my ear and says, "Again."

I help him work the strings until he's able to flip it into the pattern. He holds it up in front of us. While the top of the pattern is stretched longer than the bottom and one of the openings looks like it's on the verge of knotting, he did it.

"*Hei hei*," he says again. "I will remember this one."

His words make me frown, reminding me again he'll leave soon, taking everything he's learned with him, until I am nothing but a memory. Something he can read about in his journal to remind him of a time long forgotten.

John places the string in my lap before pointing to a pair of stars. "Gemini," he says. "The twins. They were two mortals who were granted shared godhood after death."

I sit up straighter. "We call them the twins as well," I say, excited to have found something in common between our constellations. "One looks forward, and the other looks behind."

John places one of his hands on my waist. "And is there one that looks at the present?"

I wish there were. Because the present is all that matters to me right now. I don't want to think about what has happened in the past. I don't want to think about what will happen when John leaves. I just want to prolong this moment. This now.

I clear my throat. "I suppose when you're out on the water, you need to know where you've been and where you want to go. Otherwise it doesn't really matter where you are."

He doesn't respond, and I can feel his warm breath on my neck. It causes bumps to rise on my skin. John notices and runs his hands up and down my arms to warm me, not realizing my reaction isn't from the cold.

"You have strange names for your gods," I say, trying to think of something else to talk about.

I feel him shrug behind me. "They are mythical gods. Greek gods. Their stories are perpetuated, though people no longer believe in them."

How strange to name things after something you don't believe in. I wonder if he thinks our traditions are silly, that we're fools for believing what we believe.

"Do you have a song for your stars?" he asks. "The story of your constellations?"

"Yes." He wants me to chant to him, but I hesitate. Everyone has abandoned surfing for the evening, leaving John and me alone on the beach. It's not that I'm worried others will hear, and I've sung for him before, so I'm not embarrassed, but the story of our stars is not one I want to be reminded of.

"Your people have a story for each set of stars," I say. "For each picture you see in the sky. But try to look bigger. Look at them together." I raise my arm and point as I explain. "Do you see the curve of stars that runs through the twins, stretching from the north to the south in the sky? It is the bow of a canoe, and if you were to head farther south, you could see its anchor."

"The Southern Cross," John whispers.

"The belt of your hunter is the stern, his sword is a cable, and there, stretching out to your Seven Sisters, is the sail."

"I see it," he says. "It covers the entire sky."

I nod, then take a deep breath before beginning my song. It is the story about an infant who died at birth and was buried in the ground. A great tree grew in the spot, the tree used to build the canoe in the sky. It is the great canoe, the one that embarked from our homeland thousands of years ago. It made several stops along the way, island after island. It unloaded passengers as it went until there was only one couple left, the woman pregnant with their unborn child. They landed in Hawai'i, the final stop for the great canoe.

The woman gave birth to a child, and the gods offered her a bargain. If she let them take the life of the infant, she could bury his body and a new tree would grow in that place. A tree that could be formed into another great canoe. With that canoe, her posterity could sail across the entire world, taking her descendants to every land in existence. But if she didn't allow the gods to take the child, there would be no more exploring. And this place, this destination, would be all that remained for them.

She held her infant in her arms and knew she couldn't give him up. And so the great canoe was lifted into the sky, where it sits today, anchored, never to explore again. A reminder of where we came from, of where we could have gone. A reminder of where we will always be.

I stop singing. For the first time, the story feels like a curse on my people. We are content and happy where we are, never doubting our place in the world, but the arrival of Cook and his ships has changed everything. There is obviously so much more out there than I ever imagined, and I wonder if our inability, our unwillingness, to venture beyond the safety of our islands will prove a disadvantage in the end.

"That was beautiful," John whispers.

It is sad, I think. But sometimes there is beauty in sadness. "Do you see this same sky where you come from?" I ask.

"Yes."

"And you can swim in this same ocean?"

"There are a number of oceans between Hawai'i and England," he says. "But they are all connected. The water is the same. It's how we sailed here on our ships."

I nod. "The same sun? The same moon?"

He adds to my list. "The same clouds. The same sky. The same wind." He turns my shoulders so I'm facing him. He presses his thumb against the skin between my brows, trying to smooth it out. "What's wrong?"

There's so much more I need to teach him about the night sky. About the declination of the stars and how to measure their rise and fall against the earth. He needs to know about the other starlines. Which stars are fixed and which rotate at different angles, how they cross the meridian. He needs to know about pointers and the navigator's triangle.

But all of that can wait.

I don't want to look forward. I don't want to look back. I want to live right now, memorize this moment. Seal it in my memory so I can look back on it when I'm in danger of forgetting everything that has happened.

I move closer and trace my fingers along the fabric on his chest, mimicking the scar that lies beneath—the scar I created. It ends at his heart, and I lean my head against that spot, feeling the solid drumming beat that both steadies me and excites me. I lift my head higher and bury my face in his neck, breathing in deeply, my head spinning as I do. Then I press the side of my face against his, breathing in again, relishing the smoothness of his skin. He smells wonderful.

My hands rest on his shoulders, and I pull away slightly to look at his face. He stares at me with an intensity that reminds me of the first day I saw him, standing high on the deck of the *Resolution*. I gaze back at him, not turning away this time. I match his boldness, determined to show him what I feel.

I lean forward and press the front of my nose against his, our foreheads touching. I breathe in his breath before exhaling and giving him mine. I feel his arms wrap around me and pull me tight against him. My fingers find a place in his hair, holding him close.

I draw back again, savoring the warmth in his expression as he looks at me. I was wrong about him not being a handsome man. His nose isn't too pointy—it's strong. Definitive. And his large eyes are kind and welcoming; it'd be impossible to feel afraid of those eyes. Their blue-green shade has become my favorite color, reminding me of the water I love. Of our time spent on the ocean together. I run a thumb over his lips. There are curves there I've never noticed before. They're pliable. Soft. The slight wave of his hair is the perfect shape for my fingers to hold, to grasp, to feel.

I move closer and press one side of my nose against his, and he exhales with a sigh. We share the same breath, the same touch. Then I shift to the opposite side, giving him my most intimate *honi*. We inhale each other's aroma, our life essence. We're so close I can't mark out the space where one of us is separate from the other. My heart beats fast and strong, but I'm not embarrassed because so does his. I can feel it against me. We are waves crashing into each other, merging into one harmonious surge of water.

"Maile." My name leaving his lips tickles my skin. It sounds like the resonating echo of a lover's flute, calling to me.

Remember this, Maile. Remember what this feels like.

I stand and help John rise, then I lead him into the water. It's warm from welcoming the sun all day, and so still that I can pretend we're in a pond and not the finicky ocean. I lie on my back and float on the water, John following my lead. There are so many stars in the sky, and each one is reflected on the water's surface, making it appear as if there are twice as many surrounding us. Encompassing us. Keeping us right where we need to be.

"I feel like I'm swimming in the stars," John says, putting into words exactly what I'm feeling.

This is what I wanted. To feel connected to him. To know that no matter where either of us is in the world, we are linked. By nature, by our memories. By the traditions we've shared with each other.

John entwines his fingers with mine, holding tight as we drift on the surface of the water. I close my eyes and imagine the picture we create against the backdrop of stars. Of the story that brought us here, of the chant someone would sing about us. Would it be a sad story or a happy one? Perhaps it will be both.

And as I ponder on all the things that have led us to this moment, I realize every story must have a combination of good and bad, of sorrow and joy, and I promise myself that this is one story I will never forget.

John Harbottle's Journal
3 April 1779

The natives are a people of strange contradiction.

They've been known to offer human sacrifices to their gods, but they value life above all else. They are skilled in the art of warfare but are peaceable and guided by love. They can shun and despise, yet also take someone in as they are, with no judgment. They will steal, and they will give freely.

I saw this even in the way they treated my captain. They honored him as a god then killed him without reservation. And after his death, they honored him again by preserving his bones, preserving his power.

They are a reflection of all that is good in the world, and all that is not. They are dangerous and wondrous at the same time. This is the only explanation I have for why a person could go from hating and despising me, even to the point of almost killing me, to then gifting me with what I consider the most transcendent experience I have ever felt.

It is a dichotomy I'm grateful for.

You are a constellation.
Made of stars that shine from every angle.
I could follow each line and know exactly where it leads.
The composition is perfect.
You are perfect.
But what about the unexpected?
The suddenly?
The thing you never saw coming?
Is there a place in your song for me?

iwakāluakūmākolu

Chapter Twenty-Three

Father has decided to take John and a few officers on a tour of our homestead. The combat training has ceased, the men having learned all they can about the guns and the combined warfare strategies of our two groups. And though neither of us has said it aloud, John and I both know our navigation training has stalled. I keep coming up with things to teach him, and he plays along, not minding the excuse to be with me each day. But he's ready to lead his ships home to England without the use of his traditional instruments. So we all wait for the inevitable battle to arrive, for the foreigners to fulfill their duty to fight alongside us, and then we'll part ways.

"This is the *kapa* hut," my father says. "Where the women pound the bark cloth." His voice is condescending, as though he would never be found doing such demeaning work, but John is enthralled, examining every club, every stamp, every container of dye. His interest in our customs hasn't waned in all his time here.

I stand with the rest of my family to the side, my sister and I near our mother. La'akea is pestering the other officers with curses then laughing because they don't understand what he's saying.

"I didn't realize you had to wet it," John says, motioning to the containers of water the women continually dip the bark into to keep it damp.

"It makes the bark pliable," Haukea says. "You can get it much thinner that way, before the fabric begins to fray."

"It's incredible." John glances to the skirt I'm wearing, eyeing the colorful patterns, then looks back at the bowls of dye, likely wondering which ones make which colors when the stain is applied.

Father takes him to the tattoo hut next, where lines are cut into the skin while ink is applied. It's a painful process, time-consuming, but the markings are a part of who we are and what we believe. When John raises an eyebrow at me, inquisitive, I lift my skirt to reveal a small checkered band around my thigh. It's a linear pattern of fish scales, symbolic of the tie I have to the sea and everything in it.

John's face reddens, and I think he's embarrassed to see a part of my skin that's been covered until now. I used to think it silly how adamant John is about women's modesty and treating females with respect, but it's something I've grown to like about him. It makes me feel important, special. I doubt any of the women back in England have such tattoos. I like that I'm unique in that way, too.

We walk through the banana grove among the endless green bunches of fruit hanging above our heads. Father explains how women are forbidden to eat the fruit, but that we use the giant leaves for everything from wrapping our food to thatching our roofs.

When we reach the fishponds, Haukea runs forward and points out a portion of the wall she helped mend after the storm.

"Every pond has been repaired," she says, beaming. "We

didn't lose many fish after all. Not enough to affect our harvest numbers."

"There are fish in here?" John asks, leaning over the waist-high wall made of black lava rocks. He dips his hand into the water and licks his finger. "These are freshwater ponds."

Father nods proudly. "They supplement the fish we catch in the ocean. Always here when we need it."

"We have fisheries as well, but . . ." John runs his hand lightly along the jagged rocks and the mortar that keeps them together. His eyes follow the irrigation ditch as it runs toward the mountains and a nearby spring, the source we use to keep the water level constant. "The fish just stay here, in the pond?" he muses softly.

"They are our prisoners," I tease. "I tell them we'll let them go one day, but it's a trick. They're trapped here forever."

John bursts into a laugh so loud, even his own men take a step back, surprised by his outburst. I smile widely, glad to have shared our private joke. My father looks at me disapprovingly, and the rest of my family just looks confused. I shrug as though I've no idea why the strange foreign sailor is laughing.

I stay quiet as we visit the huts where our fishing nets are being mended by the fishermen, lengths of rope laid out along every open surface.

"They are preparing for the *hukilau*," Father explains. "With the completion of our gun training, we will celebrate with a great feast. The nets will be hauled by everyone in the village to bring in a large harvest for the celebration."

As we head toward the taro patches, John slows his pace until he's walking next to me, the two of us trailing behind the rest of the group. "I love how everyone in your community is so connected," he tells me. "Everyone works together for the good of all. It's like your *hānai*. Everyone is family, no matter who they are born to."

I think about his words, not realizing until now there could be any other way. I know John lost his parents when he was young. It must have been a difficult life, growing up without the kinship we share in our village. It gives me a new sense of pride in my culture, in our traditions. There are things we do well regardless of our lack of advancements like metal and guns. Family is just one of them.

John's hand knocks against mine, and he weaves his fingers in and out of my own, reminding me of the day on the canoe when his little finger was threaded with mine. His simple touch made me feel light-headed then—like it does now.

I slap his hand away and fold my arms in front of me, lifting one hand to hide my grin. He shouldn't do such things around my family. It's forbidden for a royal to have a relationship with a commoner, let alone a foreigner. I don't know what my father would do if he found out I'd developed feelings for a white sailor.

But John doesn't waver. He rests his hand on the small of my back, then slides it along my waist to pull me closer to him as we walk. I shoot a warning glance at him, but he just smiles as he presses his finger into a spot just below my ribs, making me laugh and shout at the same time from his attempt to tickle me.

I step away from him just as a few heads turn to see what the commotion is. John laughs out loud again, and I suspect my family might think neither of us is right in the head.

Father points out the dry taro patches first then leads us to the wetland taro. Giant leaves hang in rows from taro stalks, the base and root buried beneath the surface of the water. I step into the mud, letting the rich black soil ooze between my toes. It's my turn to raise an eyebrow at John, daring him to join me.

He hesitates, then removes his boots and steps in next to me, sinking a little until his feet find something solid beneath the mud.

Laʻakea rolls his eyes, and Haukea steps back, not wanting to get dirty.

Father says, "Maile, bring him back to the beach when you're done. We're going to gather everyone to help lay out the nets."

John's soldiers leave with the rest of my family. I guess the allure of the taro patch isn't as strong as I thought. I love stomping through the fields, playing in the water that nourishes our most important plant.

"It takes several months to grow and harvest the taro," I tell John. "So we rotate through the fields to ensure we always have a constant supply."

"And you use the streams running from the mountains to feed them?"

I nod. "We divert the water into the fields, then at the lowest patch we divert the water back out. From there it heads to the ocean." I shrug. "It's how we've always done it."

He bends over, running his hand beneath the leaves and down the stalk into the water below. "May I?" he asks, wanting permission to pull the root from the ground.

I answer by bending over as well, helping him lift the taro from the water. Liquid drips from the corm and the stringy roots that dangle from the underside.

"So this is the food your people eat most?" he asks, knowing how much of it we consume.

I point to the large corm, the bulbous root at the base of the plant. "After cooking and peeling the flesh, we pound it to make *poi*, adding water to create a thick paste. That is the most common preparation, but we'll also eat it whole." I think of the day he was tied up in the prisoner hut and I fed him chunks of taro soaked in coconut milk. "We'll also cut strips of it to dry for long trips."

John lowers the plant to the ground, fingering the giant, open-faced leaves. "And you cook and eat these as greens?"

"Yes. The stems, too. Often with pork in our underground ovens." I turn the plant over, pointing to the different parts. "We use the stem on insect bites, for the pain and swelling. The root stock helps to stop bleeding, and *poi* can help stop infection or be used as glue to connect pieces of cloth together." I point to the corm. "We use pieces of the flesh for bait or feed them to our pigs to fatten them up. There are hundreds of varieties of taro, and several of them are used to make dyes." I know he's interested in the colors we make and might appreciate learning more. "And when we've used what we need, we bury the stalk back in the field where it will grow more root and leaves for us to use. The stalk is called ʻohā. That is where we get our word for family—ʻohana. Every generation reproducing and giving birth to the next, providing life, connecting us all together."

"It's all about family," he says softly. He reaches forward as though to take the root, but instead cradles my hands to help me hold it up. "And coconut, *kukui*, *kī* leaves—your people use every part of every plant." He says it with respect. "It's a marvel, really."

"And a necessity," I add as John helps me bury the plant back in the wet soil. "We don't have 'fancy equipment' and must use what nature has given us."

"Like with navigation," he says.

"Like with navigation." I lead him out of the taro patch and onto dry ground. Now that no one else is around, I let him wrap his arm around my waist. We are high above our homestead, the taro fields about halfway between the mountain forests and the beach below. From here, we can see all of our land, leading down toward the shore. Every hut and orchard. Every part of our home. "It's our *ahupua'a*," I say, motioning to everything below us.

"I don't know that word."

I bite my lower lip, thinking of how to explain it. "Every family manages a portion of land that runs from the top of the mountain down to the beach below. A strip, if you will, which contains everything we could ever need to survive. We use the mountains for wood, thatching, and rope, the upper lands for sugarcane and sweet potato, and these lower lands for taro and fish. Water, *kukui* nut trees, *koa* wood, the gardens, the plains, our dwellings, our orchards. There's no reason for us to leave when we have everything here."

John shields his eyes and scans the landscape, as though searching for all the things I listed.

"That's why another chief coming here to invade is strange," I say. "Fighting for the land of another, when your own sources on your own island have run dry or become diseased? Maybe. But to come to another island otherwise? It makes me wonder what has gone wrong with his own *ahupua'a*, or if he is only propelled by greed."

"Yes," John says. "Greed is a powerful motivator. It seems one can't escape it no matter where one goes."

I look at John and wonder what he's experienced of greed.

He brings our conversation back. "So there are a number of these land strips, these *ahupua'a*, all over your island?"

"Yes. Many."

"It's incredibly efficient. And so wise." He pauses. "You have so much abundance here."

I wait for him to put his boots back on before I say, "Now that you've seen everything, what's your favorite?" My voice is teasing, and I remember the time he listed all the things he loved about our island and concluded that he liked my singing best.

"The people," he says, smiling.

I don't know if he means certain people in particular, or all of us as a whole, but I don't dare ask. "I have one more thing I want to show you before we head back down," I say. "But it will be a bit of a trek."

"I don't mind," he says.

I lead him up the mountainside for about half an hour; the thing I'm searching for is only found in the higher elevations. Clouds gather on the high hills, and I think it might rain. The day is pleasant and warm, but a midday shower would be a welcome relief from the exertion of our hike. As soon as I spot what I'm looking for, I pause and wait for John to notice.

"It's . . . it's a vine." John sounds unimpressed. "With green leaves and . . . it's nice."

I roll my eyes and pluck off a length of vine, folding it into my palms before holding it under his nose.

"What . . . oh. Oh!" He grabs the vine from my hands and presses it against his face, inhaling deeply. "This is the most incredible fragrance I've ever smelled. Sweet and rich at the same time."

"Guess what it's called."

He lowers the greenery and waits for me to answer.

"*Maile*," I say, a warmth of blush in my cheeks.

"*Maile*?" His wide smile appears. "This is what you're named after? This particular vine?"

I nod, smiling in return.

He sniffs the leaves again. "Unfortunately, one of you smells better than the other."

My mouth falls open, and I punch his shoulder.

He tosses his head back and laughs. Then he repeats the word again and again. "*Maile*." He smells the leaves. "*Maile*." He stretches the vine out, expanding his arms from left to right.

"Even when dried, the scent remains," I say.

He gently rolls up the vine, careful not to crush the leaves as he does. "I lied."

"About what?"

"This." He looks down then back to me. "This . . . *maile*. This is my favorite thing about your island." His words are so soft, so sacred, as though he's talking about more than just the vine.

I take the bundle from him and hold it to my nose, never tiring of the sweet scent of my namesake.

"Can I keep it?" he asks, reaching for it again.

I step back and, with a mocking smile, say, "If you can get it from me."

I turn and run into the forest, my laughter echoing beneath the canopy of trees.

He shouts my name amid bouts of his own laughter, close behind me. Drops of rain begin to fall, and the trail becomes slick, but I manage to stay just out of his reach.

"That *maile* is mine," John shouts, and I don't know how much longer I can run, my fits of laughter making me weak.

When I finally slow down, turning to face him, he's gone. "John?"

He doesn't answer, and I worry he's fallen or gotten hurt. I retrace my steps, looking for any sign of him on either side of the path. The rain stops as quickly as it started, and I wipe the wetness away from my face.

I finally see him crouched on the side of the trail, his wet shirt clinging to his skin as he leans over something I can't see.

"John?" I ask, wondering why he didn't answer me before. "Are you all right?"

He stands and backs away from me, his hands covered in mud.

"Did you fall?" I reach for his hands, worried he broke something, but he jerks away from my touch. "What happe—?" My word cuts short when I see the pile of gear at his feet. The objects are wet and dirty, but I recognize them immediately. Small iron tools. Bound cloths. A sun-colored metal molded in the form of a triangle. They are the items I buried. The items I found on the stolen boat.

Several coconuts have been pushed out of the way. The outside husks are no longer green but brown, the fruit inside having long rotted. I can picture what it must have looked like as John ran past this spot—an armful of coconuts forming the simple shape of a rainbow. The shape I used when I hid what our people stole. The same shape I made over the grave of John's captain. Of course it would catch his attention, make him pause.

I finally look up at him, not knowing what to say.

"It was you." He takes another step back.

"I didn't steal them," I say, even as my guilt is unearthed in front of us. "It wasn't me."

He looks back to the coconuts, his face falling. "But you buried it."

I nod slowly. "I found it the day after the battle. In the stolen boat. I hid it to protect my father's honor."

Understanding fills his eyes, followed by a look of pain. "But you kept it from me. Why?"

I step closer, but he flinches, so I take a step back again, giving him the space he needs. With tears welling in my eyes, I say,

"You were my enemy, and I didn't want to give you what you wanted."

His nostrils flare. "After all this time. After everything that has happened." He pauses, glaring at me. "Am I still your enemy now?"

"No," I cry, shaking my head. "No, of course not. But . . ." I can't say the words.

"But what?" he yells.

But I didn't want you to leave this place. To leave me. And I wasn't about to give you the ability to do it. The words fill my head, waiting to be spoken.

"John Harbottle." A deep voice sounds from behind John, and he spins around as my father steps into view. He looks between John and me. "We've been looking for you everywhere. It's time."

"The fishnets?" I ask, confused about why he hiked up the mountain just to get us to help prepare for the *hukilau.*

"No," he says. "It's time to fight. Scouts have reported our enemy made landfall on the south edge of the island. We must leave immediately."

John nods once and begins to follow the chief beyond the forest canopy.

"Can I go?" I ask, not wanting to be separated from John after what just transpired between us. I need a chance to explain. "I can fight."

They both pause, but only my father turns back to me. "Don't be ridiculous, Maile. You know the gods will not allow it."

I wait for John to make up an excuse for me to come. To say I can help with navigation, or that my fighting skills surpass some of the men's. Anything. But he doesn't acknowledge me. He doesn't even gather the supplies he dug up because it would mean having to look at me again.

And then he and my father are gone, hurrying to a battle I am forbidden from joining.

I look down at my hands, expecting to see a golden finch from a dream I had long ago, waiting to fly free. But he was never mine to keep. All I hold is a vine, crushed from gripping it too tightly. I let it fall from my hands, a feeling of emptiness left in its wake. Then I drop to my knees, sobbing, praying for the rain to return so it can fill the emptiness inside me.

John Harbottle's Journal
17 April 1779

The scouts reported the enemy landed farther east than we anticipated, so we sailed north, around to the west side of the island, approaching them from the opposite end. We should still be able to maneuver them into position against the cliffs. By the time we reach the south end and need to make landfall, it will be dark, and they will not see our sails. We'll utilize the paddlers when we're close to shore, so the majority of our men's strength will be preserved for the battle itself.

I sit in the lead canoe with the chief. I've convinced him to leave behind the kāhili, *the feathered standards that mark his royal status,* but he refuses to remove his helmet and cape. The golden-yellow and red feathers will draw attention in the fight, but I don't argue with him. He can be as stubborn as his daughter sometimes. While his warriors and my men will easily spot him in the battle, so will our enemy, and they will target the chief. I hope our dual advantage of guns and British soldiers will keep him safe.

I watch as the sunset cycles through all the colors. It's almost too dark to write in this journal, and land approaches. I thought the imminent battle and my having to navigate us there would distract me from thoughts of Maile. How she lied to me, betrayed me.

But she is in the stars I try to read. She's in the wind of our sails and in the water that surrounds us. I've discovered the problem with learning to observe everything in nature—it means I am aware of her, always, because she is in all of it.

Will I ever be able to sail again without the reminder of her wherever I go?

iwakāluakūmāhā

Chapter Twenty-Four

When my tears are spent and I have enough energy to trek home, I gather the stolen navigational equipment into its original parcel, along with the discarded vine, and heft it onto my back. I traverse down the slopes into the village below. By the time I get there, most of the canoes have already left along with the men, including my brother, my father, and John.

It's strange to see our homestead so empty. Large fishing nets are piled on the ground, which is odd. Such care is taken with the nets, only the direst of conditions would cause them to be abandoned so haphazardly—such as a looming battle. Plans for a celebration are stalled until our men return.

I hesitate outside John's hut, not wanting to add trespassing to my list of crimes against him. But I finally decide things couldn't get any worse than they are, and I walk inside. The only other time I've been here it was dark, so I'm really seeing it for the first time. There are a few objects I can't identify, likely brought here from his room on the *Resolution*. A simple pile of mats serves as his bed, and a dozen single papers, likely torn out from one of his journals, have been attached to one wall with taro paste.

I can't decipher what's on most of them, the characters of his language inked on each surface remain elusive, but there are several with images like the one I saw him making when I held him captive. Images of a woman with long dark hair. At first I think it must be Haukea, for the girl is beautiful, but then I realize she's depicted in a canoe, or pointing at the stars, or swimming in the ocean. In one she is opening her mouth with her arms toward the sky, as though chanting a song. They are images of me.

I sit on the ground, carefully unwrapping the bundle. I lay the *maile* vine on his bed then clean off each of his tools, one by one, until they are as clean as the day I buried them. I place each object on his bed so he can't miss them when he returns.

If he returns.

"There you are."

I look to the doorway and see Haukea standing just outside.

"Are you all right?" She enters and sits next to me on the mats. "You look like you've been crying."

I shrug, not knowing what to say.

"You're worried about them," she says. "I am, too. But they've trained hard for this. They're ready. I'm confident victory approaches on the horizon."

I nod, and we sit in silence while Haukea runs her hand down my hair, soothing me.

"Do you know that feeling of stepping out of the water?" I say. "When you walk to the dry sand, and every grain clings to the skin on your feet and legs?"

"It's impossible to rub off," she says, smiling.

"Yes. And it hurts when you try."

"It's better to walk back into the water where it will rinse away easily."

"But what if there is no water?" I ask.

She pauses and looks at me, realizing we're not really talking about sand clinging to skin.

"What if the water that was once there is now gone?" I ask. "How do you get rid of the sand?"

She thinks for a moment. "You wait until your skin dries. It will rub off easier then."

"Meanwhile it will irritate and distract you, causing you to think of nothing else until it's gone."

"Or you can suffer through the pain and scrape it away," she says. "It will hurt at first, but it won't hurt forever, and at least you're rid of it sooner."

I bite my lip, not liking either option. Isn't there one that will take away the pain now? How do I get rid of the suffering before it rubs me raw?

Haukea squeezes my shoulder. "And if neither of those options are satisfactory, then you should get up and find out where that water went."

We both chuckle, and Haukea stands.

"Mother has prepared fish for dinner," she says. "Will you come and eat?"

"In a few minutes," I say, plastering on a smile.

She nods. "Are you sure you're all right?"

"I will be."

I just need to find that water.

I find a small canoe on the beach and launch it into the ocean, immediately raising the sails. I have a lot of time to make up for. It's already dark, and the battle has likely begun. At least I know where our warriors plan to trap the enemy, so I know exactly where I need to be. If things don't go in our favor tonight, if our enemy overtakes us and we are defeated, I don't want John's last memory of me to be my lie. He means too much to me to allow that. I have to find him and tell him how I feel.

The moon is hidden by clouds, and though stars scatter through the dark above, there are not nearly as many as on a clear night. When I pull my canoe to shore, I see dozens of vessels I don't recognize—'Eleu's warriors. There are so many of them. The pressure in my chest makes it hard to breathe, worry encompassing the whole of me. I can see the southern cliffs from here, but I can't tell if anyone is there.

I strain my ears to hear anything unusual, but all I can make out is the sound of water, so I move inland, away from the shore. Once within the protection of the forest, I can hear the periodic hoots of the owls that live on our island. No doubt they're the ancestor spirits of many in our company, and I pray to the gods the birds' cries will serve as warnings to our warriors of danger ahead.

When I see firelight appear on the ridge, I first think the legendary night marchers have come. They are the dead who roam the ridges of the mountains, seeking their descendants. Tonight many men will die, but hopefully they'll be our enemies.

Another flame appears, followed by several more, and I know the fires I see are torches. It could be the light of our enemies trying to find their way in the dark, and I wish I could warn our men of their location.

But when the sound of gunfire echoes down the mountain, I know it comes from the site of the battle. I can't hear the screams or shouts of those fighting, but I can never forget the sound of bullets leaving their chambers and finding a place in the flesh of another. Even from so far away, the sound is soft and barely noticeable, yet it rings through me as though it were right in front of me.

I run through the trail that leads to the cliff to which our men have led the enemy. My breath is heavy in the night air, and I take no caution to conceal the sound of my footsteps through the forest, but it doesn't matter. All warriors, no matter which side of the battle they are on, are in that fight right now. No one is looking for a disobedient girl stubbornly trying to find the man she betrayed.

When I reach the end of the trail, it veers left of where I want to go, but my only other option is a steep incline, and I can't make it alone, especially in the dark. When the curving trail angles upward again, I start to hear men yelling, their voices full of fear. The sound of gunshots has slowed. Have our men fallen? Have their weapons broken?

I hear running footsteps ahead of me, and I duck behind one of the trees hidden in the shadows, not sure if the runner is an enemy. After a grunt and the sound of someone sliding across the leafy forest floor, a feathered helmet rolls near me. My heart stalls when I see it, but it slowly begins beating again when I realize it's not my father's helmet. In fact, it's one I don't recognize, but given the feathers on it, it must belong to a high-ranking chief. The owner doesn't bother to retrieve it. Instead, I hear him stand and continue his escape down the mountain. Away from the fight. Away from his defeat.

With renewed confidence, I pick up the helmet and continue up the mountainside. The gunfire has all but ceased, but the atmosphere is full of smoke, just like the day of our battle so long ago. I step into the clearing, and through the clouds of smoke, I see our men standing tall, victorious.

I see an open box of musket fire against a tree, the bullets combined with gunpowder, ready for our soldiers to reload their weapons. I place the abandoned helmet on top of the box then scan the crowd for familiar faces.

A warrior is kneeling with his weapon standing on end next to him, helping one of John's sailors from the ground. The sailor suffers from a minor wound and will survive.

"My father?" I ask.

The warrior looks up at me then behind him toward the cliff. I don't want to think what it could mean, but I head in that direction anyway. I lift one of the torches that are anchored along the edge and peer over the side. The moon has escaped the cloud cover enough for me to see the bodies lying at the base. Hundreds of bodies. I don't realize I'm looking for my father's cape among them until I exhale in relief at having not found it.

A scream sounds to my left as someone falls over the edge of the cliff, the pitch of his terror decreasing until it cuts short altogether. I hold the torch up and see John backing away from the edge, trying to reload his gun.

He's alive.

The smoke clears enough for me to see a man, someone I don't recognize, running for John, as though he intends to drive him over the edge.

I call out in warning. "John!" But instead of focusing on the threat, he looks toward me and drops his gun, shocked to see me here. He'll be killed, and it will be my fault. I do the only thing I can think of and throw the torch toward the box of gunpowder, hoping it finds its mark. The moment the flames connect with the ammunition it explodes. Everyone instinctively drops to the ground, like I knew they would, including the man who had been running for John.

John picks up his gun and loads it in time to fire it at his enemy. Several others run from the scene, frightened by the unnatural blast.

"Maile?"

I turn to my father, relief flooding me. Just as I'm about to head for him, someone yanks my hair and pulls me back. My attacker forces my head to angle upwards, and a wooden knife is pressed to my throat.

"Back away," he shouts.

Several of our men, both sailors and warriors, aim their guns toward us. Including my father. I don't see John.

"I said back away." His arm tightens on my neck, and I can feel him shaking in panic.

They've cornered him against the cliff, which means they've cornered me as well. I squeeze my eyes closed. I don't want to think what it will feel like to fall over the edge to my death. Instead, I think of John the day of the battle, when he was in the place I am now, with a knife to his neck—my knife. It's only natural that my last thoughts are of him and the pain I caused. I regret hurting him, and I regret lying to him. But I will never regret caring for him.

I feel the distinct impact of a club against my back, or rather against my captor's back. My body vibrates with the blow as he lets go of me and falls away—off the cliff. Someone grabs me around the waist, pulling me from the ledge. It's John. He drops his gun to the ground; he must have used the end of it like a club against the enemy.

"Maile," John says simply, his eyes filled with worry. Then he steps back, looking me over like he did when I was on his ship, determining if I'm hurt. When he sees that I'm all right, his relief is followed by a wave of anger. He is upset that I came, but at least he's looking at me, acknowledging me.

The chief strides over to us. He doesn't scold me like I expect. Instead, he embraces me and says, "It's over."

I glance to the exploded container of gunpowder, where I'd left the feathered helmet I found earlier. It is gone now, destroyed in the blast. "I saw a man running away through the forest. Was it 'Eleu?"

"We let him go," Father admits. "We let many of them go."

"Why?"

"Because they will tell others what happened here. They'll speak of our powerful weapons and of the alliance we have with the white men." Father glances around at his army, both the sailors and his warriors. "The reputation of our *mana* will spread to all surrounding islands. No one will dare face us in battle again. Not for a very long time."

I understand now why my father accepted the foreigners' help. It wasn't just to protect our people. It wasn't just to win this battle—the war we all thought was unwinnable. It was to win all the other battles that would come after it. Battles we'll no longer have to fight.

As my father turns away to assess the wounded and organize his men, I look at John. None of this would have been possible without him. And despite the bold way in which I entered the fight, there's only one thing I feel brave enough to tell him.

With all the gratitude in my heart, I mouth the words, "Thank you."

John Harbottle's Journal
18 April 1779

Of all the foolish, reckless, senseless things to do, Maile has chosen the worst of them all. What was she thinking, traversing the ocean and walking straight into a battle that could have ended her life? I don't even think she had a weapon. Did she think this was some sort of sightseeing tour, a jaunt across the island to appease her curiosity?

I'm not a man who makes a habit of losing his temper. Besides a few impatient moments while dealing with the sailors, I don't think I've cursed more than a few times in my life. But there are many things I want to say to Maile right now that are not only offensive for a woman to hear, they are not the sort of thing I want her to remember me by. Even though she deserves to hear it along with a robust scolding.

She sits near me now, in the lead canoe guiding our fleet back to the bay. I should take time for my rage to settle, give my anger an opportunity to placate, before writing these words in my journal, but it gives me an excuse to not engage in conversation with her. I'll likely regret anything I say to her right now.

The chief told Maile to leave her canoe where it was for the time being, since she arrived on the other side of the southern ridge. That's another thing—she wasn't privy to the alterations we made to our original plan. What if she had run into our enemy, alone, when we weren't there to protect her? I know she is stubborn, and I know she is resilient. But sometimes I wish she was more mindful of the anguish she would cause to those who care for her most should anything happen to her.

The morning light creates a halo around her head, rays of sunshine streaming through the contours of her hair, making her look celestial. I know I will not be angry with her forever—my heart has already softened just being in her presence. She lied to me about the stolen equipment, but I killed the man she loved, which is a thousand times worse. If she can forgive me for that, I can forgive her for lying to me. The peculiar thing is, if she hadn't kept those items from me, I would have left a long time ago. And if I hadn't killed Ikaika, Maile and I wouldn't have had the chance to . . .

What I mean to say is, sometimes we do terrible things, make terrible choices, but it doesn't mean the circumstances of our lives are destined to become terrible as well. It reminds me of what Maile told me on our first day of navigational training, when she made me sit in a pool of water all day: having gone through the trial, we become stronger than we were before.

Such as tonight. Two groups of people who were once enemies came together for a common cause, and it was a wonder to see. Our men were united. Warrior and soldier. Native and sailor. It's a bond I've never experienced before, one I never thought could be achieved. And though my time on this island has brought much heartache, it's also brought the greatest joy I've ever known. I would never give up the former, because that is what makes the latter possible.

iwakāluakūmālima

Chapter Twenty-Five

I watch as John navigates our fleet of canoes without any instruments. He's learned to observe nature and listen to everything the world has to tell him. I see it in the way he continually glances from the sky to the water to the sails as they bow against the winds. He never takes his attention off the clouds or the current, and he watches the colors in the sky, the clarity of the sun, and the shape of our island as it grows larger upon our approach into the bay. He listens, he feels. He knows the signs as well as I do, and I'm both proud and sad. Proud for all he's gained. Sad for all I will lose.

John leans over the rear of the canoe and thrusts his hand into the water. We're moving swiftly, and John's hand creates a furrow in the ocean, the white water forming a line as it extends behind us. He frowns and pulls his hand back in before sitting in the base of the hull, his back against the curved end that rises slightly higher than the sides. There are lines in his forehead. He looks worried.

"What is it?" I ask. I only half expect him to answer. He's

ignored me the entire journey home, all of his attention on that journal of his.

"She feels different," he says without looking at me. "A strange calm in her. Something's changed, or is about to."

I kneel and lean over the side as well, mimicking his movement with my hand in the water. There is an unusually smooth texture to her. Like she isn't pushing against me or blocking my way, but creating an opening for my touch, welcoming me and allowing me to feel her.

"You're right," I say, withdrawing my hand and shaking the wetness from my fingers. I lean back on my heels. "You've saved us, and she's glad."

John looks up at me, glancing between my eyes. "Is she?"

"Yes." I hesitate. "How else should she feel?"

He narrows his eyes. "Nothing else? I just . . . I don't know."

"What is it?" I ask again. We both know I'm not referring to the ocean.

"It doesn't matter anymore," he says. "It's over."

I look away. Is he referring to the battle, his time on our island, or us? Perhaps all three. He's ready to return to England. He knows all he needs to lead his ships home, and with his equipment returned, there's nothing else for him here. But I don't have to say it aloud—he's already admitted it.

As we pull into shore, a conch blows, signaling our arrival. Our people are there to greet us, cheering at the news that our strategy was successful. More than that—it was a miracle, something the gods had surely favored. Though everyone is tired, preparations begin right away for the celebration we had planned for yesterday. Today we will celebrate our victory, our survival, our alliance.

Once the nets are tossed into the water and brought in, and

the abundance of fish divided among the men to be cooked, I head inland. I'm determined to keep myself busy and distracted. I don't want my despair to taint the happiness of the day. People bustle about the homestead, stringing thousands of flowers around the area. They not only bring beautiful colors and shapes, but they fill the air with a sweet fragrance. Other people assemble long mats that will hold the vast amounts of food that will soon crowd the surfaces. There is much to be thankful for.

I continue past the clearing into a large field of *kī* leaves. I help the people already there harvest the leaves and bring them under the council hut in the shade. After tearing off a thin strip of the strong leaf's spine, I thread it into a bone needle and begin to sew the leaves together, one by one, letting the bulk of each leaf hang down. Once I reach a length that fits around my waist, I tie it off. I begin again, adding another layer of leaves on top of the first. I repeat it, forming a thick mass of green that will reflect the light of the torches from every angle.

When I'm done, I stand and hold it to my body. The bottoms of the leaves brush just below my knees. I tie the ends behind me. The skirt feels heavy but perfectly measured. Atop my clothes, the weight of it pulls it naturally to settle just below my waist, clinging to the widest part of my hips. I bend my knees and kick my feet forward along the ground in front of me, one at a time. The movement allows my hips to sway from side to side, and the resulting shifting of leaves back and forth makes a satisfyingly swooshing sound.

I leave the shade of the hut and step into the sunlight. The glare of it bounces off the shiny leaves, forcing me to squint. I extend my arms to the sides and spin around and around. The momentum of the heavy leaves moving in a circular motion keeps me spinning until I feel too dizzy to stand. I fall to the ground and look up to the sky with a smile. The world continues to spin around without me until it finally joins me in my stillness.

A face appears above me, and I sit up quickly, partly in surprise, partly in embarrassment. Did John see me spinning a moment ago?

"I've never . . . I've never seen you like that before," he says.

I feel like an idiot. "Like what? Having fun? Happy?" I say it defensively, regretting the bitterness in my voice. It's not his fault there's this awkwardness between us. I'm the one who lied.

"Yes. That." He pauses. "But something else. I've never seen you look so . . . so free before. Unburdened."

I stand and think about that a moment, mourning for having lost that part of myself temporarily. "I suppose I haven't really been at ease since your ships' return." I don't have to explain the terrible circumstances of the battle on our beach, of losing someone I loved. Combined with 'Eleu's threat, my life hasn't been as peaceful as it once was. "With all the excitement in the village today—thanks to our victory—I suppose I let myself get caught up in the moment."

"I'm sorry I've made your life so difficult." I think he's apologizing not only for himself, but for all his men. His captain, even.

"On the contrary," I say. "It's because of you I've allowed myself to get carried away."

John's eyes narrow in confusion.

"I mean it's because of you and your men, your guns, that we even have this victory. It's because of you I have the luxury of releasing my worries." Of course one worry still remains—that of his departure.

John exhales. "Ah, yes. Well." He looks down to my skirt, the leaves wrapped around my hips. "Will you be dancing at the celebration?"

I clasp my hands in front of me, a bit embarrassed. "Yes. It's tradition."

"She can not only sing, but dance as well?" he asks aloud to no one, his voice reverent. "And navigate on the water. Hunt in the mountains. Fish. Farm. Sew. Heal wounds." He raises his hand to his chest, pressing against the scar that lies beneath his clothing. "Is there anything you can't do?"

I can't make you stay, I think. *I can't make you care for me. Not the way I want.*

"Thank you for the things you returned," he says. "In my hut."

I swallow hard, waiting for him to yell at me like he did when we were on the mountain. But if he's still angry about what happened or for me entering his hut, he doesn't let on.

John clears his throat. "I need to help with the food," he says. "Apparently there are sea snails on the menu." He offers a tiny smile before heading toward the underground ovens.

As I untie the leaf skirt from around my waist, I ponder what he said about me seeming free and unburdened. It's not entirely true; the thought of his departure has been at the forefront of my mind, but perhaps it's the most free I've felt for a long time. I promise myself that tonight I will not think of his leaving. Of his abandoning me for his England. Instead I will let myself celebrate that I got to meet him in the first place.

The celebrations begin before my family arrives, as is customary. When my father calls for us, we line up behind him. My mother, Haukea, and myself, followed by La'akea. The chief wears his feathered cape and helmet, and his standard bearers are on either side of him, their feathered poles high in the air. I wear a *haku lei* on my head, the orange flowers and green leaves crowning my head while my hair falls loose to my waist. The dancing skirt I made earlier is draped over my regular clothing.

We make our procession to the celebration area, where a platform has been raised for our family. The music pauses; everyone stands as we enter. Father takes his place on a stool in the center, while Mother sits next to him, the feathered crown on her head billowing every time she waves her woven fan in front of her face. The rest of us take our places alongside our parents, my eyes finding John right away in the middle of the crowd. I remind myself I won't think of his leaving.

Lit torches surround the clearing. A tangy scent of flowers mixed with salt pork hangs in the air. A cloud of smoke rises from the south end where firepits recently held cooked meat and vegetables. I serve myself mashed taro and sea snails, taro greens and fish. Passion fruit, breadfruit, and mountain apples also fill my plate. I nibble on a small salted crab from one of the platters as I head back to my spot on the platform.

While I eat, several men gather in the center of the clearing, both sailors and our warriors, holding guns and spears in their hands. They reenact the battle, showing those who weren't there how they fought with valiance and vigor, how they cornered their enemy and forced them over the cliff, and even how they showed mercy and let the rest go to tell the story to their own people. The story of how two unlikely groups of foreigners and natives came together for a common cause is powerful.

Chanting and dancing continue throughout the night, the sound of gourd drums and rattle instruments permeating the air, mimicking the beat of a heart. When it's time for me, my sister, and my mother to dance, the chief invites John to sit on the platform alongside him. It's a great honor, and John seems to understand the significance. He bows before the chief and expresses praise and gratitude before sitting next to him.

My mother, sister, and I kneel before the chief, and a holy man chants an introduction to our dance. We begin to move as he continues his song, an ode to our homeland. My hands form the sweeping green mountains, the rain that falls, and the flowers that bloom along the valley floors. I shift my feet back and forth, and my hips sway like the movement of water. I've never danced in front of John before, and I'm aware of his eyes on me. Everything moves at a slow pace. I am dizzy, like I felt earlier today while spinning, but this time as the world stops turning around me and melts into the background, John is left watching me. There's only John.

When our dance is done, I breathe hard, trying to gather air into my lungs. My head feels light. I sit on the platform next to John, fanning myself from the heat of the torchlight, the weight of my thick dancing skirt, and the exertion of dancing.

Without looking at me, John leans over and whispers, "I think I have a new favorite thing."

I laugh aloud, but he's the only one who can hear me because of the loud instruments and music. We watch as more groups of dancers take the stage, telling the stories of our people, our history, our traditions. I feel something against my hand and look down. John has covered my little finger with his own, both of our hands pressed against the mat on the floor between us.

It takes everything in me to hold back tears of relief. His words, his touch—it's a gift he can't possibly know the significance of. I thought I'd broken us, lost him before I really had him. We might not be fully mended yet, but his actions tell me it's possible.

I look at his profile and see his eyes crinkled with joy watching the dancers. His straight lips are anything but, curving wide in a delighted smile. I say nothing, just take comfort that he's enjoying the festivities. Perhaps he's promised himself to forget about his upcoming departure as well.

Smoking pipes and heavy drinks are passed around the crowd, and soon I feel a little intoxicated in the celebration. Haukea and my father have disappeared somewhere, and La'akea is laughing riotously with a group of sailors. When I hear the crunching of leaves and detect the familiar scent of a certain vine, I turn to see John holding a length of *maile* in his lap, absentmindedly rubbing a leaf between his finger and thumb. It's the vine I left for him in his hut. He must have had it in his pocket all night.

Feeling bold, likely from the smoke and drink, I take the vine and wrap it around him, pulling it tight in front.

"You are my prisoner," I tease. "You can't leave. Ever. Because you are mine."

I expect him to laugh, to smile. But his expression is unreadable, and he looks at me as though trying to see into me.

I grab the end of the vine and toss it in his face. "John . . ." I say, then I press my lips closed. A part of me thinks I've said too much. Or maybe I've reminded him about his departure, ruining the bliss he'd managed to find tonight.

He pushes the vine aside and pulls one of my hands into both of his, his thumbs rubbing across my palm as he decides what to say. "Maile," he whispers. Even with the sounds of the celebration around us, I can still hear his voice.

Haukea returns with a grin on her face, taking a spot on the other side of John. He lets go of my hand. My sister leans close to his ear and whispers something, cupping her hands over her mouth so no one else can hear. She speaks to him for more than a moment, and as his face turns a shade of pink, I wonder what she's telling him.

My father's deep voice says, "John Harbottle," and John sits tall to acknowledge the chief.

"Y-yes, Kalani?" John stutters.

"I'd like to speak to you. Now. In my hut." Father leaves without waiting for an answer.

John quickly stands and follows, but not before looking back at my sister and me. I wonder what my father has to say. The battle is over, and I can't think what's so important that it can't wait until after the celebration.

When they're gone, Haukea scoots closer to me and takes my hand like John had earlier. The smile on her face is so huge, and she looks like a young girl caught doing mischief, not the polished and well-behaved sister I'm used to.

"You're happy," I say, stating the obvious.

"Yes."

"Why?"

She shrugs. "Everyone will know soon enough."

I try to understand her merriment, but all I can think about is John. I don't like the sensation of him leaving me. I remove the *haku lei* from my head because it's giving me a headache. Then I take another swig of heavy drink and try to forget again.

John Harbottle's Journal
19 April 1779

There is a strict caste system in Hawai'i with four general groupings:

Ali'i: *the royals, including the chiefs and their families*
Kahuna: *priests and religious leaders, as well as highly skilled craftsmen*
Maka'āinana: *commoners—the majority of the population*
Kauwā: *war prisoners and their descendants who are relegated to rigorous labor*

Since we first arrived, it's been a struggle to determine where we fit within their hierarchy. James Cook was thought to be the god Lono, ranking him even higher than the chief. But what did that make the rest of us? Not commoners, but not equal to the royals or the priests, either. When Cook was killed and his mortality revealed, we were demoted to less than war prisoners. We weren't welcome within their population at all. We were asked to leave.

But as the weeks passed and a partnership grew, we were adopted back into their society. Never named or slotted into a caste, we were given a new identification—foreign allies. The barrier that was washed away had found a place in the sand again. We knew who we were to the natives; we knew who they were to us.

While their acceptance of us has been something I'm grateful for, I've never known what it meant for potential relationships, because one of the strictest rules of their caste system is that no one within one grouping could ever marry someone from another. It is strictly forbidden.

But tonight Kalani explained to me about another law, a higher law. If any man or woman completes a great feat or achieves exceptional success in warfare, the high chief has the power to alter their rank.

This changes everything.

iwakāluakūmāono

Chapter Twenty-Six

When I wake, it's strangely cold and bright. I sit up with a groan, wiping at my eyes to help them open. I look around and remember—I fell asleep on the platform during the waning hours of the celebration. The scent of smoke from dying fires combines with the dampness of morning dew, making me feel lazy and sluggish. Several others fell asleep here last night, too, their bodies sprawled around the clearing and surrounding area. La'akea is asleep next to me, his loud snores interrupting an otherwise silent morning. My parents aren't here. Neither is my sister. They were probably smart enough to return to their huts last night.

John isn't here, either.

I stand and stretch, smoothing down the leaves of my skirt. Too lazy to take it off, I walk through the maze of sleeping bodies toward my father's hut to see if anyone else is awake.

Makana, Father's scout, hurries toward me with a smile on his face.

"Have you heard?" he asks.

"Heard what?"

"Your sister, Haukea." He looks back toward the huts. "She is to be married."

"Married?" I narrow my brows. "What do you mean?"

"Now that we've won the battle, Haukea doesn't have to wed an enemy," he explains. "There will be no need for alliances once our reputation has spread. She's free from that duty."

It makes sense, but the speed of it is surprising. "Who is she marrying?" I ask.

"Lieutenant John Harbottle, hero of our war." Makana grabs my shoulder. "To show his gratitude for all John has done—his generosity of guns and soldiers—the chief has offered Haukea to be his wife, and we've just learned John has accepted."

I step backwards, letting Makana's hand fall from my shoulder. Haukea and . . . John? They are to be married? But—

"It will be a legendary alliance." Makana's voice is full of excitement. "Not just a wife for a prize, but the combining of two nations, two races. It's never happened before and will be sung in our chants for generations to come."

Something settles deep in my stomach. An emotion I've never felt before. Not jealousy. Maybe betrayal. What is the opposite of happiness? What do you call it when something you never really had claim to is ripped from your fingers anyway? I have no word to describe the feeling that consumes me. I'm drowning, struggling for air.

I see a figure in the distance. It's a man, leaving the hut of my father with a smile on his face.

It's John.

I can't stay here. I can't . . . I don't know what to do.

I turn and run. And run and run and run. Tears stream down my face even as sweat gathers on my forehead and the back of my neck. I run faster than I ever have before, the leaves at my waist creating a loud swishing noise. Slapping and tearing and scraping. It's the sound of my heart ripping into pieces. The sound of my bones crushing beneath me.

It isn't until I've reached the small clearing that I realize where I've run to without thinking. It's the place where I brought John to heal from his wound. It feels like another life, so long ago. If only there were a poultice I could apply to my own wound. If only I could heal it as easily as a slice across my chest. But this cut runs much deeper, piercing my heart. I don't know if it will ever heal.

How can John marry Haukea? How can he agree to it? She's beautiful and graceful in a way I'll never be, but I didn't think John valued such things. I thought he saw deeper than that. But having to be with me during his time here was not his choice. He was wounded when I brought him here. I kept him prisoner. I denied him any chance to leave. And Father assigned me to work with him—John didn't choose that, either.

Perhaps he would have preferred a more feminine companion. One who wouldn't think to join a battle or fight against an enemy. One who wouldn't trample through a muddy taro patch or spin in a circle like a child. Someone more delicate. More respectful.

Someone better than me.

I remember the day my sister and I watched the men training on the beach. She said then she thought John was handsome. She said she wanted to ask Father to arrange their marriage. I thought she was teasing. But what if she wasn't?

The hazy events of last night find new clarity—Haukea whispering in John's ear, the joy she couldn't hide. Did she know then? Did she know Father was going to ask John to marry her?

I storm past the small hut where John stayed all those weeks. The first place I'd noticed the color of his eyes. And his kindness.

Well, he can keep his kindness to himself.

Another realization hits me: if he's to marry my sister, does that mean he intends to stay here? It's something I once wished with my entire heart, but I don't want him to stay as my sister's husband. Every time I would look at him, every time I would see them together—I would always regret the moment I opened my heart and made a space for him. A space he apparently never wanted.

I walk away from the hut to a spot of ground covered by a simple rainbow of coconuts. I pace back and forth in front of James Cook's grave, yelling at the buried remains of a man I never knew.

"Why did you bring him here?" I ask, clenching my fists. "Why our island? Why our bay?"

I once asked the gods these same questions; they never answered me, either.

"I was fine before you brought him here," I say. "My life was set. The stars in my story were fixed." I wipe tears from my eyes. "But now this . . . I don't recognize this sky at all."

My dancing skirt scratches and irritates my skin as I pace, so I finally tear it off and toss it across the clearing.

"Maile."

I look up to see John standing a few meters away. The expression on his face is halfway between joy and apprehension. Perhaps joy from securing his new bride, apprehension for having to tell me about it. It doesn't matter, because I don't want to hear anything he has to say.

"You got your navigational equipment back, didn't you?" I

snap at him. "The war is over. You can go now. You can leave the island and never come back."

His face falls, the joy and apprehension replaced with confusion. But he says nothing.

"Go!" I stomp toward him and shove him away from me. "Leave. Now. I don't want you here."

His voice is soft when he says, "You don't want me."

It's not a question, but I answer him anyway. "I don't. I want you to go away. Go back to England."

His brow wrinkles, and he opens his mouth to say something, but then closes it. I try to move past him, but he grabs my arm, holding me back. I yank free and spin to face him.

"Leave me alone," I say. My words are broken, half in anguish, half in spite. I'm still trying to decide if I'm hurt or angry. Upset or betrayed. In truth, I'm somewhere in between.

"I need to tell you something," he pleads. "Please let me speak."

"I don't want to hear what you have to say." I take one step back, as though the distance will protect my heart from breaking any more than it already has.

"But I've come to—"

"I know why you've come!" I say, cutting off his words. "You've come to tell me you're marrying my sister. And I . . . I don't want to hear it. Not from you. Not your voice. I can't."

"You're wrong," he says, stepping closer. "That's not why I've come."

I swallow hard, worried that what he's going to tell me is much worse, though I don't know how it could be. My heart is already in pieces. There's nothing left but dust.

"Your father spoke with Haukea last night. He told her he

planned to offer her as a bride to me, as a reward for my role in the victory."

I fold my arms in front of me, trying to create a shield against what he's saying.

"But your sister suggested he offer *you* to me instead."

I freeze. I run his words through my head, again, trying to make sure I heard him correctly. "What?"

A small smile forms on his lips. "She told him she suspected I would prefer . . . She thought you would be a better match for me."

Haukea told Father that John should marry *me*? Her secret whispers to John last night, her smiles, her happiness—it was all because she was excited for me to marry John. Not her.

Tears well up in my eyes. How did she know about my feelings for him?

"So when he called me to his hut to speak with me," John says, "he offered you for my bride."

I swallow hard again, my throat swelling with emotion. "And . . . and what did you say?" I try to keep my voice level, but it shakes with uncertainty.

John steps forward and presses his hands against the sides of my arms, keeping me still, holding me steady. "I said I would be honored to have you for my wife, but only if you wanted me as your husband."

John as my husband. The sound of it makes me delirious, and I realize now, this moment, how impossible I thought it was. Yet here he is, now, this moment, standing in front of me, saying those words. Those beautiful, precious words.

John continues, "I understand if you don't want me. After everything that has happened between us—I'll leave if that's really what you want."

I think of Ikaika. Of what John did. But then I think of our time together afterward. Our friendship, our companionship. My heart expands more than I thought possible.

"I need you to know that I love you." He pauses, his admission filling the air between us. "I love you, Maile. And I want to marry you. If you'll have me."

I love him. In spite of everything, or maybe because of everything, I do love him. I love John. But I still can't make myself say the words. I am too stunned by his. Could he really love me, given all he knows of the world? Why me, when he could find someone with so much more than my own naïve existence?

He brushes a strand of hair from my face. "I loved you from the first day I saw you in the water. When I stood on the deck of my ship." He looks at me with his blue-green eyes. "Somehow I knew you would change my life. Maile—" His voice cracks with emotion. "I want you. Please say yes. Please say you'll have me."

"You will stay?" It seems obvious, but I need to know.

He nods. "I will stay here. Always. For the rest of my life."

"With me?"

He laughs. "Yes, Maile, with you."

"Even when I'm angry with you?"

"Yes."

"Even when I'm stubborn or jealous or in the foulest of moods?"

"Yes."

"What about the Northwest Passage?" I ask. "What about your England?"

He thinks for a moment. "Do you remember that day when the humpback whales came to me?"

I nod.

"You said they were voyagers, like me, but that Hawai'i, this place, was their home." John pauses. "I think . . . I think this was always meant to be my home, too. That's why your ancestors appeared that day. They weren't just greeting me or sending us a sign that it was good for me to be here. They were welcoming me home." He pulls me closer. "The Northwest Passage, England, all the places I've visited around the world—they will always exist. But they'll have to exist without me."

"You will stay," I whisper, only this time it's not a question. It's the greatest truth I know.

"I'm afraid you're stuck with me." He smiles. "I want you to be my family. Adopt me. *Hānai* me. Take care of me."

"I'm good at that," I say, a smile teasing my lips.

"Yes, you are," he says. "You're the only one I want. I love you, and I want to stay with you. Be with you."

I bite my lip, bringing my hand to his cheek and feeling the scruff there. "I love you, too," I say for the first time.

His face changes, as though I've somehow brought him back from the underworld. There's life in his expression. A hope and joy that I put there.

"I love you, John." I say again and smile before adding, "And, yes, I will marry you."

He shouts and pulls me into his arms, lifting me off the forest floor. I laugh as he places me back down, but he doesn't let go. Instead he buries his face in my neck, inhaling deeply as his fingers slide against my scalp, tangling in my hair.

I pull back and look at him, relishing the happiness in his eyes. I lean forward and press my nose against his, breathing his breath, sharing my air with him. I press the side of my nose against his before moving to the other side and doing the same, just like the night on the beach under the stars, giving him my most intimate expression of love. I meant it then, and I mean it now. I love him, and no one can take that from me.

When I feel his lips press against mine, I'm so startled by the sensation I jump back and look up at him. "What was that?" I ask, bringing my fingers to my lips, the lingering tingle of his touch making my head spin.

"That was a kiss," he says. His face is flushed, but there's no apology there.

"That was no *honi*," I say.

He chuckles. "That is the way my people kiss."

I touch my lips again, trying to memorize what it felt like.

"If you don't like it, we don't have—"

"Do it again," I say before he changes his mind. "Kiss me again."

He smiles before pressing his lips to mine, letting them linger as every nerve in my lips catches fire, burns at every point of contact. He kisses me again. And again. Each time is a little different. Each time a new form of surprise and pleasure mingles into a head-spinning bliss.

When he finally pulls away, I touch his lips with my fingers, wondering if he feels as delirious as I do.

"Will you be doing that often when we're married?" I ask. "Kissing me?"

"Do you want me to?"

"Yes. A lot."

One side of his mouth rises. "Then I will kiss you every day—a thousand times a day. Until your lips swell if that's what you want."

"Promise?"

His smile spreads across his whole face. "I promise." He kisses me again, and I moan at the sensation. I don't know if I'll ever get used to it. I don't know that I ever want to.

I slide my hands behind his neck. "It looks like you'll be my prisoner forever after all."

We both laugh so unabashedly, I know there are no more secrets between us. Nothing holding us back. No doubts.

Almost.

After we both stop laughing, I smooth my expression. "I'm sorry I lied to you."

"Maile, you don't have to—"

"Let me finish." I take a deep breath. "I'm sorry I buried the stolen equipment and kept it from you. You were my enemy, and I didn't want you to have it. But eventually, I just didn't want you to leave."

"I didn't want to leave, either. I didn't want to give up my time with you." He leans his forehead against mine. "Thank you for protecting my heart. Thank you for burying it where it would be safe."

I rest my palm on his heart and the scar that covers it. "Thank you for letting me."

John presses his hand over mine, holding it against his chest. "Now that we have the equipment back, my men can leave. They have the tools to help them return to England."

"And you will stay," I whisper.

"I will stay."

"Forever?"

"For as long as you'll have me."

I grin. "Then forever it is."

I thread my fingers with his and pull him toward the homestead.

"Where are we going?" he asks.

I squeeze his hand. "I have one more wayfinding lesson to teach you."

After spending most of the day making plans for our upcoming wedding, we paddle out into the bay, just past the *Resolution* and *Discovery*. The expanse of ocean is in front of us, the water reflecting the thousands of stars in the night sky. After placing our oars in the canoe, I scoot forward so I'm sitting next to John, staring out at the horizon.

"Hold out your hand," I say. I lengthen my arm in front of me to show him what I mean. My palm is raised, facing away from me.

He does the same.

"Good. Now keep your fingers together, just like that, but stretch out your thumb." I wait for him to follow. "Now, tilt your hand so that the line of your thumb matches the line of the horizon."

We both tilt our hands to the same degree.

"Now find the fixed star in the north," I say, "and place your hand beneath it."

He slides his hand along the horizon a little to his left.

"Where is the star?" I ask.

"It's sitting just above my index finger."

"That's right." I measure the star with my own hand, and the result is the same. "Do you know what that means?"

He shakes his head.

"It means you're in Hawai'i," I say with a quiet reverence. "It means you are home."

John slowly lowers his hand and stares up at the stars.

After a while I ask, "What do you feel?"

He grins, playing along with my navigational lesson. "I feel . . . I feel in love."

"Then you're observing things perfectly," I say, resting my head against his shoulder. "Because that is what I feel, too."

"I love you, Maile."

I know he does. I feel it in every part of me. "Then kiss me," I say.

And he does.

Acknowledgments

In 2012, I was workshopping what would become my first published novel, *Remake*, in Ann Dee Ellis's class at the Writing and Illustrating for Young Readers conference, hoping to polish that book and find a literary agent. One of her assignments was to write the first page of something we've always wanted to write. Something different, new, maybe something difficult. I knew right away I wanted to write the story of my fourth-great-grandparents: a British sailor and a chiefess in late eighteenth-century Hawai'i.

The words I wrote were personal and raw, and I remember crying while reading it aloud to the class. It stirred something inside me. But it wasn't YA science fiction—which is what I had been writing. It was so different from anything I'd ever done before, so I tucked it away. But I never forgot it.

Over the next five years, whenever I was burned out on the project I was working on, I'd pull out that little seed of a novel and write a few more words. Add a scene. Develop the characters. Daydream about their story. But that's all it was—a dream. Because I didn't write historical fiction. I didn't write for adults.

So I tucked the story away again and again, my little project that would likely always be just for me.

So one day, when my editors asked if I was interested in writing a romance with a British sailor in eighteenth-century Hawai'i, I nearly fell out of my seat. "I have just the thing," I said. And with that, I had permission to write the book of my heart.

Writing this story has been a sacred experience for me. The connection I felt to my ancestors throughout the process is something I can't describe, and I would do it all over just to feel that again. The fact that it's now a real book is just a bonus, and it wouldn't be possible without the help and support from so many people.

Thanks goes to my husband, Daniel, for your never-ending support of me and my writing. I love brainstorming through tricky scenes with you. To my daughter Emma for your valuable feedback, and Parker, Stirling, and Hailey for being patient when I worked around the clock through tight deadlines.

Thank you to my sister-in-law Mikilani for loaning me your *Iosepa* sailing journal, and to you and my mother, Susan, for checking my Hawai'ian culture, language, and history references. To my extended family, for the encouragement and excitement you've shared over this book. To my plums, Kathryn Purdie, Robin Hall, and Emily Prusso, for reading through an early draft and helping me polish this story. Also huge appreciation to my agent, Lane Heymont of the Tobias Literary Agency, for your tireless work on this book and my career as an author.

And thanks to the team at Shadow Mountain for making this book possible—Lisa Mangum, Heidi Taylor Gordon, Chris Schoebinger, Richard Erickson, Malina Grigg, and Jill Schaugaard. I'm blessed to get to work with the best publishing team ever.

ACKNOWLEDGMENTS

Finally, thank you to John Harbottle and Papapaunauapu for loaning me your story and teaching me what it means to have the spirit of Elijah—"And he shall turn the heart of the fathers to the children, and the heart of the children to their fathers" (Malachi 4:6). It has been a pleasure to walk in your shoes for a time.

Author's Note

James Cook was a captain in the British Royal Navy and made three voyages to the Pacific. He is credited with making the first European contact with Eastern Australia and Hawai'i. He was an explorer, a navigator, and a highly skilled cartographer, mapping islands and continents around the world on a scale not previously achieved. He was killed on February 14, 1779, while attempting to kidnap Hawai'ian chief Kalani'ōpu'u in order to reclaim a cutter stolen from one of his ships.

Sources report that John Harbottle arrived in Hawai'i in 1794 as a mate on the *Jackal* and was later appointed captain of the *Lily Bird*. He was instrumental in helping Kamehameha in the battle of Nu'uanu in 1795 by providing cannon fire and muskets to the soon-to-be king. John married Papapaunauapu (I used the name "Maile" to make it easier for the reader), daughter of a chief in Oahu, as a reward for his role in the battle. They had eight children, forming one of the oldest *hapa-haole* (half-white, half-Hawai'ian) families in the islands.

A Song for the Stars is inspired by these real people and real events that formed the early years of post-European life in

Hawai'i. I chose to condense the time line of these events to explore the contrast of two cultures colliding for the first time and finding a way to subsist together in a circumstance unfamiliar to them both.

John and Papapaunauapu are my fourth-great-grandparents, so writing this story was a very personal experience for me. There is something special about connecting with one's ancestors, and I'm grateful to have had the chance to explore their story and imagine what their lives would have been like.

Because this is a work of fiction, I made a few conscious changes in ancient Hawai'ian practices and history for the sake of the story. Women and men never would have eaten together, and the royal family would have had much less interaction with commoners and lived separate from the community. While the historical events took place in very specific locations, I chose to place the narrative in a more generic setting. Also, while much of what happened to James Cook in this book is true, his remains were returned to sea in a coffin after a service led by his crewmen.

Glossary

ahupua'a (ah-hoo-poo ah-ah) land division extending from the uplands to the sea

ali'i (ah-lee-ee) royalty

'aumākua (ah oo-mAH-koo ah) family gods; deified ancestors

auwē (ah oo-wEH) expression of fear or grief

'awapuhi (ah-vah-poo-hee) wild ginger

'eleu (eh-leh oo) energetic

hā (hAH) breath; life

haku (hah-koo) braided

hala (hah-lah) pandanus

hānai (hAH-nah ee) foster; adopt

hanawai (hah-nah-vah ee) urinate

haukea (hah oo-keh ah) snow

hei (heh ee) string figure

heiau (heh ee ah oo) place of worship; temple

hiluhilu (hee-loo-hee-loo) elegant; beautiful

ho'i (hoh-ee) leave

honi (hoh-nee) kiss

ho'opau (hoh-oh-pah oo) stop; put an end to

hukilau (hoo-kee-lah oo) to fish with a seine

ikaika (ee-kah ee-kah) strong

ipo (ee-poh) sweetheart; lover

kāhili (kAH-hee-lee) feather standard

kahuna (kah-hoo-nah) priest; holy man

kalani (kah-lah-nee) the heaven or sky

kapa (kah-pah) bark cloth

kapu (kah-poo) sacred; forbidden

kauwā (kah oo-wAH) outcast; slave

keahi (keh ah-hee) the fire

kī (kEE) a woody plant with narrow, oblong leaves

koa (koh ah) largest native forest tree

kōnane (kOH-nah-neh) ancient game resembling checkers

kukui (koo-koo ee) candlenut tree

lei (leh ee) necklace of flowers; garland

luhiehu (loo-hee eh-hoo) honored beauty

maikaʻi (mah ee-kah-ee) good; pleasant to look at

maile (mah ee-leh) native vine with shiny, fragrant leaves

makaʻāinana (mah-kah-AH ee-nah-nah) commoner

makahiki (mah-kah-hee-kee) ancient festival with sports and religious activities

makalapua (mah-kah-lah-poo ah) to blossom; beautiful

makana (mah-kah-nah) gift

mana (mah-nah) divine power

mikihilina (mee-kee-hee-lee-nah) ornamental beauty

nani (nah-nee) glorious beauty

nonohe (noh-noh-heh) attractive

ʻohā (oh-hAH) taro corm growing from an older stalk

ʻohana (oh-hah-nah) family

paʻanehe (pah-ah-neh-heh) subtle beauty

pau (pah oo) finish

pili (pee-lee) a type of grass used for thatching houses

poi (poh ee) pounded, cooked taro thinned with water

pōlani (pOH-lah-nee) beautiful, pure

puna (poo-nah) spring of water

u'i (oo-ee) youthful; pretty

wahine (vah-hee-neh) woman

Discussion Questions

1. James Cook's arrival was the first time Hawai'ians encountered people of another race, culture, and language. Have you ever faced a circumstance that felt completely foreign to you? Did you not know how to behave or perhaps questioned what might be right or wrong in a particular situation because of that unfamiliarity? What did you do?

2. At the end of the story, an enemy held a knife to Maile's neck, mirroring a scene at the beginning when she held a knife to John's neck. How does Maile differ at the end of the story from the start? How has her attitude toward warfare changed, if at all?

3. Have you ever traveled to Hawai'i or another tropical island? As you read the text, what descriptions reminded you of your time there? Was there something you'd forgotten and remembered while reading? Were any settings or descriptions completely new to you?

4. John said that even when foreigners do their best to minimize their influence on a native culture, it's impossible to know the extent of their impact, however innocent their intentions

are. Is there ever a cause that is worth the risk of destroying or influencing a people, whether intentional or not? How would you determine the risk versus the reward? How have perceptions about this changed since John's time?

5. There are a number of things Maile learns about John's culture that seem strange to her: wigs, corsets, dresses, writing, etc. What are some customs about ancient Hawai'ians that seem strange to you? Can you think of any practices or traditions of other cultures today that seem strange to you? What traditions of your own culture might seem strange to other people? How can learning about other cultures help build empathy?

6. When Maile discovers the stolen navigational equipment in the skiff, she decides to bury it to protect her father's honor. What do you think would have happened if she had returned the stolen supplies that day instead? What would you have done in the same situation?

7. Today, half of all marriages in Hawai'i are interracial, by far the highest percentage of any place in the United States. Do you think the national rate will increase? What are some of the benefits and challenges an interracial couple faces today? How are those different or similar to the challenges you think Maile and John had to face?

8. Some of Maile's frustrations in the story stem from her dissatisfaction with the gender roles her culture perpetuated. What are some ways she challenged gender expectations? What are some ways she followed them? How do you challenge or follow society's expectations of your gender today?